THE
Corpse
WITH
THE
Opal
Fingers

CATHY ACE

FOUR TAILS PUBLISHING LTD

PRAISE FOR THE CAIT MORGAN MYSTERIES

"In the finest tradition of Agatha Christie…Ace brings us the closed-room drama, with a dollop of romantic suspense and historical intrigue." – *Library Journal*

"…touches of Christie or Marsh but with a bouquet of Kinsey Millhone." – *The Globe and Mail*

"…a sparkling, well-plotted and quite devious mystery in the cozy tradition…" – *Hamilton Spectator*

"…If all of this suggests the school of Agatha Christie, it's no doubt what Cathy Ace intended. She is, as it fortunately happens, more than adept at the Christie thing." – *Toronto Star*

"Cait unravels the…mystery using her eidetic memory and her powers of deduction, which are worthy of Hercule Poirot."
– *The Jury Box, Ellery Queen Mystery Magazine*

"This author always takes us on an adventure. She always makes us think. She always brings the setting to life. For those reasons this is one of my favorite series."
– *Escape With Dollycas Into A Good Book*

"…a testament to an author who knows how to tell a story and deliver it with great aplomb." – *Dru's Musings*

"…perfect for those that love travel, food, and/or murder (reading it, not committing it)." – *BOLO Books*

"…Ace is, well, an ace when it comes to plot and description."
– *The Globe and Mail*

Other works by the same author
(Information for all works here: **www.cathyace.com**)

The Cait Morgan Mysteries
The Corpse with the Silver Tongue
The Corpse with the Golden Nose
The Corpse with the Emerald Thumb
The Corpse with the Platinum Hair
The Corpse with the Sapphire Eyes
The Corpse with the Diamond Hand
The Corpse with the Garnet Face
The Corpse with the Ruby Lips
The Corpse with the Crystal Skull
The Corpse with the Iron Will
The Corpse with the Granite Heart
The Corpse with the Turquoise Toes

The WISE Enquiries Agency Mysteries
The Case of the Dotty Dowager
The Case of the Missing Morris Dancer
The Case of the Curious Cook
The Case of the Unsuitable Suitor
The Case of the Disgraced Duke
The Case of the Absent Heirs
The Case of the Cursed Cottage
The Case of the Uninvited Undertaker

Standalone novels
The Wrong Boy

Short Stories/Novellas
Murder Keeps No Calendar: a collection of 12 short stories/novellas
Murder Knows No Season: a collection of four novellas
Steve's Story in "The Whole She-Bang 3"
The Trouble with the Turkey in "Cooked to Death Vol. 3: Hell for
the Holidays"

Family and friends – that's what it all boils down to

Down Under

"I never thought I'd see this for myself," said Bud quietly. "Not in my wildest dreams."

The sky was aflame above Sydney's iconic opera house – the perfect sunset. Which was just as well, given that we were on a sunset dinner cruise.

I hugged my husband tight, happy that we could share the wonderful moment. "I'm sure we'll make it to Siân's home in Perth one day, but with her and Todd coming here for his annual mining conference, and us being able to make it over from Canada, you're right…this trip is special in so many ways."

As though my mention of her name had conjured her into existence, my sister was suddenly at my side, looking anxious. "We'll be heading back to the dock at Barangaroo soon," she announced. "Do we have a plan for when we get off?"

I didn't want the magic of the evening to end, so replied, "Don't know…oh look, what's going on over there?" I hoped Siân would be distracted enough to leave me and Bud alone.

My sister followed my gaze. "That Mob from the Kimberley are at it again – the ones who build roads through the Bush and the Outback for mining companies. They're settling in for a few yarns, I'd guess. You've bumped into some of them earlier during the conference, right?"

I nodded. "Hard to miss, really, aren't they?" My sister rolled her eyes in agreement. The group of about twenty men who were rambunctious at best, and rowdy at worst, had become a bit of an item at the annual get-together, making their presence felt at every gathering – and not just because of their matching corporate shirts, which were an eye-watering yellow with a massive red and black S & S logo on the back. None of them seemed capable of doing anything but shouting, and they all shared an inexhaustible love of beer, it seemed.

"I was ten years old when I found a murder weapon," said a gravelly voice from somewhere within the crowd.

My curiosity kicked in immediately, of course, and I craned my neck to try to spot who'd spoken.

There was a cheer, a couple of shouts of "Good on ya, mate", and the canary-shirted men began to congregate, with expectant faces.

Bud smiled at me indulgently and said, "That's an opening line it's too good to ignore, right?"

I grinned at my always understanding husband as we gravitated toward the huddle that was gathering around a few tables, which were already littered with empty bottles and glasses.

A voice called from the edge of the crowd, "How d'you find this so-called murder weapon, Lennie, mate?"

Lennie Orkins – a man I'd already encountered a few times during our days in Sydney – leaned in, his weathered face and raisin eyes glowing with the promise of a tale that would be worth hearing. His colleagues shifted closer on the pastel-orange banquet seats, then a couple gallantly rose so Bud and I could sit within the circle.

Lennie scratched his face thoughtfully, then began, "It was summer, and all the local waterholes had dried up – except one, the biggest, and deepest. When the water was high, no one could ever reach the bottom. That was the dare, see? Get to the bottom and pick up a stone to prove you got there. Like I said, no one ever managed it. But with the levels so low? I reckoned I could do it. So I jumped from an outcrop that hung over the water, got all the way down, and made a grab for…anything, really. Came up with a big stick in my hand, or so I thought. Turned out to be a rifle. It proved I'd got to the bottom, see?

And, on top of that, I was a hero because I'd found a gun. Huge excitement for a bunch of young fellas, as you might imagine. I washed it off and took it home with me. Handed it to my grandad, who gave me a pat on the head for my trouble. I didn't find out it was a murder weapon until about twenty years later, when he died. Turned out he'd kept it rolled in a blanket in a tin trunk at the foot of his bed all that time. I was clearing out his place after he'd gone, and there it was. I handed it in at the local cop shop and thought that would be the end of it. Then it turns out they'd been looking for it for all that time."

He paused and drank almost half a bottle of beer in one draft, with many in his audience matching him gulp for gulp.

"Who'd the gun killed, mate?" asked someone.

"The Girl with the Opal Fingers," said Lennie ominously.

There were a few gasps of disbelief, and several knowing nods.

"You're kidding," said someone just behind me.

I turned to see who'd spoken, but my view was blocked by a young man I'd already met a few times. Neal was the "baby" of The Mob, the son of Big Stan, who owned the company they all worked for. In his mid-twenties, Neal had swagger, good looks, and a winning crooked smile, which he'd used – twice – to get in front of me at the breakfast buffet at the conference hotel.

"Bloody oath," said Lennie, sounding wounded that someone thought his claim unlikely.

Bud and I stared at each other, round-eyed and clueless.

Neal stage-whispered, "She was a kid who got shot, out in the Bush, a long time back. Before I was born. Sad story. Had this weird ability – like magic, they said. You could give her a map and she could point to exactly where you should dig to find opals. Just that, nothing else. Couldn't do it for gold, or coal, or salt…just opals. Not that they aren't worth digging for, of course. Especially the black ones. She made a lot of money for a lot of people, I heard."

"She was almost twenty when she died, son, not a kid really." Big Stan leaned his great bulk toward us, then addressed the group as a whole. "A tragedy. They never got the bloke who did it until Lennie found the rifle. Then she finally got justice."

"Yeah," agreed Lennie. "All those years my grandfather had it tucked away. Cops came to his place three or four times after I'd handed it in. Chapter and verse, they wanted. I've got a pretty good memory, but I couldn't give them exact dates or anything. Like I said, I was only ten when I found it. They reckoned the rifle must have been in that waterhole for at least a year before I pulled it up. They matched the bullets they'd...um...you know...found, and they easily worked out who it belonged to. And that was that."

A man I knew only as Dan piped up, "It was one of those stories I always told my young 'uns when they was growing up. Everyone said her father had killed her because she wouldn't do what he told her to. Not that I wanted my lot to think I'd shoot 'em if they didn't listen to me – but it gets to a point where you've got to get their attention somehow or other."

"You should know, mate, you've got enough of 'em," came a chuckling reply from somewhere behind me.

Big Stan called, "And Dan's only got himself to blame for that, right fellas?" Raucous laughter followed. He added, "But it turned out it wasn't her father who did it...the bloke she refused to work for shot her down, right?"

Our storyteller, Lennie, nodded sagely. "Yeah. It was his rifle – big, old, double-barrelled thing, it was – and me finding it again sewed it up for the cops. Thanks to my grandad, it took them far too long, but they got him in the end."

It looked to me as though Big Stan was about to comment, but a voice cut in, "Good yarn, Lennie – but I can go one better."

The man who'd called out was standing right behind where Lennie was seated; he was about twice his breadth, and squat, with a head that reminded me of a bulldog.

Lennie chuckled. "Go on then – you're up next, Shorty. Can't help yourself, can ya, mate? Got to outdo everyone, right?"

Shorty cleared his throat. "I didn't just find a murder weapon – even if it was used in one of the most infamous murders ever – nah…I saw an actual murder happen. Right in front of me."

This announcement brought a round of applause and lots of hooting; I felt my right eyebrow shoot up, which led Big Stan to observe, smiling, "All in good humor, Cait – don't go getting your knickers in a twist. Yarning's a harmless way for us to have our fun, right men?" He waved an arm. "Get on with it, Shorty, mate. Lennie's right, you can't let anyone spin a yarn without having a better one, can you? But he's good 'cause he gets to the point. Take a lesson from him."

Shorty rearranged his shoulders, looking somewhat slighted, then stuck out his broad chin and said, "It was summer in Alice Springs, just before Christmas, a few years back." The man had decided to adopt a dramatic tone, and stepped forward, waving his arms above Lennie's head.

Once he was certain he was the center of attention, Shorty continued ominously, "It was too hot to want to do anything but suck on a beer. The arvo this all happened, there was a storm on the way – you could feel it on your skin. But it wouldn't break. You know what I mean? The sort of weather only the flies enjoy. The boozer was full, someone knocked over a beer, and it all kicked off from that. Fists flew, then a knife came out, and it got serious, fast. I saw a bloke get stabbed, and I saw who did it. Wished I hadn't. Brutal. Nasty. The bloke on the floor didn't get up, and we're all backing off, but there was this kid who used to hang around the pub who had a few kangaroos loose in the top paddock, you know? The only one stupid enough to pick up the knife that had been dropped by the mongrel who'd stuck it in in the first place. So there's this bloke on the floor, dying, and the kid's just standing there – the knife in his hand – and, of course, he got grabbed. By everyone. Thought they'd tear him apart, I did. Now, as you all know, I'm not one to dob a man in, but I couldn't say nothing, could I? So I shouted that I'd seen who'd really done the stabbing, and eventually they let the kid go. He wasn't too crook, but it could have gone real bad for him. Then the boys in blue turn up, and cart off the scumbag who'd really done it. Nasty piece of work, he was. Everyone knew it. Always just on a simmer, ready to boil over. The town was glad to see the back of him. Me too, to be honest. For some reason he seemed to think we was mates, though I'd cross the street to avoid him. Of course, they drag me down the cop shop too, to swear to what I'd seen. Had to do it. Too many people had heard me speak up."

"Is that even really murder?" Neal sounded skeptical.

Shorty replied, "I think the family of the dead bloke reckoned it was. Besides, even if you call it manslaughter, or something else fancy, the bloke's still dead. Anyway, I had to stand up in court and say I'd seen who'd stuck the knife in. Ricky 'Carver' Richards. And he wasn't called 'Carver' because he whittled wood."

A few colorful comments were shouted about Shorty having to wear a suit to go to court, and then more followed about how difficult it must have been for him to find one that would fit.

"I can do even better than that."

Heads turned toward the only other twenty-something in the group; his slight figure was hovering to one side of the main huddle. I knew his name was Ditch, and I'd felt sorry for him on more than one occasion as we'd attended various functions; he'd always looked uncomfortable, and – other than Neal – no one took much notice of him, until they needed him to fetch beers…which was why I'd heard his name called out so often.

Neal said, "Go on then, Ditch, tell us. What?"

Ditch didn't raise his eyes as he spoke quietly, "I know about someone getting away with murder – because no one even knew it was one."

A young female server passing by with a fully laden tray tripped, sending a shower of bottles and glasses crashing to the floor, which tore everyone's attention away from young Ditch. She looked horrified, but got the biggest cheer of the night.

Neal moved to clear the debris and called Ditch over to help. They carefully collected shards of glass, and the crowd began to break apart.

"Fancy watching us come into the dock, Cait?" Todd, my brother-in-law, was at my side.

I couldn't imagine anything less engaging.

Todd's mousey comb-over signified his inability to admit to his incipient baldness, and the poor chap looked about ten years older than my husband, even though he was only my age – fifty – so seven years Bud's junior. It's amazing how much more youthful a full head of hair can make a man look. Of course, Todd was also rail-thin, and somewhat sallow, which didn't help matters – especially when he was standing so close to Bud whose deep tan set off his piercing blue eyes a treat, all helped by the hyacinth shirt I'd picked out for him to wear.

The sun we'd been enjoying during the past few days, as well as through the summer months at home on our little mountain in British Columbia, had silvered my husband's hair more than usual, and I acknowledged silently that the sight of Bud Anderson made my heart flutter; I found it hard to believe we'd been married for almost two years.

"We need to make a decision about what we're doing when we get back to Barangaroo, Cait," said my sister. *Again.* I stood and looked up at Siân – who's three inches taller than me – and smiled sweetly; despite the purse of her lips, she meant well. She was looking as annoyingly cool and collected as ever, with her neat, gray-blonde bob, her willowy frame hidden beneath a shift of palest lemon cotton, and her hint of make-up an acknowledgement that even a "casual" dress code required a bit of lipstick and mascara.

The forecasts I'd researched before our trip had suggested we'd need jackets during the day and maybe waterproofs too, but the unseasonable September warmth in Sydney meant I was overdressed for the weather, and the boat we were on had massive windows to allow for panoramic views; they'd been letting in the heat of the sun until it had set, so the place felt airless, and I was more than a bit clammy.

All of which meant that I felt like a gray-haired, greasy lump.

I stared at my skinny sister, wondering how she managed to make looking good appear so effortless…then forced myself to push aside my feelings of inadequacy, replying, "Tell you what, you all decide what you want to do while I powder my nose. See you in a tick or two."

Needless to say, there was a queue at the ladies', so I waited patiently, and tried my best to not listen to an alcohol-fuelled conversation taking place between two young women, part of a hen party that was also on the dinner-cruise. I failed, because I was absolutely entranced by the slang, the accents, the boldness of the descriptions of the various wicked plans they had for the bride-to-be later that night, and their inability to whisper.

They took absolutely no notice of me, of course; as my sister had noted more than once since we'd arrived, my hair has taken on a more salt-than-pepper sheen in the past couple of years, and I've found that fewer people seem to pay any attention to me these days as I go about my business in the world. As a psychologist, I find the concept of the invisibility of the older woman in society to be academically fascinating, but I haven't found a way to shoehorn its study into my chosen field of criminal psychology…yet.

"They said they'd let the stripper in through the side door at the club, so he can come to the private room where we get him all to ourselves," said one of the girls dressed in vivid lime green.

"Good. He's costing an arm and a leg…though I hope we get to see more of him than that," replied the other, also kitted out in neon sequins. "Did you text him?"

The door opened, and it was my turn to go inside, so I never heard the reply. However, the idea that at least one of the girls had a stripper's number on her phone intrigued me…though not quite as much as the three stories about murder that had been shared a little earlier. Especially Ditch's. I hoped I'd have a chance to ask him about it later on, or even at the next day's breakfast gathering, the last of the conference.

Off Out

In my time as a professor of criminal psychology at the University of Vancouver I can't say I've been to a lot of conferences, but I still feel I've been to too many. I am not a fan.

I've always noticed that the so-called "last day" of these things leaves one with an odd feeling – it's always just a bit of a whimper, as folks wander off throughout the final morning to catch planes, or trains, or jump into their automobiles. Thus, the seven o'clock breakfast gathering was a good way of bringing all the delegates and their guests into one place, allowing everyone a final hurrah – literally – then setting folks free to do…well, whatever they wanted.

Siân, Todd, Bud, and I were staying on at the hotel for one more night before decamping to a house we'd rented for a few days near a place called Katoomba, in the Blue Mountains, about seventy kilometers away.

It turned out that quite a few of the other delegates had plans that also included taking advantage of the low price offered by the hotel for the next couple of nights, allowing them a chance to see more of Sydney. They'd come from all over Australia, as well as other countries, and – for some – this would possibly be the best chance they'd ever have of enjoying the sights, since the location of the conference was usually Melbourne; a booking snafu had led to it being moved on this one occasion.

I've never been to Melbourne either, so Bud and I had planned this trip believing it would be there. At least, I'd agreed we'd join Siân and Todd for the next possible conference when I'd last seen her, at my wedding, and I only got around to telling Bud about it when Siân emailed me the dates and told me about the shift to Sydney.

To be fair, Bud had been quite happy about the entire thing, and had then thrown himself into his role as travel agent – which had only really amounted to booking our flights and finding the house to rent, because the hotel was sorted out by Todd, on our behalf.

With Todd fully involved in either attending, or giving, presentations every day, Siân, Bud, and I had done the full-on tourist thing. Our hotel overlooked Darling Harbour, which turned out to be a fantastic location – not only because of the delights of the restaurant-rich waterfront around the harbor itself, but also because of the ferry terminal at Barangaroo. Until I'd arrived, I'd had no concept of just how much use Sydney made of its waterways; it was a revelation, with affordable ferries that took us everywhere we wanted to go. Because of our hotel's location, most of our trips took us beneath the Sydney Harbour Bridge and past the opera house at least twice every day. It was…well almost unbelievable, to be honest, because it started to feel normal, as opposed to an arm-pinching experience.

The only downside, as far as I could see, was that we also had to go right past a place I'd never even known had existed before my arrival. Luna Park. From the minute I'd set eyes on it, it had terrified me in a visceral way I'm not sure I can even explain to myself. It conjured thoughts of Stephen King's Pennywise, with its massive clown's mouth through which the public entered a fairground, where I often saw motion, and lights…but, weirdly, never any actual people. It freaked me out. Completely. Bud couldn't understand why I hated it so much, and swore he'd seen human beings inside there enjoying themselves at some point. Me? It was one place I knew I'd never go, because I was convinced it was the sort of place from which one never returned.

That probably says more about me than the place itself; as a psychologist, I could – and possibly even should – dwell on that at some point, but sailing past it with the sun on my face, and my heart full of the prospect of seeing places I'd only ever heard about before this trip, I'd decided to set those thoughts aside, and return to them when I wasn't having such a wonderful holiday.

The last time Siân and I had spent any time together had been when she'd traveled to Wales when Bud and I got married. It hadn't been an easy week, and we'd both learned a great deal about each other in a pressurized situation, when we'd found ourselves trapped in a creepy castle with a killer. It was only then that I'd discovered that my sister was suffering from spinal osteoarthritis, which finally explained what I had always imagined to be her chosen lifestyle with a strict diet, lots of exercise, and a need to get things done with an inexplicable sense of urgency. I'd also discovered that – at the time – Siân hadn't been exactly happy with her life at home, though our days in Sydney together had finally convinced me that she and Todd were now seeing eye to eye about the number of business trips he took, and that she was, finally, feeling fulfilled both within, and beyond, her roles as a wife and mother.

Mattie and Beccie, my nephew and niece, were staying with two different families in their home city of Perth – each with a special schoolfriend; Siân Face Timed with them every day and felt comfortable that they were both safe, and keeping out of trouble. The other thing I'd discovered since our arrival was that she'd finally managed to wean herself off the terrifically strong painkillers she'd been prescribed that had led to her mood being less than predictable during the week of my destination wedding. It had taken a great deal of effort on her part, and she was now relying upon a blend of acupuncture, yoga, and meditative techniques to help manage her pain, though we all knew her prognosis meant she'd have no respite from it in the long run.

Our days in Sydney had been a kaleidoscope of sights I'd only ever imagined. Bondi Beach was…well, a very nice beach with a great deal of wind, and surfers, but – despite its worldwide fame – it reminded me of Porthcawl, near Swansea where Siân and I had grown up.

The historic Rocks area had been fascinating – if terribly depressing, in some ways, because of the tragic tales of some of those who'd arrived in Australia by that route. However, our tour around the opera house had been…well, a bit overwhelming; it's so much bigger than I'd imagined, and yet smaller, too – simultaneously. The amazing story of getting the thing built was a lesson in determination on the part of many, overcoming the challenges of the laws of gravity, physics, and known engineering.

And the Australian National Botanic Gardens had Bud and me amazed by how many plants they had growing there that we had at home, like forest pansy trees and rhododendrons, as well as exotic specimens with multicolored bark, or striking foliage we knew would never survive on our mountainside property in British Columbia.

The only trip Siân didn't take with us was to the zoo. In fact, our plan to go there had led to what my sister and I had called a family discussion…which Bud had later assured me was an argument. As a volunteer at the zoo in her home of Perth, Siân had some strongly negative opinions about Sydney's Taronga Zoo, which mainly focused on the way they used concrete at the place. I was desperate to see a koala, so wouldn't be swayed. When I got within feet of one, during our pre-booked, exclusive "Koala Encounter", I cried. With joy. It had been a once-in-a-lifetime experience that I'd dreamed of since I was little; I'd never had a teddy bear, but did have a stuffed koala, and I knew in my heart that the photo of me, my husband, and a koala would end up somewhere on display at home, however bad I might look in it.

However, Siân had been right; there was an awful lot of concrete at the zoo, and not nearly enough natural-style habitats for my liking. I'd left there with my already ambivalent feelings about the whole concept of zoos not assuaged, and I'm pleased to say that my sister appreciated it when I told her she'd been right about the concrete.

Now it was our last day and night in Sydney – and Todd finally had the chance to spend time with us. We'd all agreed to go to Manly; Siân had told us she'd heard about a place Todd would adore for lunch. We'd also half-planned to have a final evening meal at a restaurant we'd enjoyed already, on the way back to the hotel, but we hadn't really firmed anything up, nor booked a table, knowing that at least Todd would welcome the chance to not be tied to a timetable for the day.

And so it was that we found ourselves waiting for the next ferry to Manly from the Circular Quay, making a bit of a nuisance of ourselves by standing around one of a series of brass plaques set in the walkway, this one commemorating the English writer Nevil Shute.

Siân was reading aloud, "'It's a funny thing,' Jean said. 'You go to a new country, and you expect everything to be different, and then you find there's such a lot that stays the same.' Who's Jean? Is she in *A Town Like Alice*? I haven't read it. Is it good?"

"My new wife's from the Philippines, and she reckons it's an inspiring read." The voice was the unmistakable rumble of Big Stan, and there he was, his massive arms outstretched, a beaming smile, and surrounded by The Mob.

Despite the fact we'd all been in the same large room sharing a breakfast buffet just a few hours earlier, this felt like a coming together of old chums who'd been apart for a long time. I reasoned it felt that way because the glue that had held us together – the conference – had dissolved, and we were now all just separate human beings, making our way in the wider world…and happening upon each other.

"What are you lot up to?" He smiled and bowed, then winked. "Nothing naughty, I hope."

"Off to Manly," said Siân.

"Great – so are we. The next ferry's in ten minutes, let's all go together." And, just like that, it was settled; Big Stan had a force about him it was hard to deny – besides, I didn't really want to, because he and his employees were fine, if boisterous, company.

Todd tutted, which I suspected was because he'd been hoping to leave all connections with the mining industry behind him for the day. However, I was quietly pleased, because I knew I had an unexpected chance to try to wheedle some information out of young Ditch who was bringing up the rear, once again.

We all tapped through the barriers, using our credit cards, and entered the holding pen to wait for the ferry to dock. As we hovered, I managed to sidle toward Ditch.

"That was an interesting story you started to tell last night," I opened. "Do you really know someone who got away with murder?"

Ditch shuffled and studied his shoes, which were oddly sturdy for a man about to jump on a ferry to go to a beachside town, as was his long-sleeved jacket, and hoodie. "I shouldn't have said anything. My mum said not to. Stupid of me, really. But I'm always stupid. Can't help myself."

I felt sorry for him. "Come on now, you can't be that stupid, Ditch; I bet Big Stan wouldn't keep you on if you were incapable of doing what you're paid to do. What is it you do for S & S Roads, precisely?"

Ditch seemed surprised that I would be interested. "I'm an equipment specialist."

He spoke as though he'd given me an illuminating explanation of his responsibilities, but I was none the wiser. "Equipment specialist?"

Ditch kicked a bit of gravel. "I help work out what terrain we're facing when we're making a road." He nodded skywards. "We get satellite images, but we need a closer look. I'm the one in charge of the equipment we use to do that."

I replied, "Really important, I'd have thought. So you're clearly not stupid at all."

Ditch's eyes darted. "I was stupid to say what I said last night. Shut up now."

There was a sharpness in his voice that surprised me.

He leaned in and whispered, "This lot call themselves The Mob because there's a lot of Aboriginal blood there. All different amounts in everyone, and all from different places. The name? Use it to make a point. We're us. Special. You know... *The* Mob. Big Stan's got rights because of his blood. Some of the others have, too, even if you can't tell that when you look at them. That's why the S & S shirts are yellow, red, and black – colors of the Aboriginal flag of Australia, see? But me? I'm all white, me, not a drop of their blood in me. I'm not the only one in The Mob like that, of course, but I'm just here because Neal always stuck up for me when I was bullied at school. Even in kindie. Now he looks out for me here. I've got a job with him, and a lifestyle that suits. And Neal doesn't let anyone pick on me too much. Leave me alone. I'm happy."

He beetled off, looking anything but.

I pondered his claim from the previous night: surely if he'd seen one of his workmates getting away with murder, he'd never have mentioned it the way he had done...in front of them all? Or maybe he'd had one beer too many, and had wanted desperately – just for once – to be the centre of attention? Was that why he was saying he'd been "stupid" to say what he had?

Up Top

"Will you go on ahead, and keep a couple of places for me and Todd if you can, Cait?"

Siân wasn't able to get onto the ferries as fast as I could, and certainly wasn't able to get up to the top deck for the prime spots quickly because of her back problems – so Bud and I did as she'd suggested, only to find that Neal and Ditch had beaten us to it, and were lying across entire benches. They laughed, stood, and gallantly waved us to the best seats.

As we set off, I found myself sitting next to Lennie, who was the only one in the group with hips slim enough to fit onto the half-space available beside me. He was almost slipping off the edge of the bench, so I squished as close as I could to Bud, and we all hung on, laughing and enjoying the jollity of a day out.

The top deck was playing host to a great number of tourists, all of whom were eager to get the best possible photographic angles of the opera house, the bridge, and any number of other points of interest as we headed out into the bay at what felt like a pretty high speed. Having realized days earlier that the only way to see anything on a ferry was to tie back my hair, I'd got used to it. However, The Mob had only seen me with my hair down, during breakfast, or at the cocktail parties and dinners where we'd joined Todd and Siân, so I wasn't surprised when Lennie commented upon it.

"Your hair suits you, up like that," he said. Then he turned to Bud and asked, "Can I say that to your wife?"

Bud's reply: "I suggest you ask her, not me," was greeted with surprise by Lennie, and gratitude by me.

"Is it alright for me to say that?" Lennie sounded like a small boy who wasn't sure how to address an adult.

"I'll take it as a compliment," I replied, and he smiled.

"I never know what to say to women about anything. Don't mix with them much. Know they're different, but not sure how. Best to ask, I reckon." He grinned boyishly, then looked away.

"Fascinating story about that rifle you found," I commented. "Tell me more about that girl – the one who could locate opal deposits on a map. She sounds…unusual."

Lennie's eyes were almost completely black, encased in what looked for all the world like folded old leather, and his wild, wiry hair was streaked with just a little gray; I wondered how old he was. Forty'ish? Fifty'ish? His manner in company was often acquiescent, and I'd only really seen him come to life when he was telling a yarn.

Now? Now his eyes burned as he spoke. "She was a very special girl, they said. Older than me by more than ten years. So not a girl when she died, really, like Big Stan said last night. A young woman. But everyone spoke of her as a girl. Out of pity, I reckon. For a long time, the talk was that her father had killed her. He certainly killed himself. Couldn't live with the guilt, they said. Everyone whispered about her death, but I was just a young 'un…didn't think the old-looking rifle I found in a waterhole could be anything to do with her death. Then, when I found the gun again and handed it in, all hell broke loose. The bloke who really did it? Head of what had become a big mining firm by the time they got him for it. Fair threw the croc in with the hens that did. I…I didn't dob him in, or nothing, just handed in the rifle, see?"

I couldn't resist. "Why do you think your grandfather kept it all that time? Do you think he was hiding it?"

Lennie looked as though the thought had never occurred to him. "Probably put it in that trunk the day I brought it home and forgot about it. Reckon he used thing for storing old stuff he didn't want – it was almost rusted shut, so he probably forgot the rifle was there."

I couldn't imagine someone not looking inside a trunk at the end of their bed for twenty years, but I let it pass; after all, who was I to judge the organizational regime of a man living alone…*where?*

"And where did your grandfather live?"

Lennie stared ahead as we rounded yet another picturesque point, bouncing across the wake created by one of the many other ferries and pleasure craft zigging and zagging madly across the bay.

"Northern Territory. Bush country. No more than a shack, I suppose you'd say, by city standards. A Bush man through and through, my granddad. He couldn't even live near the town, let alone in it. Outside it by a long walk, he was. The fewer people he saw, the better he felt. He raised me. Taught me to read, write, and do my numbers. A good man. A gentle man. I was sad when he died. It…it took me bad. I was pretty crook there for a while."

The bravado with which Lennie had told his yarn the previous evening had evaporated; he peered toward the horizon as if trying to see beyond it, then blinked, and refocused on me.

He sighed. "He knew I had to go to school to be able to make anything of my life, so sent me to live with a family near the schoolroom. But, by then, it was too late for me – I couldn't stand being with people, either. So I left. Walked back to his place. Stayed. Word came that a group of young fellas was off to do a bit of digging for gold, and I joined them – for the adventure, you know? And I knew I'd found my calling right away. Finally found something that interested me. All those lessons my grandfather gave me? They took. I gobbled up everything I could read about gold. I got jobs panning for it, and digging for it. Travelled about. And now? Well, The Mob needs someone who's worked just about every type of mine there is, and I've done that – branched out a bit after the gold, you know? It gives them credibility with all sorts of clients. Gold, salt, opals, coal…you name it, I've dug it up. Though I have to admit to a bit of a soft spot for gold. First thing I ever got out of the ground. There's nothing quite like it, is there? It never changes. It's always…the same. Constant. Quite something. Did you know that a bloke once pulled a massive nugget right out of the Ovens River, in Victoria? Out for a dive, and he finds nearly twenty ounces of pure gold, worn to a shape a bit like a dinosaur. I've seen it in the museum. Beautiful. Over a pound of it. I know a pound doesn't sound like much, but when you've got a pound of gold in your pocket, you feel like you own the world…I bet."

He seemed to be lost in wonder for a moment, then snapped back to reality, adding, "I know exactly what sort of equipment needs to travel the roads we make because of my experience, so I can help them make the right kind of roads."

I could see a glimmer of concern in the dark, glinting eyes, and wondered how Lennie felt about bobbing about on the sea. I suspected he'd rather have his hands in the dirt at that very moment.

As if he'd read my mind, the man said, "Don't tell anyone I'm enjoying this ferry ride, because it would break their faith in me. They all reckon I'm going to get crook, you know? But I'm fine on water, or on land. It's being in the air I'm not happy about; I wish we could drive back from here, but that would take too long, so we'll have to get into that big lump of metal again, and I'll just have to suck down enough beers that I can take it. My grandfather never flew, ever, nor went out onto the sea. If he could see me now. He was a good man. Respected every form of life, he did. But even he was…taken. When he died? I was lost for a while, yes, but then…then I decided he'd want me to get on with living, so I did. In his memory." He chuckled ruefully.

I'd been thinking that, if Lennie had lived alone with his grandfather, then who else could have been "whispering" about the dead girl, so I asked, "And was he the one who told you about this girl? The one who was shot? Did she come from where you lived?"

Lennie shrugged. "No. Ended up in our general part of the world because she was on the run. Had family in our area. Thought she'd be safe there. Never went outside. Hid in the home. Like that for months, so they said. Then she's found dead. Out in the Bush. Shot. In the back. Twice. Terrible. The bloke who found her took her body into the local town in the back of his ute. He was her cousin. I didn't know any of this at the time, of course, because I was only a kid. I knew about it in the way a child does – everything patchy, not joined up, because it doesn't make sense."

"It must have been awful," I said, hoping he'd continue.

"Not really. I didn't know her. Like I said, she was someone people whispered about. Didn't know until much later that she'd been written about in newspapers at the time, because of what she could do. I really found out all about her at the trial, where they talked a lot about how she was known for being able to mark the locations of deposits of opals on maps. Seems a load of money went missing when she died, too. She was paid a lot for her skills, and no one ever knew what happened to it all. Another reason everyone thought it was the father."

"What was her name?"

Lennie smiled sadly. "She was called Lowanna. But that can mean 'woman' or 'girl' in some of our Aboriginal dialects, so no one was ever sure if that was how she was referred to, or if it was her name. There were no papers for her. Nothing. She just was, and then she was not. Her father refused to speak about her after her death. Then he was found dead, too. Shot himself. Guilt, everyone said, because he'd killed her. But when they arrested the man who'd really done it, then everyone wondered why the father killed himself. I reckon it was because no one ever bothered to find out who'd killed his daughter. That would be a heavy burden for a father...not that I've got any kids."

"And who did they arrest for killing Lowanna? You said he was involved in the mining business. Did you know him?"

Lennie looked surprised. "Philip Myers, the one who started up Myers Mining. Todd Anderson, your brother-in-law, used to work for him...was his right-hand man, at one time. I thought you'd know that."

I didn't.

Surf Side

When we disembarked through the fabulous art deco pier building at Manly, the entire Mob waved as they headed for a pub they'd heard about, Bud strolled ahead with Todd, and I hung about and waited for my sister, which meant I had her to myself.

"That was a bit bumpy for me," she noted as she stretched out her back. "But I'll do my best to walk through it; it's all nice and flat here at least, which helps. Todd's keen to get to that restaurant on the seafront I told him about. I'm so pleased that he and Bud are hitting it off. Two Mr. Andersons, nattering like nobody's business."

When I'd married Bud but had chosen to keep my own name, Siân had joked that it was a shame, because the coincidence of both of us marrying someone with the surname Anderson wasn't lost on either of us: true coincidences are so few and far between that it's always worth noting them.

Bud's family was Swedish – in fact, so was Bud, properly speaking; he'd been born there, then taken to Canada as an infant by his parents, both of whom were still hale and hearty, thank goodness.

Todd's family had been British, migrating from Hull in England to Perth in Australia long before his birth, and they'd been keen to put their Britishness behind them. They'd made sure he was raised as "a true Aussie", through and through. But it seemed he'd inherited his father's love for all things mining oriented, so he'd taken his engineering qualifications and had applied them to the field. This much I knew – but Siân had never been more forthcoming about Todd's work…and I realized I'd never asked. Given what I'd been told by Lennie on the ferry, I thought this stroll along Manly's broad, shop-lined main street,

The Corso, with its lovely mixture of Victorian and art deco architecture, would be a good opportunity to put that right.

"It's been interesting to see and hear so much about mining these past few days, even if only as table conversation. It's been Todd's whole career, hasn't it?"

Siân gave me a sideways glance. "Yes. Not that it's any interest of yours, I know."

I slapped a cheeky grin on my face. "You know me, Sis – not one to pry."

Siân laughed. "Not one to pry? Your whole life's all about prying – trying to work out why people do what they do. What you mean is that you're not interested in anyone else unless from the point of view of solving some puzzle about them. You've never really been one to connect, Cait. You just see, wonder, dig, solve…then you move on. It's who you are. You've never been any different. If I brought friends home, when we were growing up, you'd ask them loads of questions about themselves, then – if they seemed normal, or boring, to you – you'd grunt and leave. But if they were a bit off in some way? Oh, those were the ones you'd keep at until you'd worked out what made them tick."

I did my best to not snap back, because I knew there were a few grains of truth in what Siân had said, though I baulked at her overall characterization of me as being someone who only liked to solve puzzles, rather than getting to know people; I honestly think that's often one and the same thing.

Oblivious to the fact that I was almost literally biting my tongue, my sister continued, "It's funny…Todd having a career in mining makes sense – his father did it, and then, so did he. What took everyone aback was you deciding to work in advertising and public relations; there couldn't have been a job less well suited to your personality. I'm surprised you didn't analyze all your clients to death, and tell them what you thought of them. I suppose at least you ended up working out who murdered your ex-boss, so that was something. Now? Now I couldn't imagine you ever having a career other than the one you have – being a criminal psychologist who specializes in profiling victims. It's what you were made to do, Cait. Good on ya for getting there in the end."

I smiled as winningly as possible at my sibling's back-handed compliment, then tried to think of a way to get back to the topic of Todd's working history, when Siân did it for me.

"Todd's had some great jobs, and some terrible ones. All I can say is that the role he's got now, on the board of a mining research company, means he has to travel less, and for shorter periods, and that's the best thing of all. I want him to be around to enjoy the children, and for them to be able to have him as a part of their lives. They're getting so big now, they won't want anything to do with either of us before we know it."

I knew that Mattie had just turned seventeen and had recently sprouted significantly, which had proved useful for his great passion of playing Aussie rules football – despite my sister having done her best to get him to throw himself into rugby, instead. Beccie was a petite fifteen-year-old who excelled at gymnastics. Both were, apparently, also gifted golfers, which I found hard to reconcile with them being teenagers, because I always associate golf with poor taste in knitwear and a middle-age paunch. For me, my niece and nephew were faces on a video call screen, or photos in a card or two each year. I wondered if I'd ever get to know them as people…wondered about what it felt like to be a normal teen growing up in middle-class suburbia, in Australia – but my imagination wasn't that elastic.

"This is a new company he's with now, right?" I tried to stay on topic. "Smaller than the last one. More specialized."

Siân stopped and stared. "I would say 'good memory, Cait' but we both know that's ridiculous. You might have a memory that retains everything, but you have to have bothered to remember it in the first place, I know – so, yes, good job recalling what I put in last year's Christmas letter. What that *means* is that he's more local, more of the time; lots of online work, not as many trips away for weeks on end. It's a completely different way of life for all of us."

I thought I'd check: "And that's good, right?"

Siân nodded. "For the main part, yes, though the kids have been used to him letting them have their own way when he comes back from a trip, so that's a whole different dynamic to cope with. No wrapping Dad around their little fingers any longer, for them. Todd and I used to argue a lot about how strict I was with them – now he gets it. He sees how they test their boundaries, and how they understand exactly which of our buttons to push. He's getting used to having to dispense punishments, too. Though he seemed to think that making them stay in their rooms was something that would get them to toe the line; it took him weeks to work out that they can live their entire lives inside their rooms. Now he knows that it's no video games for Mattie, and no phone for Beccie that really gets their attention."

"And you? Good having him around more?" I thought I'd ask sisterly questions.

"Yeah. Not bad. He's surprised by how much time I'm out of the house, to be honest. Started asking if I could give up a bit of volunteering so I'd be with him more often."

"I dare say that went down like a lead balloon?"

Siân nodded. "You could say. But we're working things out. By the way – where did our husbands get to?"

I looked along the street – but couldn't see either of them, anywhere. "They must have gone along a side street, or into a shop."

I spotted Bud's head popping out of a doorway, then he beckoned for us to join him. We two wives dutifully responded, and walked into a shop that seemed to sell anything and everything to do with surfing, or the beach lifestyle. I couldn't imagine why Bud was there.

"Decided to take to the waves, Husband?" I asked brightly.

"Todd's buying a top that's got built-in sun protection," announced Bud. "He's just waiting to pay."

"Nothing here appealing to you, Bud?" Siân smiled as she surveyed the range of clothing and surfing accessories.

"Not really. Though I have been wondering if I might invest in a really good hat while I'm here. I noticed on the internet that there's a famous shop called The Hattery in Katoomba, and I thought I'd check it out. Got some special hat designer who only sells through them. They looked like they might suit me. Some are even made from kangaroo leather." He grinned, and I replied with a raised eyebrow.

That's the first I'm hearing about it, was what I thought; "It'll be fun to go hat shopping with you," was what I said.

Bud chuckled and we hung around just outside the door as Todd paid for his purchase. Gazing up and down the street, I spotted Ditch at the tail end of a straggling formation of The Mob. It looked as though they'd left one pub, and were heading for another. I waved, but all I got from him was a scowl.

Deciding I had nothing to lose, I asked Siân, "Did Todd once work for a bloke by the name of Philip Myers?"

Siân glanced furtively toward her husband, who seemed to be discussing the merits of various surfboard waxes with the young woman at the cash desk. I couldn't picture Todd on a surfboard. Not upright, anyway.

My sister hissed, "I knew you'd find out about that." She sighed heavily. "Whenever anyone mentions that poor girl who died, like that blessed Lennie did last night, they always end up getting to Philip Myers…and then someone mentions Todd, too. The mining world is so small – for all that it employs thousands of people across the country. Yes, Todd did work for him – but it was long after Myers had killed that girl. She died almost thirty-five years ago, donkey's years before Todd had even heard of Philip, let alone agreed to work for him. So don't go down that rabbit hole, Cait, I'm warning you. Todd was distraught when he found out about it all, and he never ever mentions Myers anymore, so please don't bring it up. It was bad enough that Lennie did last night; I bet they all know that Todd used to work for Myers…they were joined at the hip, and wherever Philip went, Todd went with him."

"Did you know him too?" I could see that the sales assistant was painstakingly wrapping up Todd's hoodie thing, and knew we'd soon be on our way.

"Of course – a bit." Siân seemed to shrink. "Todd was working for him when we got together, so I was introduced. Vetted, even. Philip and his late wife, Cindy, came to our wedding. You met him there yourself. Tall chap, white-blond hair. Very dashing."

Once Siân had described him, I recalled him, of course. I put my eidetic memory to good use and replayed every interaction I'd had with him on the day, which didn't amount to much. "Ah. Him. He looked…wealthy, glossy…polished."

"Yes, it always shows, doesn't it? Nothing to do with the department stores, of course, but worth a lot by then."

My sister's response confused me. "Department stores? No, sorry – don't understand."

Siân shrugged. "Aussie department stores: Myer. All over the place. He's not connected to those people. Nothing to do with them at all. But, by the time he was a guest at our wedding, he'd made a bundle for himself."

"He seemed…affable," I added.

"Weird word. What does it even really mean?" Todd commented as he rejoined us. "And who was being it?"

"Cait was talking about Big Stan," lied Siân.

"Big Stan? Affable? Maybe," said Todd, sounding skeptical. "Now, how about we head for lunch – I'm starving. I hope this place is as good as you said it would be."

We reached the sea front, and crossed the busy road to walk along the paved area that ran atop broad steps leading down to the golden sands. The wind was gusting, the surf rolling, and the glinting sea was dotted with dozens of bodies and boards. It was such a joyous sight that we stopped for a few moments, drinking it all in. The happiness was infectious: youngsters strolled past carefree and barefoot, wearing board shorts and rash shirts, or else with wetsuits rolled down, rubber arms flopping about around their legs; dogs scampered joyfully beside their humans, or were even pushed in buggies; children sat with parents and extended family members sharing food at picnic tables beneath the trees. The cries of the gulls – so many gulls! – and the roar of the surf mixed with the happy shrieks of those playing volleyball and soccer on the beach, and everywhere there were smiles…and the intoxicating smell of the sea. It was magnificent.

"Nice beach," said Todd, rather underwhelmingly. "I don't like seagulls."

Bud and I exchanged a furtive eye roll.

"Let's walk along this side until we get to the restaurant," suggested Siân, grabbing her husband's hand and setting off.

Bud and I dawdled.

"I could live here," I said quietly.

"Me too, I think," he replied. "But places can be so different on a day like this, when you're on vacation. I bet we'd get sick of the tourists. I mean, we're neither of us going to be in that sea every day, are we? You can't swim, so you couldn't even paddle – those waves would cut your legs from under you and that would be that. And I don't think I could cope with it either. I guess you've gotta be raised in that sort of sea to ever be able to be as comfortable in it as all those folks are. Look at them – like fish, the lot of 'em."

Bud was right – it was something we'd commented on so many times; the people who were in the sea seemed to be more at home in the water than on land.

"Like penguins, more than fish," I said.

Bud grinned. "Yeah, I know what you mean."

We strolled for a while, then he asked, "What were you talking to Siân about back there at the store?"

I told him about Philip Myers having been the man who'd eventually been convicted of killing the girl named Lowanna, and about Todd having worked for him.

"Another killer you've met, Cait? And not one you even knew about. Well, at least there aren't any murders for us to investigate on this trip. Let's be thankful for small mercies, eh?"

"Quite big mercies, actually," I replied. "Look, we're there. I hope this lunch is good; the prices my sister mentioned sounded a bit steep, so it had better be worth it."

Bud pointed across the road. "If we can get a table at that window so we can stare out at this while we eat, I wouldn't mind just sucking on a few ruinously expensive lettuce leaves while we did it."

But lunch was so much more than just lettuce, and after I'd devoured my luscious mussels and plump prawns, tender barramundi with a zingy orzo salad, and refreshing raspberry sorbet, I was still hungry for the view, so everyone agreed to join me in having coffee, just so that we didn't have to leave our table beside the open window.

Siân had popped to the loo, Bud and Todd were involved in an ongoing "discussion" about who would pay the bill, and I was drinking the last dregs of my coffee – and drinking in the last few moments of my eyrie view – when I noticed Ditch wandering along the beach, alone.

He wasn't hard to spot; with his heavy shoes, thick jeans, and almost wintry outerwear he stood out among the more beach-ready figures down there. He wasn't so much walking as kicking his way across the sand. He rubbed his eyes, then dragged his sleeve across his face. I suspected he was crying…yes, his movement suggested he was sobbing. Then he stopped, turned, and ran toward the sea, not breaking his stride when he hit the surf, his arms windmilling as he bounded through the waves, fully clothed.

I stared out of the window, and shouted toward the bar, "I just saw a man running into the sea fully clothed. What do we do? Who can we alert to help him?"

I didn't have a clue…I just hoped the people who worked on the seafront every day would know.

On The Beach

The day had certainly taken an unexpected turn, and not just for me; I spotted a group of girls sitting on the beach who'd obviously noticed a young man running into the waves, fully clothed. They didn't hesitate: they followed Ditch into the sea where they managed to surround and support him, and – despite the fact he'd already disappeared beneath the surface – they lifted him up and floated him back to the shore, where they dragged him away from the pounding surf.

I abandoned Bud and Todd at the bar, leaving them to pay – and wait for Siân. I dashed out, then across the road to the beach where, by the time I arrived, the group of girls had Ditch on the sand. He was spluttering, and they were explaining everything that had happened to a couple of cops who'd materialized.

I was able to tell the young officers about Ditch – to the extent that I knew his name and that he was with a group who were bar-hopping their way around Manly. I gave the younger of the two cops as many of the names of the members of The Mob as I knew, and he relayed the information into his walkie-talkie.

"We'll phone a few places, see if they're there," he said, which seemed eminently sensible to me.

"Will he have to go to hospital?" I thought this an equally sensible question.

The cop looked puzzled. "We'll get someone to check on him here."

I leaned in. "But I think he was trying to kill himself. Don't you have some sort of duty to try to stop him trying again?"

"I wasn't trying to kill myself. I don't want to die." Ditch was on his feet, looking pink and healthy – if completely soaked and covered with sand.

"Well you nearly drowned, whether you wanted to or not," snapped the tallest of the group of girls who'd rescued him. "I'm a trained lifeguard – not on duty, of course, but I know what I'm talking about. You're lucky to be alive."

"I'm sorry," said Ditch timidly. He began to cry. "I'd maybe had one too many, and wanted a swim, but I didn't have my bathers, so I just went in as I was."

Not what I saw, was what I thought; "You can't have imagined it was a good idea to go into the sea the way you were dressed. Even if you didn't have a swimsuit, you could have taken off your boots," was what I said.

"I…I didn't think. Sometimes I don't. All my mates say I have my moments. I just had a moment." Ditch smiled weakly, just as Bud, Todd, and Siân joined us on the sand.

"Everything okay here? What's the situation?" Bud still isn't used to not being in control when there's an emergency, and his career in law enforcement, including heading up Vancouver's integrated murder squad – when he contracted me in as a profiler of victims of crime – as well as his role in a command post with an international gang-busting task force, means he automatically switches into a specific gear when faced with such circumstances. His posture changes, the tone of his voice and even his choice of vocabulary shift, and he develops a distinct aura of authority…none of which was lost on the two young police officers, both of whom became immediately, and weirdly, deferential. It was as though Bud had hypnotized them.

"G'day, sir. All under control, now, thank you. This young gentleman decided to go for a swim. Very poor decision, as it turned out. Fortunately, these young ladies came to his rescue. We'll have him checked out, then make sure he's got the support of friends we believe are in the area."

Bud nodded at the girls. "Good job."

They all smiled politely, and I felt oddly comforted to see that they, too, appeared to automatically trust my husband.

The arrival of an ambulance and The Mob happened almost simultaneously, leading to far too many people clustering around Ditch all at once. They were either trying to find out what had happened, or wanting to check to see that he hadn't been injured. The girls were hailed as heroes, and Big Stan forced them to accept a healthy wedge of cash in thanks for saving Ditch's life. They only accepted once the officers – and Bud – gave them the nod, and they agreed it would be spent on a dinner they could share as a group.

Standing aside, I managed to say to Big Stan, "I saw Ditch run into the sea. He wasn't going for a swim. You need to make sure he gets some professional help."

The man's reaction shouldn't have surprised me; he poo-pooed the idea that Ditch had any intent other than taking a drunken dip, and promised he'd make sure he got sobered up. The medicine he prescribed – loudly – was a pot of coffee at the pub The Mob had just left.

I wasn't happy about the situation, and pressed myself upon the more senior of the two officers – or, at least, upon the older of the two – and reiterated my observations from the restaurant. He handed me a couple of cards for a suicide prevention and support helpline.

"I've given the young man one, and I'll give you a couple too. Do you know him well enough to encourage him to phone the number?"

I had to admit that all I could promise was to do my best.

"Follow my lead?" I whispered to Bud as I approached Ditch. I said loudly, "We're taking the next ferry back to Sydney. We wondered if you'd like to come with us, Ditch. We could pick up a couple of things on the main street for you to change into. We'll see he gets back to the hotel safely, folks, you can all stay here and keep the pub crawl going, if you like."

"Absolutely," agreed Bud, scooping up Ditch by the arm. "I saw a pair of board shorts in a store nearby that have your name on them, and I bet you could do with some flip flops – sorry, *thongs* – too, couldn't you? See you guys back at the hotel later tonight, eh?"

A ripple of shrugging ran around The Mob, with all eyes turning toward Big Stan. "Great idea," he said, slapping Ditch on the back as Bud led him away. "You get some shut-eye, young 'un, and we'll see you in the morning."

Neal had hovered on the edge of the group as everyone had peppered Ditch with questions, now he scuttled toward Ditch and Bud as they headed for the steps to the road. "You take care, Ditch. Don't go doing anything daft, mate. I'll rock up to your room when we get back."

Ditch nodded, but didn't stop moving away from the crowd. "See you at brekkie, if not," he said quietly.

The three of us caught up with Bud and Ditch at the surf-gear shop, but we waited outside as the pair went in alone. Ten minutes later, a freshly attired Ditch emerged, carrying a couple of already-wet paper bags containing his soaked clothes, no plastic carrier bags being available.

As Bud passed me, he said, "Tipsy, not drunk. I'll stick with him. He's not saying anything about anything. I'll follow a listening brief, will speak up about professional help if I get the chance. Leave us to our own devices for now, okay?"

I nodded, and allowed the two men their privacy, while I followed on with Siân and Todd, to whom I explained the entire situation.

"But why on earth would he want to drown himself?" My sister's question was one that had been bothering me since I'd seen Ditch sobbing, then running toward the sea.

"I don't know him well, but he seems a few cents short of a dollar, if you ask me," replied Todd.

Siân tutted. "Oh, come on, Todd – you know suicide is a national problem, especially among certain groups – it's been all over the news, recently. Young men taking their lives in record numbers. Look at where we live. Think about what he does. Months on end out in the Bush with just The Mob for company. It's enough to challenge anyone's good mental health. I know I was a surgical nurse, but I was a nurse nonetheless – and nurses get to know all sorts of things when they work the wards, and we do like to share stories. Poor mental health's behind a good many problems that can end up putting someone in a hospital bed. That boy? I bet he's picked on all the time. Probably as miserable as sin, poor thing."

Todd paused and snapped, "He's not married to Big Stan…he could always get another job, you know. A lot of us have had to make changes in our lives, or have had changes forced on us. You know that. If he's unhappy, he should do something about it."

Leaping to my sister's defence I said, "I think what Siân means is that he might not have many choices. He's very close to Neal, and I think he believes Neal keeps him safe – he told me he did in school, and maybe he just can't imagine life without him."

Todd glared at me. "Sometimes there's someone you think you can't live without who gets ripped away from you, and you've got no choice but to just keep going. That boy needs to take a good look at his life. He's got it made, being in with the son of the bloke who owns the company. Probably got work for life, that one."

He stomped off.

I turned to Siân seeking insight with a shrug.

"His mother died a few years back – I think he's still coming to terms with it," she said – unconvincingly, I thought. In fact, I couldn't help but wonder just how close my brother-in-law, Todd and the convicted killer, Philp Myers, had once been.

Over And Out

Bud and Ditch sat downstairs, inside, on the ferry ride back to Sydney, while Siân, Todd, and I, once again, enjoyed the warm weather and glorious sights from the top deck. I realized as we did it that this would be the last time I'd sail into Sydney, because the next day we were travelling to Katoomba. It had been agreed that Siân would be the nominated driver for the car we'd rented, and that she and Todd would make their way by road – transporting all the luggage – while Bud and I would take the train: we knew we could do with some time alone, as well as giving Siân and Todd the same opportunity.

I took my last chance to admire the famed opera house as we approached it; with the sun glinting off the bizarre roof, the beauty of the shapes, the shadows, and the textures of the place, I couldn't understand why folks hated it…I'd fallen head over heels in love. I wondered if I'd ever get the chance to see it again, but was grateful I'd seen it at all. As we docked and prepared to disembark, I could see Bud leading Ditch toward the exit, then Ditch broke away from him, and mingled with the throng, his sun-kissed, tousled brown hair disappearing into a sea of similar heads.

We caught up with Bud, who was none too pleased about Ditch heading off alone, then we all made our way to board the next ferry to Barangaroo. Bud and I hugged at the railing overlooking the opera house to our right and a massive cruise ship docked to our left; a piece on the local TV news the previous evening had talked about how lucrative the local business owners were hoping the coming cruise-ship season would be for them all.

"We could do that again one day," said Bud quietly. "Cruising can be relaxing."

"Only if we could be certain there'd be no dead body, unlike our blessed honeymoon cruise," I replied.

"There might not be. We're having a wonderful time here and not a corpse in sight – hurrah for us."

"If you forget the girl who pointed out opal deposits on maps…the one who was shot in the back by Todd's ex-boss, that is," I replied.

Bud nodded and rolled his eyes. "I'd let that one stay where it lies, Cait – in the past."

"Then there's the murder witnessed by Shorty," I added.

"And someone's been convicted for that one too."

"Or what about the person who got away with murder, that Ditch knows about?"

"I think he made it all up – just seeking a bit of attention," said Bud dismissively.

"What if he didn't? Did he tell you why he ran into the sea like that?"

Bud squeezed me, then said, "Cait, sometimes people are suffering in ways we can't imagine. That Ditch? He's not a happy camper. Got something weighing him down, that's for sure. I urged him to talk to someone – even if it was only on the helpline number I know the cops gave him. But he was sticking out his chin and saying it was all just a stupid idea. He wasn't going to let me in at all. He was polite – thanked me for the new 'clobber', but made it clear he wanted to get back to the hotel as soon as he could. And, no, before you ask – he didn't as much as mention the identity of the person who 'got away with murder', so let it go. Okay? Let's just have a nice time with Todd and Siân. Please?"

Todd made us both jump when he spoke loudly behind us. "We thought an early dinner at that restaurant on King's Street Wharf, along from where we get off the ferry, then back to the hotel to pack."

"Fine by me," I said, my heart sinking at the thought of packing. "They've been really good to us at that place while we've been here. That eggs Benedict dish with braised lamb we had for breakfast on our first morning was amazing. I might have to get the recipe," I said.

"I might try the churrasco tonight," said Bud, rather cavalierly, "I cannot imagine there's such a thing as too much barbecued meat on sticks." He grinned impishly.

"Meat on a stick it is then," I replied, "though it has to be said that those sticks are massive metal skewers, and the mountain of meat those blokes were tucking into as we walked back from that incredibly fancy dinner up in the Crown Tower the other night looked…well, as though it would take a lot of scaling."

As we embarked on what was likely to be our last trip under the Harbour Bridge – and past the chilling Luna Park – Bud whispered, "It only looked like a lot of meat because you were already full."

I nudged him in the ribs – playfully, of course – as I replied, "They haven't yet invented the Michelin-starred tasting menu that can fill me up, Husband, so, no, I wasn't full by any means. We might have enjoyed seven courses that evening but, come on – be honest – how can you call a mouthful of fish with a foam of wild mushrooms a 'course'? Nope, not filling, just rich, and leaving me in need of Tums. So tonight? Plain and simple…meat on a stick, and loads of it, please."

We arrived at the restaurant in time to see the dinner cruise boats being boarded, then setting sail. It was fascinating to watch literally thousands of people milling about, many gaggles and groups pretty much matching those who'd been on our boat the previous night, all meeting, greeting, then forming orderly queues to walk up the gangplanks. I was impressed by how well-dressed so many of the young men and women were: even the men wearing mini-skirted sailor suits, which marked them out as the groom within a stag group, wore them smartly.

When I grabbed Bud's hand, he squeezed back…though he couldn't have possibly guessed why I was doing it. Then he said, "So lucky, Cait, aren't we?" Proving me wrong. Again.

We enjoyed cocktails made with a wonderful Australian gin and grazed on some olives and nuts; the air became cooler as the sun descended, and Siân pulled a wrap from her little backpack, putting my organizational skills to shame.

What I hadn't realized, until I'd studied the menu, was that the churrasco offering was limitless…which sounded like a great idea until the reality kicked in. It turns out there really is such a thing as too much barbecued meat on a stick – and it only took us about an hour to discover that…well, it took about twenty minutes in Siân's case, when she put in a special order for a green salad, claiming we would all regret not having done the same as her the following morning.

Eventually, our eating rate began to slow, and we were discussing the question of where all the seagulls – of which there'd been many, prior to sunset – went to sleep after dark…with some enjoyable and bizarre suggestions. Then an unmistakable sound drifted along the wharf.

"It's The Mob, isn't it?" Siân sounded less than enthusiastic.

Todd stood and said, "Maybe not. Just off to powder my nose," and disappeared into the restaurant proper.

We were seated at an outdoor area between the restaurant and the waterfront, surrounded by planters with a vine-covered gazebo above our heads, so we were easy prey as The Mob passed by. To say they had been drinking would have been pointless – because you'd have needed to be deaf and blind to not know it. Indeed, they were so raucous that the manager adopted a protective stance at the entrance to our enclosure to ensure they didn't come in. Luckily, frantic waving, and a few choice comments, was all we got, and we smiled and waved back in return.

Neal held back as the group meandered in the direction of our hotel. Peering through the foliage in the planters like some comedic spy, he exaggeratedly beckoned to Bud and stage-whispered, "Did you get Ditch back in one piece, Buddy Boy?"

Bud was truthful. "He gave me the slip at Circular Quay — but said he was headed to the hotel."

"Good on ya, Buddy Boy. He'll be right. He was after the last time he tried it. I'll get Dad to talk to him again," slurred Neal, then he extricated himself from the greenery and lurched off, whistling something that might have been a tune.

The manager seemed surprised that we knew such a rowdy bunch. "They have been drinking, I think," he said, displaying an admirable talent for understatement.

Todd returned to our table with a crisp, "Was it them?"

Siân nodded.

"Drunk?"

"As Lords," replied my sister.

Todd settled himself. "That must have taken some doing; I've spent a lot of time with miners all over this country, and you'll have to trust me when I tell you they know how to drink. But this lot? Never seen anything like it. And what's really amazing is how much they can tuck away without it even looking as though they've had any. Quite something. It's a real problem, alcoholism — a scourge."

He finished his glass of wine and refilled it. The irony was not lost on anyone at the table, except, maybe, for Todd himself.

As if she knew what I was thinking, Siân said, "It makes a nice change for Todd to not be driving, doesn't it, love? And a few glasses of wine never hurt anyone, did they?"

Given what I'd seen him guzzle down at lunchtime, and now at dinner, I would have said he'd had a few of bottles of wine, rather than a few glasses, but I knew better than to throw stones; Bud and I had commented on how our own drinking had certainly taken an upswing in the warm weather, with so many excellent beers and local wines to try out. Siân, on the other hand, had given up all alcohol – for the sake of her back – so I was pretty sure her perspective had shifted.

"Big Stan's liver must be shredded by now," said Todd, almost with an air of satisfaction, I thought. "He's always been the same, I've heard – drinking like a fish, even when he's out doing a job, which cannot be safe with all that heavy equipment about. But who's going to know? Out there in the Bush, they're on their own. Anything could happen and no one would be any the wiser."

"I wonder if that's where Ditch saw someone get away with murder." It was out of my mouth before I had a chance to stop it.

Bud sighed, Todd looked puzzled, and Siân pushed away her plate. "I knew you'd pick up on that, Cait," she said crossly. "You just cannot help yourself, can you?"

Bud's expression suggested he was thinking the exact same thing. Todd still looked confused. "What are you talking about, Cait? Ditch saw who…do what?"

I pictured the way the yarns had developed the night before, and realized that Todd had probably been out of earshot when Ditch had spoken; he'd made himself scarce after Lennie's talk about finding the rifle that had killed the girl Lowanna, which – now that I knew more – made sense.

"Last evening, Ditch said that he knew of someone who'd got away with murder, because no one knew a murder had been committed," I explained.

"Young Ditch?" Todd sounded surprised.

I nodded.

"Sounds like the kid's a few stumps short of a cricket match, if you ask me," commented Todd. "Unless he knows something no one else does about what happened to Bruce Walker about a year back. But my money's on that having been down to someone having a few too many pops, even if it was the night before. Tragic. Massive piece of equipment flattened him – and I mean that literally. No one knew how it could have happened…it shouldn't have."

Bud leaned in. "Are you saying that a member of The Mob died in a work-related accident last year?"

Todd nodded, and his naturally glum expression matched the topic, for once. "You never get used to it, you know…the loss of life because of work…because of mining, and all the ancillary jobs related to it. Mining is one of the most dangerous undertakings in the world. Always has been. Deaths still happen, even though there are safety protocols, training, so-called fail safes, even. Yes, accidents will happen – though most of them are down to human error. Which is what they said must have been the case for Bruce Walker. Human error: didn't engage the brakes properly. The machinery involved is so massive it doesn't have to move far to kill you, as he found out."

Siân sounded horrified. "Did someone run him over – by mistake?"

Todd shook his head. "Not exactly. He was alone, at the head of the road they were making, and his own machine ran him over. He was the one who didn't engage the brake properly, and he paid the price. They found him the next day when the rest of the crew caught up to him. Said they thought he'd decided to have a night in the Bush."

Siân asked gently, "Did you know him?"

Todd nodded. "I met him first…oh, about twenty, twenty-five years ago."

Siân touched her husband's hand tenderly. "I'm sorry, love. You…you never mentioned it at the time. Was there a funeral? I don't remember you going to one."

Todd appeared to pull himself back from some reverie. "I know how you get when there's a death – you worry about me enough as it is. I'm desk-bound these days, not in the mines themselves, anymore, and I didn't think it worth causing you more stress. I sent flowers. The services were up in Port Hedland."

"Did you know this Bruce from when you were working with Philip Myers?" I had to ask.

Todd nodded. "Like I said, I met him a while back. Didn't ever work with him, but folks spoke of him. Knew him by reputation, more than anything. He was a good man, by all accounts. Never said no to any job, however menial or even overwhelming it might appear. Saw the value in every task associated with the business. Philip trusted him like a brother – gave him a good start, put him on some big projects, then Bruce set up on his own – helped by Philip. Did alright for himself, as far as I knew."

I wondered how someone who'd worked in important roles, and had his own business at one time, had ended up driving a piece of roadbuilding equipment for Big Stan, but didn't have a chance to ask, because our wonderful host for the evening – who'd picked up on the fact this would be our last meal at his establishment – had decided to treat us to the most incredible passion fruit mousse I had ever tasted. He called it *mousse de maracuja*; the texture and flavor were exquisite and, despite the fact I'd been holding my tummy and claiming I might never eat again just half an hour earlier, I managed to squeeze it in, somehow.

By the time we got back to our hotel, the idea of packing was a non-starter, so Bud and I agreed to set a horrifically early alarm on each of our phones – just to make sure we actually got up – and pack in the morning.

Of course, me being me, I couldn't help but mutter, "It's interesting that Lennie found the gun that got Philip Myers convicted – albeit twenty years after the murder he'd committed – and that one of his colleagues, who also used to work for Myers, recently died tragically…while another of his colleagues claims to know about someone getting away with murder. Don't you think?"

Bud was facing away from me, but I could still tell he was gritting his teeth when he replied, "No, I do not, Cait. Good night. Please go to sleep – we've only got six hours before the alarms go off."

All Aboard

Having spent a fair amount of time cursing my seemingly tiny suitcase, and the huge amount of stuff I needed to pack into it, Bud and I were nonetheless able to join Siân and Todd at reception to hand off the luggage by nine o'clock after all, then we headed toward the railway station.

We enjoyed the walk, even though a lot of it was uphill to begin with, and it was fun to be able to amble through the magnificent old Strand Arcade as we killed time until our train was due. I'm not one for shopping, and nor is Bud, but this was something we'd both agreed to not miss: we enjoyed the original Victorian tiled floors, and marvelled at the glass roof arcing three floors above us, the wonderfully ornate iron balustrades, and delightful shop frontages – all offering boutique-style, posh stuff, in the main, so not posing any threat to either of us in terms of adding to our already bulging bags.

We left, then indulged in treats: one of my most pleasant surprises upon our arrival in Sydney had been the discovery that coffee shops didn't just offer sweet pastries, but also sold meat pies, and that it wasn't seen as at all weird to have one for breakfast. Even better? They were the British style of pie, hot, with meat and a bit of gravy, perfectly portioned for one, and with a taste and texture that took me back to my university days, when I'd been lucky enough to live just around the corner from a chip shop in Cardiff that sold the best pies. Ever. These were almost as good. I'd tried the local habit of squirting tomato ketchup into the hole on top, but it wasn't to my taste, so I chomped away on an unadulterated pie, and sipped a double espresso.

Finally ready for the off, we orienteered our way around the railway station – which wasn't easy – then got our tickets, and eventually found the right platform. We boarded our train with just two minutes to spare, then clambered up the stairs to the top deck where we managed to find a bench that was empty, and tipped the back support to allow us to face the direction of travel.

I always find railway trips to be instructive because you're not seeing the parts of a place that face the public, but the backs of everything: the rundown, graffitied, weedy parts – the bits the town or city council would rather keep hidden – and I adore it. You also get to peep into the windows without curtains that those who live backing onto the tracks always seem to believe will not be peered into by the folks on passing trains – or else they just don't care that they are being seen; and the joy that brings me is almost immeasurable.

Bud reckons it's all because I'm naturally nosey; I tell him it's because I'm a psychologist, so humanity in all its glory is what interests me. We usually agree to differ, then move on. On this occasion, I commented upon gingerbread Victorian railway stations and compared them with those I knew from Wales or England, and Bud enthused about them himself. Indeed, one of the reasons Bud had wanted to take the train was just so he could see all the little towns with what he called strange names as we travelled.

"Parramatta, Emu Plains, Warrimoo, Bullaburra – don't they sound great? So exotic." Bud's eyes were alive with anticipation.

I chuckled. "There's also Strathfield, Penrith, and Woodford," I replied, "which all sound quite British." Which they did.

We enjoyed the little stations we stopped at, or sometimes passed by, with their small brick buildings, and well-tended gardens in many cases. The views from the train were also extraordinary, the landscape undulated gently, or looked bleakly craggy, by turn – always familiar, yet a little strange. We both snapped away with our phones; the plan was to return to Sydney by road with Todd and Siân, so we couldn't be sure if we'd get the same views on the way back. Besides, the railway had a prime location on high ground, and we had the additional advantage of being on the top deck.

As we stared, and snapped, I said, "I've been thinking, Husband."

Bud chuckled. "As you are wont to do, Wife. And what's your massive brain been contemplating, eh?"

I smiled sweetly. "Death, to be honest. If Ditch saw a murder, and has tried on more than one occasion to commit suicide, don't you think there might be a connection?"

Bud sighed. "What makes you think that Ditch has tried to kill himself before yesterday?"

I was surprised. "Didn't you hear what Neal said last night? When he was peering through the shrubbery he mentioned 'last time'. I took that to mean there'd been an earlier attempt by Ditch. And to say that's 'not good' is a terrible understatement."

Bud raked his hand through his hair – always a sign he's a bit stressed, or focussed. "Look, Cait, I did my best with Ditch yesterday, but he wasn't going to open up to me; I'm a complete stranger, after all. But I did impress upon him how it might help to talk to a professional, and he sounded pretty good when I talked to him this morning."

Another surprise. "You spoke to him this morning? When?"

"I phoned his room, when you were in the bathroom. I know it's not really our business, and he's certainly not our responsibility. However, I just thought I should follow up a bit. He sounded…contrite, and even a little cheerful. Said he was off to meet Neal, for breakfast."

I considered Bud's words – unhappily – then we exchanged a look that told me we were both thinking the same thing: two suicide attempts meant the possibility of a third. We both sat in silence for the rest of the journey, and, while I couldn't be sure about what Bud was thinking, I certainly dwelled upon the hope that Ditch would seek out some help.

Finally alighting at Katoomba Station, we both snapped each other sitting on a bench below a sign that informed us that we were now 3,336 feet above sea level – as probably every other visitor to Katoomba who arrived on the train did.

"Not as high as our Coquihalla Pass, on the way to Kelowna," observed Bud.

"And about four hundred feet less than the top of Snowden in Wales," I replied.

But high enough to be going on with, we both agreed.

I was glad to have my jacket as we made our way up the steps to find ourselves a taxi, because the warmth of the morning in Sydney had become a cool afternoon in the Blue Mountains.

We gave our taxi driver the address of the house we were renting, and he knew exactly where we were headed – out of town a bit, he informed us, but within about a twenty-minute walk to restaurants.

"Any places you'd recommend?" Bud was grinning from ear to ear as he chatted, his eyes darting as we drove along the main street of the town, which had a mixture of Victorian arcades and some snazzy art deco frontages, all mixed in with more modern blocks of low-rise offices, where coffee shops – with pies! – rubbed shoulders with bookstores and antique shops. We even spotted The Hattery, which Bud had mentioned; it was a beautiful place with attractive Victorian windows, filled with an amazing variety of hats.

"What sort of places do you like?" The taxi driver asked, quite sensibly, I thought.

"Not too stuffy, not too rough, but authentic." Bud was starting to sound as though he'd never traveled before.

"Nice spot just along here, on the right – the one with the green awning. *Winnie's Place*. They'll see you right for a good piece of meat – with some veggies to act as cover, if you need them. Heavy on the meat. And the beer's good, too."

"Excellent," Bud replied enthusiastically. "Sounds just like us, right?"

I nodded, knowing in my heart – and arteries – that my sister had done the right thing the previous night when she'd bailed on the meat fest and stuffed a few greens inside her instead. Not that I had the slightest intention of ever admitting that, of course.

When our driver said, "I wonder if you'd mind a quick detour?" I was surprised. He added, "I need to use the...you know...and there's a public one for the tourists at the lookout point for the Three Sisters – and taxi parking. You two could take a quick squint at the view while I...you know."

Bud and I agreed, and happily hopped out when we reached our destination, which was a large circular area, a bit like a roundabout. It was busy, with dozens of tourists huddled in jackets standing along the rail, which we approached. The view was magnificent: the famous outcrops of rocks – The Three Sisters – were bathed in pale sunlight, and a haze hung in the air. The vista was staggering – as far as the eye could see there were undulating layers of gradually bluer, tree-covered mountains, fading into the distance. Of course we posed, took photos of each other, then selfies, and swapped photographic duties with a Japanese couple who, like us, were struggling to get themselves and the best view into their shot.

We made our way back when we spotted our taxi driver waving furiously – a man with a cap and epaulettes was trying to move him along, so we jumped in, and thanked him for our unexpected sightseeing opportunity.

A few moments later, after a couple of turns along residential streets, he announced, "We're here, not that you'd know it from the street. She's back a good way, she is. And with a better view because of it, so the rumors go. Have a great time. And tell Winnie that I sent you – she might shout me a beer the next time I drop in. I'll take it slow along the drive...you never know what might jump out of the Bush at ya."

"Is any of the wildlife around these parts deadly?" Bud sounded concerned.

"Only the ones that can bite or sting you. So always look where you're putting your feet, or your bum – that's a piece of advice my mum gave me, so I'll pass that one on."

The large SUV we'd rented was already parked in the car port; the drive and the train journey took about the same time, and we'd taken a couple of hours for ourselves in Sydney before we'd set off. The idea had always been for Siân and Todd to buy some essential groceries before they arrived, and then get things set up while we were on the train. The plan appeared to have worked, though I could see that my suitcase was still in the back of the vehicle – which, given its weight, I thought was fair enough. I understood the decision better when I realized the only way into the house was via a daunting wooden staircase which led up beside the car port to a deck that appeared to wrap around the entire building.

After a few calls by us of "Cooee" – which Todd and Siân habitually used to hail each other – Todd ambled around the left-hand corner of the deck, smiling.

"Come this way," he beckoned, "everything's around the back."

When we got there, we could see he wasn't wrong: massive sliding doors led into the open plan kitchen, dining, and lounge area of the house, that much was true, but beyond the deck was the most incredible view out across the Jamison Valley, with its blue-green foliage, and the undulating layers of the mountains in the distance.

"It's so much better than the photos online," said Bud, sounding awestruck.

"You picked a good 'un," said Todd, smiling and patting Bud on the shoulder. "Good on ya, mate."

Siân bustled out of the kitchen. "Cait, it's brilliant. It's got all the mods and cons, everything we need, loads of bench space for food prep, and they left some soft drinks in the fridge. Oh – and the bathrooms are lovely. And both our rooms have big beds, huge robes, and this view. Isn't it fantastic?"

We all agreed how fortunate we were going to be for the next few days. Bud and Todd agreed to work together to get my bag up to our room, then – finally – I was able to flop onto the bed and gaze out at the wonders of nature. Through the window I'd opened – protected by a bug screen – I could hear exotic bird calls, and nothing else. It was wonderful.

"You can't be tired – all you've done is sit about today," said Bud as he wiped his brow. "That suitcase is never getting onto our airplane the way it is, so you're going to have to either get an extra bag, or get rid of whatever it is you've got in there that weighs a ton," he remarked. "And for all that it's cloudy and cool out there, it's humid. I need a drink. Fancy a beer? Todd picked some up with the groceries. They're good and cold, he said."

I couldn't for the life of me work out how my bag had become heavier; I'd hardly bought anything, and what I had couldn't have weighed more than a couple of pounds. But I knew Bud was right. "I'll sort it, and, yes, I fancy a beer too. Come on, let's go."

I poked my head into a couple more bedrooms we weren't using; we'd all agreed this looked like a great house, so we'd also agreed we didn't mind paying extra for something bigger than we really needed. The place could sleep eight, or ten if the pull-out bed in the sitting room was in use, and there was even another apartment below us that could sleep six, but it wasn't being rented for the few days we'd be staying, thank goodness.

Bud popped into our ensuite bathroom as I wandered off toward the kitchen. The house rambled a bit, and there was the odd step up, then down. It was nicely appointed with modern "casual rustic" furnishings, and bedecked with what I thought were completely unnecessary, though attractive, dress curtains at all the windows. *Why dies the place need curtains? It isn't overlooked at all.*

The wooden structure of the building was visible on the inside, and there were even ceiling fans in the hallways, as well as every room I'd seen. Pieces of art hung on most of the walls; the prints were well framed and represented the work of Australian artists, many of whom had used Aboriginal iconography, I noted. I looked forward to having a bit of time to study them during our visit – there's so much to learn about Australian art. I'd found the Wi-Fi password in our bedroom, and had taken a moment to set up the internet connection to my phone, so I was able to check the name of the artist Charlene Carrington, prints of whose work were displayed along one wall of the main hallway. I was pleased there were such lovely pieces for us to enjoy, with their undulating ochre and brown tones, and delicate tracery of dotted lines; I bookmarked the site so I could take some time, later, to fully understand the meaning of the pieces, but – for now – I knew I wanted to get properly settled into the house.

However, rather than beetle into the kitchen, I paused – because it sounded as though Siân and Todd were having at least a heated conversation, if not an actual row. I didn't want to walk into a situation where they'd either have to shut up and seethe silently, or where I'd be required to take sides.

"I can't undo my past," Todd was saying…quietly, but angrily. "Of course it's always going to haunt me, but if I can't convince you I have no idea what's going on, then who can I convince? Not the boys in blue, that's for certain. So, no, I will not be speaking to them about any of it any time soon. I don't know how I'm going to get through this. But I will."

I felt my tummy clench with anger as he spoke: so spending time with Bud and me was something he felt he had to "get through"? Lovely.

I stomped into the room, ready to explode, only to discover that Todd was alone, and on the phone; he hadn't been talking to Siân at all. He glared at me and disconnected.

"Sorry, a work thing." He smiled weakly. "Now, how about a couple of cold ones?"

I couldn't help but wonder who he'd been talking to. And about what.

On The Town

We sank into comfy lounge chairs on the deck with some refreshing drinks, and chatted with delight and wonder about our surroundings. Bud and I enthused about our train journey, and I could tell we were all settling in nicely. I was enjoying spending time with Siân gabbing about this and that; we'd really not done enough of it over the years. Rather than any of us having to think about preparing a meal – and we all agreed we'd prefer to eat sooner, rather than later – Siân and Todd accepted our suggestion that we try the taxi driver's recommendation.

It was a short car ride, but finding somewhere to park when we got to Winnie's Place proved challenging. It wasn't until we'd taken five minutes driving around that we spotted there was parking available behind the building, so that's where we ended up, then entered via a rather grotty back door. We shuffled along a narrow corridor that took us past the toilets, and I was beginning to wonder about the wisdom of having taken a taxi driver's word about a restaurant recommendation, then we entered the building proper, and it was as though we'd been transported to a different time. Yes, the place was casual – it was mainly a bar with tables to one side, as opposed to being a restaurant with a small bar – but the décor was entrancing.

The Victorian theme Bud and I had enjoyed in Sydney, and on our railway journey, was continued in spades: heavily embossed wallpaper painted in glossy teals and greens made for a cozy atmosphere; the tiled floor looked original and was intricately laid; a brass footrail along the entre length of the impressive oak bar was being used by several men perched on stools, dangling their legs; bentwood chairs set around wooden tables beckoned invitingly beside what looked to be antique wall sconces which glowed with something more reminiscent of gaslight rather than modern LEDs. It was a delight.

Bud and I exchanged a smile – of relief – and Siân gave me two thumbs up. We settled at a table, with Todd convincing us that we'd be served there, and we waited.

After five minutes, Bud and Todd went to the bar themselves, came back with four menus and we all made our choices. As our cabbie had promised, there were any number of meats on offer, including kangaroo, all of which would, the menu promised, be perfectly grilled to order. However, after the excesses of my meal the night before, I ordered a salad with duck, which I thought might mean only a small amount of meat. After a lengthy discussion within which "Skippy" was mentioned several times, Bud and Todd decided on kangaroo steaks, and Siân plumped for something with tofu, which didn't appeal to any of us.

Beers, and a fizzy water for Siân, all duly arrived courtesy of Bud, and we raised our glasses and began to plan the next day's outings. Lots of time was spent discussing whether I could be persuaded to take the world's steepest railway and then a cable car in order to see some of the best sights around at Scenic World, but I held fast, knowing I wouldn't be able to cope with the vertigo.

A young man brought our food, with all four plates on one very large tray, which he popped onto the empty table beside us. As he placed our meals in front of us, I couldn't help but notice that he worked out – quite a lot, by the looks of it – and that he not only smelled wonderful, but was extremely clean-cut, too.

As he moved to place my plate in front of me his hip started to beep, with a tone that sounded…urgent. He was clearly startled – so much so that he abandoned my plate just a second too soon, and my duck ended up on the table itself. But he didn't notice; he was ripping off his apron, and running toward the bar – then he disappeared, using the corridor to the back door.

We all stared at each other, confused about what had just happened. A redhead in her sixties bustled toward us, her slacks almost creating sparks as she marched across the room at speed.

"Sorry about that. I'll bring you another." She scooped up my plate, and my duck, and said, "G'day, all. I'm Winnie. This is my place. That's Timbo, my grandson. He's an on-call firefighter. Got beeped, so he has to go. I hope it's not serious; I hate the idea that he might be in danger, but he's such a brave boy. Anyway, it's what he wants to do with his life, so all me and his parents can do is support him. I dare say someone will phone me to let me know what's going on…he'll be far too busy. Now you just hold tight, I'll be right back with another one of these."

As Winnie headed off, Siân leaned in and whispered, "Is it just me, or does she remind you of Chris, from The Imperial, in *Blue Heelers*?"

I covered my laugh as I saw what my sister meant about the woman: a redheaded proprietor of a rural Australian pub. We enjoyed our moment together, though Bud and Todd had absolutely no idea what was going on.

Eventually able to speak through our giggles, we explained how Siân had tipped me off about Australia's favorite TV drama that had run for more than five hundred episodes over a dozen years which focused on the police who lived and worked in a small rural Australian town, whose jobs and lives proved to be a magnet for millions of viewers of all ages across the entire country. She'd suggested I watched it to pick up on some Aussie flavor and to improve my grasp of "Strine", or Australian slang, before our trip. I'd poo-pooed the idea…then I'd become addicted. Bud had held firm about not watching such a series; having spent so many years in law enforcement, he finds it difficult to watch anything on the screen that involves policing.

Todd, it seemed, had managed to miss the entire phenomenon because of his work schedules.

Once all that was sorted, Siân managed to regain her composure to note, "It's worrying that there's a fire hereabouts: it's been such a dry August and September in this area that they have to take anything seriously, I suppose. It shouldn't be wildfire season yet, but you never know, these days. It starts earlier and ends later now. Global warming; it's a worry."

The irony that Todd had spent at least some part of his career involved with coal mining wasn't lost on me as my sister nibbled at her tofu thing, and Bud and Todd demolished their steaks. I'd insisted that no one should wait for my replacement meal to arrive, for fear theirs would spoil…though I wasn't convinced it would be possible for tofu to get any worse. When Bud assured me that the kangaroo was tasty, I tried a bit and had to agree that it was delicious. I pushed all my childhood memories of cute, helpful Skippy to one side, as I accepted another chunk.

We were the only guests seated at a table in the entire place, the half a dozen or so other patrons preferring to sit at the bar itself. However, even though they weren't really within earshot, I could sense a change in the atmosphere in the restaurant; everyone appeared to have their phone in their hands, and most were texting like mad.

"The fire's at the old Wilmott house – the one they rent out now," called an older man.

One of the younger men asked, "That's the one on the Lower Jamison Road, right?"

Another of the older men at the bar shouted across to us. "Where are you lot staying?"

"We're on the Upper Jamison Road," replied Bud, "a rental house called The Overlook."

"You never told me it was called that," snapped Siân. "Why would you pick a house called that?"

Bud looked puzzled.

I explained, "It's the name of the hotel in *The Shining*. The Stephen King book? The movie with Jack Nicholson? Siân always hated that one."

Bud nodded. "Yes, I know the one you mean, it just hadn't occurred to me, is all. Does it matter? I mean the house does look out over the Jamison Valley…so, Overlook…you know?"

Siân had tensed and Todd was…well, off in a little world of his own as far as I could tell – certainly not engaged.

"I'm sure it won't develop the characteristics of the place you're thinking of, Siân," I said, using my most comforting tone.

Continuing from Bud's comment, the older guy at the bar relinquished his perch and ambled across to us, smiling, with his hand held out.

Bud rose and shook the man's extended hand.

"I'm Frank Tipton," he said, with a gap-toothed smile. "Sit. Eat. Don't let it spoil. I built the new upper deck around the place you're renting. The old one had rotted out. The new one? That'll see you right. Hope you enjoy it."

We all congratulated Frank on a job well done. "It must have been a challenge to build," observed Bud. "I had a nose around, down the steps that lead to the lower apartment, and there's a pretty sheer drop down there. You must have a good head for heights."

Even though I don't deal well with high places, I'd managed to cope with the deck by staying close to the walls of the house and looking ahead, rather than down – which I had to believe hadn't been a possibility for anyone actually constructing the platform we'd been using.

Frank laughed. "You'd be right there, mate. They had one bloke come to take a look at the job and he ran away from it – terrified him. Me? Like a tree-kangaroo, me, all my life – so it was right up my street. Got it done fast, too. I even had time to rebuild the top deck on the place that's gone up in flames tonight as well…both the same design, both built by the same bloke, see? On two different roads and about a mile apart, mind you. May was a dry month, and I needed all of it. Got both of them done."

I recalled that the deck hadn't looked that new. "This past May?"

Frank nodded.

"Oh right," I added, "the new deck's been stained darker to make it look more 'settled in' rather than brand new. Good idea."

"She's sharp," commented Frank to Bud and Todd.

"She could count the flies on a roo's tail," said Todd, surprising me – both because I hadn't thought he was listening, and due to his dismissive tone.

Siân must have picked up on that, too, because she gushed, "Cait's good at what she does, Todd."

Frank laughed again. "And what's that then? You count flies for England, do you?"

I smiled politely. "If I did count flies, I'd do it for Wales…or even for Canada, but probably not for England."

"You're Welsh?" Frank looked pleased, for some reason.

Siân and I nodded, then chorused, "Born and raised."

"So's Jonesy over there," said Frank. He called, "Hey, Jonesy – some Welshies here for you, mate. Jonesy's from a place I can't pronounce. Been here forty years and sounds as though he's never lived anywhere else…come over and say g'day, Jonesy."

Jonesy turned out to be the younger man at the bar who'd made the announcement about the location of the fire. He slid off his barstool and wandered across to us.

"G'day. William Jones of Ystalyfera, as was. Now known by all as Jonesy, and proudly of Katoomba – New South Wales, rather than the original 'old' South Wales. You Welsh then?"

Frank was right, I'd never have guessed from Jonesy's accent that he came from the same part of the world as me and my sister.

"Cait and Siân Morgan, originally from Swansea." I held out my hand.

Now that he was close, I could see that Jonesy's muscular frame and upright stance was what had made me believe he was younger than his eyes told me he was. He greeted me and Siân heartily. "What part of Swansea?"

"Manselton – do you know it?"

He shook his head. "We all came over when I was about ten, so, no, I don't really know the area, but I do remember The Slip, and Swansea Beach – magnificent. Oh, and Oxwich Beach in the Gower. There's an old church there where we went to say goodbye to my great-grandparents – well, their graves, you know – before we left."

"There you are, see?" I observed, "You call it 'the Gower' like a proper local – you never lose that turn of phrase thing, no matter how long you're away, right?"

Jonesy grinned. "I've given up 'over by here', and 'over by there' because no one ever knew what I meant," he said with a chuckle.

Siân and I told him about our extended family members who'd also been laid to rest in the same graveyard as his forebears – which made the entire "coincidence" thing, that Bud and I dislike intensely, feel real.

I saw Winnie come out of what I assumed was the kitchen carrying a plate I could tell was for me, when three men almost fell through the entrance to the pub. I was taken aback to recognize Neal, Big Stan, and Shorty. I hadn't imagined I'd ever see them again.

I accepted my plate, and nodded toward the door, getting Bud's attention. "Should I worry that we might have been followed?"

Frank, Jonesy, and Winnie turned to see what all the fuss at the door was about, and I could sense Winnie's tension increase. "Not serving you lot," she said loudly. "Get back to wherever they got you into that state."

The three of them moved as one toward the trio at the door, who righted themselves, all trying to adopt sober expressions – but failing.

Unfortunately, once they spotted us, Neal called, "Hey, it's Oscar! G'day, mate. How's you?"

We shared confused glances at our table, then Neal lurched toward Bud and greeted him like a long-lost relative. *Oscar?*

"Hi there," said Bud, getting to his feet; the chances were high that Neal might have ended up face-first in Bud's lap, otherwise.

"You know this lot?" snapped Winnie, every ounce of bonhomie having evaporated.

"We've been at a conference in Sydney together for a few days," replied Todd, also rising, and preparing for an incoming Big Stan. "We hadn't expected to see them again – here, or ever."

Clearly Todd was doing his best to distance himself from the three representatives of The Mob, which I had to agree didn't seem like a bad idea at that moment.

"You can be responsible for them, then," said Winnie. "One schooner each, then they're out."

Shorty headed straight to the bar, where he managed to wobble up onto a stool, and appeared to immediately engage the poor bloke he'd chosen to sit beside, while we were joined by the extremely inebriated father and son duo. I did my best to wolf down my dinner – all the others having pretty much finished theirs. Frank and Jonesy retook their stools at the bar, and it felt as though the barriers between us and the locals had not only shot back up, but had been reinforced…barricaded, even.

"It's jumped to the trees and it's going down into the valley," shouted Jonesy, up on his feet again. "I'm off. Got to be ready in case the wind shifts. They've got eight fire engines there. They're calling them in from all over. They'll have the rural volunteers out by now."

The effect of Jonesy's words was electrifying; everyone at the bar – except Shorty, who looked completely bemused – finished their drinks and headed for the doors, anxiety etched on each face. None of us was sure what to do. I looked across to Winnie, who was behind the bar clearing away empty glasses.

While Bud and Todd got Neal and Big Stan safely onto a couple of hurriedly pulled-over chairs, I darted to the bar.

"Winnie, as you know, we're staying at a rented house out on the Upper Jamison Road. If the fire's going down the valley from the lower road, will the house we're in still be safe? Should we be trying to get in touch with the homeowner?"

"You're at The Overlook?"

I nodded.

"You can try to reach the bloke who owns it, by all means, but I know for a fact he's in Bali at the moment. He'd tell you what I can – if you lot want to get your stuff out of there while it's safe to do it, then go ahead. There'll be places here in town that'll have a couple of rooms, I'm sure – but we haven't had any alerts yet, and it sounds as though they're doing all they can to knock it down, so you might be good."

"How would we even get any alerts if we're just visiting?" I asked.

Suddenly, Bud was at my shoulder. "We're all sorted, Cait. Our host sent me details of the Hazards Near Me app, and I've got it on my phone. I guess we should all download it now; it means we can check our location for warnings. It's not registering anything at the moment – though I'm sure the locals know a good deal more about what's going on because they'll all keep in touch with each other. I do suggest, however, that we get back to the house and maybe do a bit of repacking, in case we have to make a quick exit."

Winnie said, "Good to know one of you's prepared," then she carried a couple of small glasses of beer across to Neal and Big Stan.

Shorty had already almost finished his drink, and was beaming at us from his precarious position on a bar stool; it looked far too high for him because his stumpy legs didn't reach the brass rail. The expression on his face suggested he could barely focus on us, however, that didn't stop him from slurring, "You wanna hear a real good yarn? I could tell you a tale or two that would knock your socks off…"

Bud and I smiled, but politely declined, and headed back to our seats.

"How come they've shown up?" I asked Bud quietly.

"They arrived on the train before ours, it seems," he replied. "They all split up, with Neal and Big Stan taking a suite, if you please, at that swish hotel near the railway station – remember we talked about how fancy it was? It sounds as though the others have rented a house – hopefully Shorty can remember where it is, because neither of those two can…which isn't surprising, given their state. Big Stan reckons they're not used to wine, and had 'a few bottles' through the afternoon – so that might explain why they are the way they are. Do you think Winnie might be able to organize a cab to get them back to their hotel? Especially if we're leaving; I don't feel comfortable abandoning them."

Winnie overheard Bud as she returned to the bar. "No taxi would take them, not like that. It's a straight shot along this road to their hotel – though whether they'll let them back in, I don't know. They've paid through the nose for a posh sleep, so I dare say the hotel has no choice. No idea where this galah is staying – maybe they can let him sleep on their floor for the night."

"Not our responsibility," said Bud firmly as we approached our table, where Big Stan seemed to be intent upon telling Siân how wonderful her eyes were.

"Why did Neal call you Oscar?" I hissed at Bud.

Bud chuckled. "He said I look more like an Oscar than a Bud – and I don't think there's any point debating it with him at the moment, do you?"

I agreed there wasn't, then we explained to the father and son, who were clutching their half-empty beer glasses, that we had to leave.

Both Big Stan and Neal assured us they'd be able to get themselves back to "their place" with no problems, and were most insistent that Shorty would be "fine", so we left them – and Winnie – to it. I felt a bit guilty about leaving them there, especially as I could overhear Shorty already trying to bend Winnie's ear with his yarn about seeing a murder take place. However, I also knew I'd feel a lot more comfortable if we did all we could to be ready to leave in case the fire took hold, and began to threaten our rented house.

As we got into the SUV, Todd was quite scathing about the men we'd just left behind. "If I'd known that lot were going to be in the area, I'd have suggested we changed our plans."

It seemed a bit extreme to me, and I said as much.

Siân replied, "Todd's been telling me about The Mob, Cait, and – while I don't think we need to go into it now – there's a lot about them that you don't know. So just trust him on this. He's known of them for a long time, and their reputation for causing chaos wherever they go is well-earned. Let's just hope we don't see or hear any more of them."

Bad News

We couldn't see the fire from The Overlook, but we could most certainly smell it. The weird thing was that there was also the tang of eucalyptus in the air, giving the night a strangely medicinal quality; it made me think of the essential oils I used to put into boiling water to sniff under a towel, hoping to clear my sinuses when I had a cold.

We all packed away what we could, and went to bed quite early – but I don't think any of us expected to sleep well. Both Bud and I had our phones plugged in to charge, and had them set up as close as possible to our ears because we didn't want to risk not being woken by the alarms we'd set to be received if there was a safety alert for our specific area. However, I was surprised to find myself waking around eight the next morning, not even having got up to use the bathroom.

Bud and Siân had already made coffee by the time I emerged – showered, dressed, and ready for whatever the day might hold.

"Good news: the fire's out," said Bud.

"They're still working on hot spots," added Siân, "but they said on the news that they'd stopped it spreading."

I nodded. "No one hurt, I hope."

"Not that they've said on the TV," replied Bud. "Though the house where it began has gone completely. Wooden structure, just like this place, like Frank at Winnie's Place told us last night," he said. "They showed before and after photos a few minutes ago. I feel sorry for whoever owns it."

"You have to wonder how it started," said Siân. "They didn't say on the telly if anyone was renting it, did they?"

Bud shook his head.

We heard swearing coming from the direction of Todd and Siân's bedroom.

I suspected something like a perfectly natural response to a stubbed toe, but Siân's reaction didn't support my theory. "Good grief – what's happening? He never uses language like that." She scampered off.

Bud poured coffee for me, knowing I'd need it, whatever might happen next.

When Siân rejoined us, her face had lost all its color.

"What's the matter?" I could tell that something was horribly wrong. "Are the kids okay?"

She nodded, dumbly.

"Todd alright?"

She shrugged.

"What's the matter, Siân?" Bud used his calming voice.

"That house fire. Last night. Three dead." Her voice was flat.

"That's terrible," I said, and instinctively pulled my sister into my arms. If anyone had ever looked like they needed a hug, it was Siân, right then.

I clung to her for a moment or two, then realized she was shuddering. Sobbing. I held her tight, wondering why it was that Siân had got the genetic code for overwhelming compassion, and I'd got the bits of the family DNA that gave me an eidetic memory, and the desperate need to know how everything works. Same parents, same home, same schools even – and yet we were so different.

"Okay now, Siân, come on, let's get you a hanky, shall we? I know it's tragic, but I hate seeing you get this upset about…well, you know…about three complete strangers dying like that." I let her go and headed toward the bathroom, where I knew there was a box of tissues.

I was already out of the door before Siân was able to speak, so I wasn't sure what she'd mumbled. I returned, and said, "Sorry, I didn't catch that."

Bud's expression told me that whatever she'd said, it hadn't been good.

Siân wiped her eyes with the heel of her hand. She almost-shouted, "I said, they just announced on the radio that three men died last night, but that they weren't giving out names until the families had been contacted. But Todd got a phone call from one of the blokes who was presenting with him at the conference in Sydney, and the word is out already that the men were Leonard Orkins, Richard Early, and Daniel Entwistle."

"Who?" I stared at Bud who had his eyes closed tight.

"Lennie, Ditch, and Dan…from The Mob," replied Siân.

I grabbed the doorframe. "That's…awful."

Siân sobbed. "I know. We were just with them. They were so alive…" She started crying again.

Todd cantered along the corridor. He looked…*terrified?*

"Siân's just told me the news," I said. "It's shocking. Awful. What a tragedy. She's terribly upset, I'm going to get some tissues for her."

Todd grabbed my arm, leading Bud to take a couple of wary steps toward the pair of us. Todd's voice broke a little as he said, "Cait – you're good at this stuff. You and Bud. I need help. And I need protection."

Bud and I were completely at sea.

Placing a protective arm around my shoulders when he reached me, Bud said, "You're going to have to explain yourself, Todd. I mean, of course, this is terrible news – such a dreadful loss of life – but why on earth do you need 'protection'?"

Siân sniffed. "Tell them everything, Todd. You have to, now. I'm alright, really, Cait, I'll get some kitchen roll. Come and sit down – my husband has a story to tell you, and maybe then you'll both understand…though I'm having a hard time getting my head around it all myself, to be honest."

Step Back

Bud and I squished together on a seat that had clearly been designed to hold one and a half normal-sized people, while Todd and Siân perched awkwardly on the large sofa, their fingers entwined, white-knuckled.

Todd's voice cracked. "You know I used to work for Philp Myers, and that he was convicted of killing Lowanna, the girl who could locate opal deposits on maps?"

Bud and I nodded, and my brother-in-law's face pinched with resignation before he continued.

Todd swallowed, then pushed on. "Right, well, needless to say, the whole thing came as a great shock to me – to everyone who knew Philip, to be honest. The person I knew – *thought* I knew – was corporately clean, and personally pleasant. Both I, and the whole industry, believed he'd had a lucky find of several big opal deposits early in his career, and that had set him up to build his company. He moved from opals to gold, to coal, then had a finger in so many mining operations that he was almost unstoppable. But it all came crashing down when that rifle showed up. His businesses were either bought out for cents on the dollar, or collapsed altogether, so, in a matter of months, hundreds of people were out of work. I was one of them – but I was fortunate enough to have met a lot of people over the years who could give me jobs here and there, so at least I was one of the ones who managed to keep their head above water. Just. Siân and I had a lot to get through. She was brilliant. Went back to her nursing, working extra shifts, juggling everything at home, and so on. Anyway, after Philip was convicted, I managed to get myself back onto the corporate ladder, and continued to work my way up it again."

I wanted Todd to get to the point, and noticed Siân staring at my foot, which I was doing my best to not jiggle with impatience. *She knows me too well.*

Siân squeezed her husband's hand as she added, "It was hard; we had the kids by then, of course, but I had to go back to work. It was only once things had settled down, and Todd was certain he'd really have a future in mining again, that we decided it was the right time for me to give up work – for the second time."

Bud and I nodded.

"Now I'll tell you this truthfully," said Todd, "to start with, I couldn't believe that Philip could have shot that girl. But as more and more came out at the trial – stuff that was clearly true about him, but that he'd kept hidden – the more I wondered if he might have had it in him to do it, back then, when he was young. See, he'd have been about twenty-five when he killed her, and I didn't even meet him until he was about forty. I met a mature, successful businessman, who wanted to take me under his wing – and I was only too keen to let him do it. I went from a fresh-out-of-the-box mining engineer, to the person the lauded Philip Myers had by his side at every meeting. Which, at the time, meant I was the Golden Boy. Not so much when Philip was convicted of a brutal murder, of course. I…I never once visited him, nor kept in touch. Because…because I felt so conflicted about it all. I almost loved him, like a father. I certainly admired him. And yet he'd done this terrible, unforgiveable thing to another human being. I couldn't bring myself to look him in the eye ever again."

So far, I was with Todd; an often-underestimated part of being a criminal psychologist is to understand not just those who commit crimes, but those who are impacted by crime, too. Indeed, that's my specialism – profiling victims. The girl Lowanna was the murder victim, but the ripples created by a violent act always spread much further than most will ever acknowledge; Todd – and my sister – had been impacted by the murderous actions of his employer, too.

"I'm so sorry," was all I got out before Todd shook himself, like our beloved black Lab, Marty, does when he's wet from swimming in the pond. A vision of Marty happily cavorting with Jack and Sheila White's dogs at their place, where our lovely boy was staying, flashed into my head, making me smile…which Todd must have taken the wrong way.

"I don't want your mock pity, Cait, I need your help," he snapped. He took a moment to compose himself, then added, "You see, I got a letter from Philip a few weeks ago. He wrote to me at work. In the letter, he asserted his innocence, claimed he'd been fitted up – you know, framed – and suggested he knew who'd done it, and why. Pleaded with me to visit him urgently, so he could tell me everything…but…but I didn't go. I put the letter in a drawer in my desk, and left it there."

I shrugged. "You could go and see him now, couldn't you? Put your mind at ease, somehow?"

"He died last week." Todd sagged. Siân put her hand on his thigh.

"Todd only told me all about this last night," she said quietly. "He's been holding himself together through the conference, knowing the news about Philip's death could break at any moment. In fact, Todd only knows that Philip is dead because the man went and named Todd as his next of kin, so they had to tell him."

The fact that a convicted killer had named my brother-in-law as his next of kin hit home. Maybe Myers' family had ostracized him because of his crime? Maybe he didn't have one? But there'd been a wife…I forced myself to stop running unpleasant scenarios in my head.

Bud said, "So what's the issue right now – concerning you?"

Todd sighed. "Lennie Orkins was the one who found the rifle that got Philip convicted. I…I think now that Lennie fitted him up him for some reason. I never could work out why someone like Lennie ended up driving earth-moving equipment for the likes of Big Stan. He was good at his job, once upon a time, and generally known as a man who wouldn't say boo to a goose…you know? But he developed a reputation for being a bit too fond of the sauce. No one hires a drunk as a driver, do they?"

"Who exactly is 'Big Stan', anyway?" I realized I really knew nothing about the man.

Todd replied, "Big Stan Swan? He's well known in our business. How he got started is a bit of a legend: he teamed up with a friend of his and they struck a deal to rent equipment on the cheap to make a road that was needed by a sheep farmer who was getting some big electrical plant installed at his station. Stan was called Big Stan from the time he was about thirteen; the bloke he was always seen about with was a head shorter than him, and also named Stan. Little Stan had the gift of the gab – everyone reckoned he must have some Irish blood in him somewhere – and he was the one who got the deals done, while Big Stan got the crew together to do each job. They set themselves up as S & S Roads. Their jobs got bigger, and they invested in their own equipment. They specialize in providing services to companies either exploring for minerals, or else extracting them – whoever needs roads to access remote and inhospitable sites. And trust me when I tell you that every mine in Australia is located in the most inhospitable place you can imagine. It's like the joke of the universe: whatever you want is here…but you've got to go through hell to get at it."

"So Big Stan's a Big Noise in mining nowadays?" I quipped, regretting my levity the instant I saw my sister's face. "What happened to Little Stan? Doesn't he come to things like the conference in Sydney?"

Todd sounded grim. "Had a massive heart attack while giving a presentation in Melbourne in front of a couple of dozen people…when the conference we just attended took place there last year, in fact. Dead before he hit the floor, they said. Great way for him to go, I suppose, but awful for everyone left behind. The whole business took it badly. Massive memorial service. They came from all over. That was the last time I saw Big Stan before this past week. He was in bits. I was surprised he didn't speak at the memorial. Not that he'd have been able to say much, because he sobbed and shuddered…and coughed…through the whole thing, with his son supporting him. That said, the eulogy was incredible: an old friend of Little Stan's, named Ryan McCready, gave it. He told some fantastic yarns about the two of them over the years. Amazing. Little Stan certainly lived life to the fullest. Absolutely wonderful, it was. Everyone was crying by the end of it. I'll never forget Ryan McCready's name because of that; it takes something to get hundreds of Australian men to break down in tears. That wasn't long before The Mob lost Bruce Walker, in that so-called 'accident' I told you about. And now? Look, I'm worried. I think Philip might have been telling the truth in his letter to me – that he *was* framed. I don't like it. I feel…connected to the whole thing because of how close I was to Philip, and I don't want Siân or the kids in any danger. Me neither, of course." His voice had lifted by an octave.

"Tell them about the email, Todd." Siân shot a worried smile at me.

Todd sagged. "I got an email. Don't know who from. The address looked very similar to one I'm used to seeing – a trade publication, online – but it had an 'rn' in it where there should have been an 'm'. In my defence, that's an easy mistake to make – scammers and phishers use it all the time, and I got hooked. It was addressed to me personally, so I opened the email and the attachment. It said I was to keep my mouth shut about Philip Myers and his claims to be innocent. Or else. It didn't specify what else…which is what's worrying me."

"And when did you get the threatening email, in relation to receiving the letter from Philip himself?" Bud was on the edge of the seat, and not just because the two of us hardly fitted on it.

Siân's pinched face turned toward her husband, as he examined the ceiling. "I'd say a week later?" His voice was guttural.

"I don't know the vetting procedures for the Australian prison system, though I do at least know that it's called Corrective Services, Australia," said Bud, "but I guess there's a chance that the letter Philip sent to you was legitimately read before it was mailed – or maybe someone illegitimately gained access to it before you did. It could be that the letter was 'allowed through' because it had to be…but the warning you received was because someone would have preferred that Philip didn't say anything more to you. Who knows what might have happened if you'd gone to see him."

Siân grabbed her husband's hand. "Oh my God, Todd – this isn't good, is it?"

Todd shook his head.

I had a thought. "Who were you talking to on the phone when I walked in on you yesterday, Todd?" I had to know, because I suspected it was somehow connected to what Todd was telling us.

Todd's ears turned pink at their tips. "I said. Just a work thing."

Siân looked at her husband in disbelief. "Your ears are telling me otherwise, Todd Anderson – you know they always give you

away when you're lying. If you want Cait and Bud to help you –
to help *us* – you have to be honest with them."

Todd swallowed. "I was talking to a colleague at work, that
much is true. But we were talking about…all this."

"And?" Siân pressed.

Todd sat very upright. "I have a personal assistant – well, no,
she's more than that really, because she's better trained in
management techniques and all the management-speak that gets
used these days. I rely upon her, and trust her. I told her about
the letter I received from Philip. She worked with Philip back in
his early days. Then she took a break to raise two kids. They
grew up, left home, she got divorced, and she rejoined the
workforce about five years ago. She got in touch because of my
history with Philip; I'd been told all about her by him – when he
used to hold her up as the person to whose work ethic I should
aspire. Of course I hired her – I'd have been mad not to. To be
honest, the only reason *I'm* not *her* assistant is because she took
a twenty-year parenting break."

"You mean Joyce? Joyce Trimble?" Siân sounded surprised.
Todd nodded. "But you said she was new to the industry, that
she was still learning the ropes. Your exact words. What's been
going on? Todd…"

"Nothing's been going on," snapped Todd sounding hurt.
"Nothing, other than I've been more reliant upon her skills for
the past few years than I've let on. I'd never have made it onto
the board without her support. We're a team – not a couple,
Siân. Never that. You're my wife, she's just my colleague. That's
it. But…yes, I'd told her about the letter, and the email, and she
knows about Philip's death, and I told her about the yarning
Lennie was doing the other night. We all knew about the link
between him and the rifle…but I didn't know he was telling the
tale over and over again, as entertainment over beers."

I stood – I had to, because my bum was getting numb. "So, to be clear, Todd: you and your very able assistant Joyce think that Lennie – he of the wonderful yarning ability – fabricated the entire story about finding the rifle when he was a boy, then rediscovering it when he cleared out his dead grandfather's house? Just so there'd be evidence to point to Philip Myers having been the person who killed Lowanna?" Todd nodded, his eyes downcast. I continued, "By the way, what was the girl's family name?"

"Lowanna Swan." Todd blanched.

"The same family name as Big Stan?"

Todd nodded.

I asked, "Is that a common name? Are they related?"

Todd shrugged. "Quite common. There's even the beer named Swan. But Siân will be better at answering about names and all that than I ever could."

I was intrigued.

Siân said, "I used to do a bit of volunteering for the Australian Institute of Aboriginal and Torres Strait Islander Studies – entering data for them, at home, several years ago. I learned that individuals might have several names throughout their life: their traditional name, their European name, their nickname or nicknames, and a kinship name. Lowanna might not have been the girl's registered, legal name – she might not even have had one, but it was the one she was known by, so that – de facto – becomes her name. Especially since it was the one she became known by in the press, after her death, and in the courts when they were looking into her murder."

Todd added, "And as for the surname of Swan? I can tell you that her father wasn't called Swan; he was Pamkal, Guy Pamkal. Her mother was dead, and went unnamed in the court proceedings, but maybe she was a Swan? Or maybe the family members who took in Lowanna in the Northern Territory were

Swans, or had a connection to the name. It's impossible to say if she and Big Stan are related, right, Siân?"

My sister nodded. "It's an incredibly difficult situation for members of Aboriginal and Torres Strait Islander families; so often they've become disconnected across generations, and their chances of finding their ancestors – of ever really understanding where they come from, or belong – are slim."

"So you're saying there's no way to know if Lowanna Swan and Big Stan Swan have anything in common but a name?" Bud sounded disappointed.

Todd smiled weakly. "We're both named Anderson, and we're not connected at all – other than by marriage…to two sisters."

Siân shook her head, ignoring her husband's comment. "But Big Stan himself might know if they belonged to the same extended family – or believe he does. With oral histories, sometimes people are able to make connections – eventually."

"So," I mused, "maybe Big Stan Swan discovers he's related to the murdered Lowanna Swan, and he comes up with a plan to frame Philip Myers for her killing…using Lennie Orkins to plant evidence. But that only makes sense if Big Stan had a reason to hate Philip Myers, or had another 'good' reason to get Lennie to frame him for a murder he didn't commit…*if* Philip really didn't kill Lowanna, that is."

"I…don't…know," said Todd. "I thought that's where you and Bud could help, see? No one ever knew why Philip set up Bruce Walker in business the way he did, but I know they knew each other around the time that Lowanna was killed. Maybe that suggests Bruce knew something about how Philip got his money? There were rumors mentioned at Philip's trial that a great deal of money – in the form of gold, which was how her father got paid for her services – went missing when Lowanna died. See, I've been thinking…oh, thinking so much about all of this since I heard the news about Philip being dead, and the letter, and everything…and I thought that maybe Bruce knew that Philip really *did* kill Lowanna to get that fortune, and he got paid off to keep his mouth shut."

Todd's eyes were flicking from side to side, not focusing on anything within our immediate surroundings, and his hands were flapping about madly. My reading of his body language suggested he was quite literally searching for meaning, and understanding, as he spoke…without much luck, it seemed.

I was about to try to give him some direction, when he pressed on. "Maybe Lennie *was* telling the truth about finding the rifle when he was a kid and his grandfather keeping it shut up in an old tin trunk for all those years. But Philip's dead. And Bruce is dead. And now Lennie's dead, too. What if whoever it was who emailed me that threat thinks I know something about it all and tries to kill me too? They might have killed Lennie by setting that fire. That's what Joyce and I were talking about on the phone…not about Lennie and the fire, because I didn't know about that then, of course. She said I should go to the cops with my concerns…my suspicions. But why would anyone believe me that I know nothing? If I say anything to anyone, maybe they'll suspect I know more than I'm saying…and I don't. I really don't. Please help me. Help *us*. This has all been rolling around inside my head for so long, now, that I'm lost inside it. I can't get any of it straight. It's been such a long week since they told me that Philip was dead…and now this news about Lennie…I'm exhausted with it all."

All I could manage was: "I need to have a think – because what you're saying really does sound a bit scrambled, Todd. It seems the only way we might clear this up is to go right back to the beginning and work out who really killed Lowanna Swan all those years ago…though maybe finding out what we can about the fire last night could point us in the right direction. Right –

let's get this timeline sorted, folks…because something's not adding up here."

Get It Sorted, Mate

It took some time for me to find paper and pens, and to sketch out the timeline I'd gathered from what Todd had said about everything so far. And my assessment had been right – the various references were not well aligned. I lay the papers across the dining table, then peppered Todd with questions, getting things sorted out for all of us.

Gradually, parts of the story of Lowanna Swan's life, tragic death, and its aftermath, began to emerge. However, it was clear that Todd's knowledge was spotty; it helped that he was able to clarify bits of backgrounds for all the "players", but I decided it was best to try to access whatever records existed about Lowanna for myself.

Of course, none of us had a laptop with us except Todd, who'd been using his for his presentations, so I hijacked that and set myself up at the table on the deck – the valley ahead, and the forest all around me.

Todd absolutely refused to take up Bud's suggestion that the three of them should continue with their planned excursion to the high-altitude delights of Scenic World. To be fair, I was with Todd on that one; I wondered if the day after a deadly blaze was the right time to be zooming over – possibly – the site of the fire itself, in a cable car.

However, rather than have them all mooning about the place while I concentrated on reading anything and everything I could find online in terms of the press reports of the trial of Philip Myers, I suggested that we ate a hearty lunch – which everyone could prepare as a group. That resulted in a trip to buy supplies, which got all three of them out of my hair for a good hour. Todd was only prepared to leave the house if Siân was with him, and

Bud accompanied them both to "keep an eye on them" – which I thought ridiculous, but it suited my needs.

By the time they returned, then got going with some pizza-making in the kitchen – my request, because I knew it would take ages – I had managed to pretty much wrap my head around the overall picture. I thought it best if we discussed it on full stomachs, so was delighted to leave them to set the table while I fussed about in the bathroom.

Of course, our lunchtime conversation was anything but normal; we'd all agreed to hold off talking about Lowanna Swan's death until I was ready to do so, but the trio had managed to glean some information about the previous night's tragic fire when they'd been out shopping, and we talked it through while we ate.

Siân told us that there was general agreement among those she'd spoken to at the shops that it was either a drunken inability on the part of the men who'd died to turn off something that had started the fire that had killed them, or else it had been arson. Apparently, there'd been a few other "unusual fire incidents" over the past several weeks in the area, though no one locally was certain if they'd been arson or accidents, nor if they were even linked to each other, let alone to the fire the previous night.

Todd didn't have much to say for himself at all.

It seemed that word had got out about the shenanigans of Big Stan, Neal, and Shorty at Winnie's Place – as well as some surprisingly detailed accounts of just how badly behaved they'd been when they'd turned up at their hotel. Once it became common knowledge that the men found in the burned-out house were connected to them, the assumption was made that they must have all been drunk before they ended up dead, just because of the state Neal, Big Stan, and Shorty had been in.

I was fascinated to hear how quickly facts, opinions, and theories had begun to swirl around the small rural town, and I could imagine the increasing number of rumors that would ensue, until the fire department – or whomever – released some actual news about the incident.

I'd already established that the names of those who'd died still hadn't been officially released, however, because word travels so fast in the "social-media-verse", all the victims had been identified by friends or family on various sites long before newscasters would ever speak their names on mainstream media. The online tributes told of three men who were all apparently adored and admired by everyone who'd ever met or worked with them, who each had the most magical smile, and great work ethic. Crowdfunding for funerals couldn't be far behind.

From my point of view, at least all the social media activity and comments helped fill in the blanks in terms of the men's backgrounds, and I mulled that as I chomped through the most delicious pizzas – two of them – that I suspected had ever been produced in the kitchen of The Overlook.

"These are really excellent. You could sell these." It had to be said, so I said it.

Both men nodded at Siân.

"I keep telling her they're good," said Todd, sounding almost like a normal husband for a moment. "The kids and their friends can't get enough of them, and when she makes them for fundraisers, they fly off her stall. She's got a secret, haven't you?"

Siân blushed. "I do – but if I tell you lot it won't be a secret for long. However, I'll just say that it's got something to do with the olive oil I choose, and what I add to it."

"And we hunted down the exact brand, didn't we, love?" Todd beamed.

Siân replied with a smile, "Indeed we did – though I still managed to keep my *real* little secret, I think." She winked at me, and I smiled back. I couldn't imagine what it could be; I love to eat, and I'm not a bad cook, but making pizza dough is not part of my repertoire, so she could have hurled diesel fuel into it for all I knew. I'm an instinctive cook, not a baker who follows, or amends, recipes.

After we'd cleared up – I felt I had to do my bit – everyone settled down and looked at me expectantly, so I stood to make my little presentation. Looking at Todd's haggard face, I decided to start brightly.

"Right then, I think I have it all sorted now – well, at least in terms of who was doing what, where, and when, so…I wanna tell you a story." I waggled my hands about and faked a London accent.

Siân clapped. "Yay, Max Bygraves – brill." She explained to Todd and Bud, "English variety performer – sang, danced a bit, told jokes. Never really said, 'I wanna tell you a story', until an impersonator called Mike Yarwood put it into his interpretation of Max Bygraves…who picked it up for himself."

My husband and brother-in-law exchanged an indulgent shrug.

Siân added, "Him and his wife ended up living in Queensland, up on the Gold Coast. I wonder if he was here long enough for his Cockney accent to take on an Aussie twang? Him and his wife both died here. Did you know that two of his three illegitimate children even came over to visit him before he died? His legitimate children knew about it, and said it was alright by them. People lead such complicated lives, don't they? I mean, if you made it up, someone would say it was ridiculous."

We shared a "truth is stranger than fiction" chuckle, then I began in earnest. "Okay, here we go: as I understand it, Lowanna Swan was born approximately fifty-three years ago…somewhere – this is one example of a gap in information I can't fill from publicly available sources, sorry. There'll be more. Anyway, at 'some point' in her pre-teen years, her father, Guy Pamkal, discovered she had a unique talent – she could look at a map and point at a place where opals could be found. It appears – from what I could gather from newspaper stories about her – that she could only locate one dig site at a time…which I have to say seems odd. In any case, her father quickly saw a way to capitalize on her skills. He'd already used her abilities to unearth small deposits for himself, then he used that money to promote his daughter's abilities – presumably seeing that as a much easier way to earn a steady income. Over the next ten-ish years – at least, up until she was about nineteen – their lives progressed with her creating a good income stream for her father and herself. He 'rationed' how much 'work' she would do, so her fees went up and up – and every single time she was paid to point at a map, there was a hit. She was a phenomenon."

Todd raised his hand sheepishly. I nodded, and he said, "She was more than that – she was a legend. She's been talked about in our business since I've been part of it. Everyone has their point of view…their stories. Imagine knowing exactly where to tell people to dig for something as rare and precious as opals? But you're right, her father didn't let her do it often – so when there was a strike, it was big news…everyone talked about it. And – just in case you didn't get this from your research, Cait – what I can add is that her father also kept her largely hidden from the world. I have no idea what her life was really like, but she was a mystery figure who could do magic – that was about the size of it."

I pounced. "Do you know where he 'kept her'? There's nothing I can find out about her working life, other than it seemed fairly peripatetic."

Todd shrugged. "Rumor was they moved from hotel to hotel, all around the country. Well, not all around the country – not much point in her moving outside the area of the artesian basin, really. Though…maybe they did. Even before she scarpered to the Northern Territory…to her family."

Bud raised his hand. "For those not in the know – what's the 'artesian basin'….and why does it matter?"

I glanced at Todd. "Want to give a quick primer on opals, Todd?"

Todd obliged. "Opal occurs in very few locations in the world because a very specific series of geological and other phenomena have to take place for it to be formed. About one hundred and forty million years ago, right up until about sixty-five million years ago, what is now the great desert region of central Australia was an inland sea, and the Great Artesian Basin was formed when the sea receded. Then, about thirty million years ago, soluble silica formed – due to weathering – and this solution traveled along faults in the ground, filling cracks and voids. It hardened to form common opal, and in rare circumstances it formed precious opal. It takes about five million years for an opal to form one centimeter thick. Nowadays, Australia produces around ninety percent of the world's precious opal."

Bud looked suitably impressed. "Thanks, Todd. Interesting. I had no idea. Sorry to interrupt – but, yeah, thanks for that. Okay – off you go again, Cait."

I grinned my appreciation at my brother-in-law. "Now, as far as I can tell, Lowanna Swan headed off to hide out about thirty-four years ago," I said, "and she died thirty-three years ago, so she'd been in hiding for about a year. The reporting of Philip Myers' trial says he and she first met just before she went to the Northern Territory, and then onto East Arnhem Land, and evidence was given by her extended family that her father took her there to avoid being hounded by Myers. The investigation immediately following her death was unable to find a culprit for her shooting, but fingers in the community pointed to the father. However, Guy Pamkal was never arrested nor tried for the crime, but – there again – nor was anyone else. I have to say, right now, that I could find almost no reporting about this initial investigation, so I might be missing a lot that really happened, or it might be that as little happened as I've just mentioned. Anyway, roughly two years after the death of his daughter, Guy Pamkal walked into the Bush and shot himself in the head – at least, his body was found with a fatal wound, and the gun used was found beside him. There was no note, but assumptions ran that he'd succumbed to guilt about killing his daughter."

"It's awfully sad, isn't it?" Siân looked grim. "So much death."

"It is, you're right," I replied. "Now – moving on…the year after Lowanna's death – so, while her father was still alive – Philip Myers had a few big opal strikes. One example that he dug up is still sitting in a museum; they paid him handsomely for it because it was so notable. Following his liquidation of his finds, which netted him a 'substantial' amount of money – various sums are bandied about in several online sources – he set up his own mining company, and, according to Todd, that's when he also set up Bruce Walker with his company. Right?"

Todd nodded. "As I recall from what I gathered at the time I joined Philip. It wasn't something that ever came out in court – why would it? I gather that Bruce was only in his early twenties back then and it's funny now I think of it, but no one ever seemed to question how such a young fella could get set up the way he was. I wasn't even in the business at that time – still studying for my engineering degree. I didn't meet Philip until I was just getting going in the business. He hired me and we…clicked. The twelve years I was by his side I learned a lot. Everything my career today relies upon. If he hadn't taken me under his wing, I couldn't have achieved what I have."

Siân sounded disgusted, rather than supportive, when she sniped, "So your career is down to Philip Myers and Joyce Trimble, is it? Nothing to do with all the hard work and months and months away from home that you've given the companies you've worked for?"

Todd gave a flash of a weak smile. "That too, love, that too. And your support, of course."

Siân sniffed, and I thought it best to press on.

"Okay folks – so Lowanna's been murdered, Philip Myers and Bruce Walker are nicely set up for life, and her father, Guy Pamkal, has apparently killed himself. You, Todd, met Philip, and worked successfully with him for a dozen years, then – about thirteen years ago – Lennie Orkins' grandfather died, and he rediscovered the rifle he'd pulled out of a waterhole twenty years earlier, and hands it in to the authorities. They arrest Philip Myers pretty sharpish, there's a trial, he's convicted of the murder of Lowanna Swan, and he's spent the past dozen years in jail. A year ago, Big Stan Swan's business partner Little Stan died of a massive heart attack on-stage in Melbourne, and not long after that Bruce Walker – who had somehow fallen so far in life as to have become a driver of earth-moving equipment for Big Stan – is found dead, killed when he didn't properly apply the brakes to his vehicle. Three weeks ago, Todd received a letter from Philip Myers, asking Todd to urgently visit him in prison; a week after that Todd received an anonymous threatening email, and, finally, Philip Myers was found dead in his jail cell a week ago. There – I think we have it."

Bud gave me a round of applause, which apparently amused my sister.

"And now Lennie Orkins is dead, as is Ditch Early, and Dan Entwistle," added Todd glumly. "And I might be next."

"I think you're being a bit dramatic, Todd," I said. "There's nothing to connect a fire here in Katoomba last night with anything that's gone before. Except, of course, that it was Lennie who first discovered the rifle – or else it was Lennie who used it to frame Philip Myers thirteen years ago. But, if there was an unknown person behind the possible frame-up – if that's what it was – and they were afraid that Lennie would give them away, then they'd have done better to kill him off right after he'd given his damning evidence at Philip Myers' trial, not wait until last night...thirteen years later."

Bud offered, "Too suspicious-looking? I know I'd have investigated if one man who'd provided evidence that convicted another had died suddenly thereafter."

I replied, "But only if you – as a homicide detective – had been given the case. It might be that last night's fire will be ruled as accidental – and 'accidents' can be arranged, at any time."

"Very uplifting thought," said Siân.

"Sorry –" I patted my sister's hand – "I didn't mean to imply that you and Todd might be next to have an accident. You see – and with all due respect to you, Todd – I've read every press account of Philip Myers' trial, and there was compelling evidence, in the shape of witness testimony, that he had been pursuing Guy Pamkal to allow him to buy Lowanna's skills to help him with his dream of striking opals. What was also interesting was the evidence given about the reasons why Lowanna – or at least her father – refused to sell Philip her skills."

Todd sagged. "Yes, I know what you mean."

"What reasons?" Siân snapped. "I know you followed the trial, Todd, but I was too busy. Why would Lowanna Swan not agree to do her map-pointing thing for Philip Myers? Wouldn't he pay enough? He was always a bit cheap, you have to admit that, Todd."

Todd shrugged. "Careful, not cheap."

Siân shook her head. "He was as cheap as chips. I bet he'd have cut every corner going."

I took my sister's observation on board, but replied, "It wasn't anything to do with money – at least, that's not what those who gave evidence said. The reason Lowanna Swan wouldn't point her magical opal fingers at a map for Philip Myers was because she'd met him a couple of times, and didn't like him at all. Newspaper reports noted that the jury was told to disregard comments made that were hearsay, but several people who were related to Lowanna testified that Philip made unwanted advances toward her when they first met. 'Put the hard word on her,' they said. They also said that Lowanna told her father she found Philip creepy, and wouldn't go anywhere near him. Now look, I know I met him briefly at your wedding, and I certainly didn't feel my creep-o-meter jangling, but you knew him better than me, Siân – what did you think of him? Was he the sort who'd get handsy with a twenty-year-old? He wouldn't have been much older at the time, of course – only about twenty-five himself – so I'm not suggesting we're wandering into 'dirty old man' territory. But might he have been one to not understand that 'no' really does mean 'no'?"

Siân stood and stretched. "I...I don't think so. Not a predator. Not even a creep. A bit smarmy maybe, and like I said, cheap. But, remember, by the time I met him he was doing very well and was married. No kids, but married." She paused, then added, "And I know this is all very important but I'm gagging for a cuppa. If I put the jug on, does everyone want tea?"

"Beer for me," said Todd.

Bud stuck up his thumb. "I'm with him."

"Me too," I added. "Just you for tea, so you do that, and I'll get some beers."

Bud stood. "No you don't – I'll get them, you do this."

With Siân and Bud bustling in the kitchen, Todd whispered, "Back in a few," and headed toward their room.

I gazed out of the sliding doors toward the forest, and marvelled again at the exotic and plaintive birdcalls I could hear.

When Todd screamed, Siân dropped a mug, sending shards of china pirouetting across the kitchen floor, and Bud swore loudly as three cans of beer landed on his foot.

A Bird In The Hand

All three of us sprinted toward Todd and Siân's room, but I got there first. The sight that met my eyes wasn't what I'd been expecting – though I wasn't really sure what that had been. Todd seemed fine, though he was clearly shaken, and his thin hair was sticking out all over the place, as though he'd been dragged through a hedge, backwards. There were signs that someone had dislodged the bug screen on the window and had tried to rip down one of the curtains, by the looks of it, and there were things out of place around the room, and unexpectedly on the floor. Then I noticed a dribble of blood roll down from Todd's receding hairline.

I blurted out, "You're bleeding. Are you alright? What on earth happened."

"Bloody bird. A corella – a white cockatoo type of thing. I came in to go to the toilet and it had somehow managed to get itself into the bathroom. Flew right at my face. Frightened the life out of me. Then it grabbed my hair and started flapping. I ran to the window and tried to smack it off and out with the curtains. But..." He looked at the bloodied hand he'd just rubbed over his head. "It got me. The little bugger."

"I'll get the first aid kit," said Siân, taking charge. "We'll need to sterilize that and get some antibacterial cream on it. Goodness knows where its talons have been."

"Digging into my scalp, that's something I can be sure about," snapped Todd, holding his head.

"Glad it's nothing too bad, Todd," said Bud. "How about we let these two get sorted here, Cait, and we'll grab those beers?"

He limped along the hall ahead of me.

"Will you live, Bud?" I whispered.

Bud smiled sweetly. "Thanks for the sympathy. My foot will be just fine. Nothing broken. Sore, though. And it'll probably bruise."

I sighed – dramatically. "Go and put it up, and I'll bring you a beer." I mugged loping to the fridge. "Which ones did you drop? These?" Bud nodded, so I chose a couple of different cans and stuck each one into an insulated "tinny".

I handed him one. "Can sir manage to drink his own beer?"

"L.O.L. Ha-ha, Cait." He snapped open his can and glugged.

I leaned close to his ear and whispered, "I don't suppose you could wangle some way to find out about the cause of last night's fire from the local bobbies, or even your secret squirrel colleagues at ASIS, could you, Husband, dear?" I batted my eyelids until I nearly had a stroke.

Bud leaned back and shook his head slowly. "You only want me for my contacts, don't you?"

"My turn to L.O.L., Husband. No, I want you for your sweet disposition, loving nature, *and* your contacts."

"Well, I should warn you that I have none at all in this part of the world; I don't think local Aussie law enforcement is likely to tell a retired Canadian homicide detective anything. And – as far as they are concerned – that's who I am, because, as you very well know, I'm not allowed to tell anyone about my role with the international gang-busters' task force. And as for contacting the Australian Secret Intelligence Service? Nope. Not happening. Just because I've worked for CSIS doesn't mean I'm linked to any Aussie counterparts at all."

"You're a spy?" Siân was almost on top of us, having slithered silently into the room on bare feet.

We both jumped, and Bud snapped, "No, I'm not. And don't go saying I am."

Todd joined us, flattening down his hair, and asked nonchalantly, "Don't go saying you're what, Bud?"

Siân bubbled, "A spy. Bud's a spy. I just heard him and Cait talking about it."

I said, "He isn't, and we weren't. You both know that Bud had a big job heading up a homicide squad, but he also had to do a few things that needed CSIS clearance. That's all."

Todd looked confused. "What's *seesis*?"

Siân said, "C.S.I.S., pronounced *seesis,* is the Canadian spy thingy, isn't it? I saw it on…something on TV. Like the ASIS, but Canadian."

Bud glared at me – which I felt was quite uncalled for, since he'd been the one who'd mentioned it at all – then he said, "Sit down, both of you, and listen up."

Todd and Siân sat obediently and waited, open-mouthed and wide-eyed.

Bud rather pointedly sipped from his can of beer. Slowly. "I am not a spy. Cait's right when she says I have carried out some duties to serve my country that required me to have special clearances from the Canadian Security Intelligence Service, CSIS. But – and I must emphasize this – I am not a spy. I was an officer of the law, and that is all I have ever been."

I was amazed at how well my husband lied – though, given what he was lying about, it wasn't really a surprise.

Todd looked confused. "And why are we talking about this? I mean, it's interesting, true enough…but why did the topic come up?"

Siân nodded meaningfully at me. "These two were talking about it when I came in. Do you think there's something like espionage going on here, Bud?"

Bud shook his head. "No, I do not. I think Cait's put together a timeline of occurrences – many of which are horribly tragic – but I cannot see why Todd thinks he's in danger at all."

"But Philip named me as his next of kin…and the letter…and the threatening email. And now Lennie's dead. That must mean something." Todd was bleating, and I sort of felt sorry for him. At least, I did until he stood, his little fists clenched, making his knuckles turn white, and squeaked, "You've got to help us. We're...we're *family*."

I was at a loss, and allowed my face to show it as I looked at Bud. "Other than having dug up what I have online, there's no more I can do. There's no real way forward."

I could have added, "because everybody's dead," but that would just have made things worse; I silently congratulated myself for clicking my underused internal EDIT button.

My darling husband rolled his eyes and tutted. "I can put out a few feelers, I suppose. But just because Australia and Canada are part of the Commonwealth, it doesn't mean I've got any automatic connections to the ASIS lot. They've got much more in common with the USA than with Canada, to be honest; that massive Pine Gap information gathering place they've got together at Alice Springs being a good example. So don't hold your breath. Besides, I have no idea why ASIS would know anything useful about the murder of a young woman in the Bush over thirty years ago, even if it did turn out that the guy who killed her was a successful mining operations owner. Anything pertaining would be much more likely to be under the purview of the police, where I have zero contacts. Though, again, I'll reach out to a couple of guys I know back in Canada to see if I can forge a bond – cop to copper...so to speak."

I hesitated then whispered, "What about John Silver – might he know someone?"

Bud chuckled wryly, "The John Silver who won't answer my calls, you mean? Hardly surprising after what we know he's been through...largely because of us. So, no, I don't think John's an avenue worth pursuing."

"But you'll try?" Todd was pleading.

Bud nodded. "I will, Todd, I promise you that. Now – if you're all going to be waiting on me finding out more than Cait's been able to, why don't I make myself scarce and hit the internet with a few emails, and make a few calls, while you three discuss any potential paths forward?"

Bud left, and Todd, Siân, and I all grabbed cool drinks and sat out on the deck, surrounded by nature, and silence. Todd did his best to not keep touching the sticking plaster Siân had put on his forehead, but I could tell his fingers were desperate to fiddle.

"Did the original investigation into Lowanna's murder throw up anything that might be useful? Anything at all that you can remember, even if Cait wasn't able to find anything online," Siân asked her husband. "If it was thirty-five years ago, I'd have still been in school, back in Swansea."

He shrugged. "Wasn't much of one at all, I don't think. Remember, like you said, she died almost thirty-five years ago, and she was an Aboriginal girl, shot while out in the Bush. Can't imagine anyone did anything much about it, can you?"

Siân sighed. "Sadly not. It's so awful…I'm glad folks are finally acting more humanely when it comes to the people who've inhabited this land for over sixty thousand years. We're all just newcomers, yet we're so disrespectful of their place here. So, no, I also wouldn't be surprised if there'd been little effort put into finding out who'd killed Lowanna Swan immediately following her death. I know the rifle showed up again about thirteen years ago, as Cait said, and I also know things had improved somewhat by then – but what was it that made it headline news then? Was it because a successful white man was being accused of killing a young Aboriginal woman? Was that it, Todd?"

Todd looked unusually thoughtful. "To be honest, I think it was because Philip Myers had made it his business to put a few journos' noses out of joint over the years. He was a letter-writer – you know, back when newspapers were printed and they published 'Letters to the Editor', that kind of thing. Had some strong views on…well, lots of topics. Mainly about the way we all pay too much tax. I reckon when there was a chance for them to stick the knife in, they did – then turned it. Best way for them to do that? Splatter him across the front pages when he was on trial for murder. Revenge served hot and steaming."

I wondered if Todd made a valid point; my own views about newspaper journalism had been tainted by my experiences in the UK when I'd been arrested on suspicion of murder after the police found my ex-boyfriend Angus dead on the floor in my flat in Cambridge. The fact that I was never charged, and was entirely exonerated, carried no weight at all with the so-called journalists; they'd continued to hound me, and it was one of the reasons I'd taken a job at the University of Vancouver, where a professor of criminal psychology wasn't seen as cannon fodder for the tabloids.

Mirroring my thoughts, my sister said, "You'd know all about that, wouldn't you, Cait? Those sharks never let up on you, did they? So maybe Todd's right – they went for Philip's jugular during the trial, not caring what the outcome might be. Did they calm down at all after he was convicted? I hate to say it, but I can't remember. I suspect I was too busy juggling the kids and having to go back to work at the time."

I was able to answer that one. "There was almost nothing I could find about the original investigation, but the coverage of Philip's trial was extensive, as was the raking over of his entire life's work after the conviction was handed down. Indeed, one of the things I noticed was that the papers followed the demise of his businesses, gleefully reminding readers that whichever business they were writing about that had been bought up, or had gone bust, had been originally built and owned by the convicted killer, Myers."

"They're looking into arson as a real possibility for last night's tragedy." Bud burst onto the deck looking pleased with himself.

"Who's 'they'?" Todd turned to speak.

"The local fire service, and the cops," replied Bud. "All I had to do was phone the police station to find that out." He grinned. "I told them who we are, and where we're staying, and they were only too happy to fill me in. Said it was information they'd already released. I didn't take it further via that route, but I've emailed a guy I know in Toronto who might be able to send me a useful contact: he knows a guy who now works in Sydney who used to be a cop in the Blue Mountains, so there might be a sniff of a local connection there. Maybe we can get some insights not available to the public…as a courtesy."

"Thanks," I said, smiling at my husband, who seemed more excited than his news should have made him. "There's more, isn't there?"

Bud nodded, and plopped himself onto a chair beside me. "I know I said I don't have any contacts inside ASIS, and I don't, but it turns out that someone I happen to know is in Canberra on secondment from Ottawa. She's going to get back to me. Small world, eh?"

"Have you been vetted by CSIS, Cait?" Siân seemed suddenly fascinated.

I shrugged. "Yes. They did it years ago, when Bud and I first worked together, it seems – without me knowing about it." I arched an eyebrow at my husband.

"Had to be done, Cait," said Bud soberly. "Though, as you well know, all they did at that time was pull together a bunch of information about you that already existed. It's not as though anyone was tailing you, or anything like that."

I agreed. "Few people ever think about how much information is available about themselves. The idea that CSIS has 'a file' on me doesn't mean they possess any novel insights into my life, just that they have everything that exists elsewhere, all in one place. Plus a few interviews I did with them – voluntarily – after Bud and I were married."

Siân placed her empty glass on the table beside her. "I don't like the sound of that very much. Would they have investigated – or gathered data about – me or Todd? Because we're related."

I looked at Bud, who replied, "Can't imagine why they would."

"I like the way you say 'they' not 'we', Bud," said Siân snottily. "Like to distance yourself from all that governmental prying, do you? Not that I'd blame you; none of us like to think there's a Big Brother looking over our shoulder, do we?"

I wondered how we'd got from possible arson to Big Brother in just a few moments, and was about to try to reset the conversation, when Bud's phone rang. He looked at the screen, nodded toward the bedrooms, and took off again.

"Is he always like this, Cait? Dashing about, taking secret phone calls?" Siân sounded quite put out.

"Not really. In fact, to be honest, not ever – unless we've needed help with something we've been looking into, in the past," I said, a bit cagily.

Bud reappeared. "Just a quick question: does anyone have any objections to a visitor?"

Todd replied, "How do you mean?"

Bud answered airily, "The...um...person who's over from Ottawa is on a walking trip at the Gardens of Stone national park, which is – apparently – not too far from here. She'd like the chance to see what's in this area too. She asked if I knew of somewhere she could stay. So – I was thinking – since we have unused rooms in this place could we put her up for a night or two?"

Bud and I shared a glance that told me I should speak up. "That's a great idea, Bud. I don't mind sharing this big place, and I'm sure Siân and Todd feel the same, don't you? Especially for someone who might be able to help us, right?"

They both shrugged, noncommittally.

"Great," said Bud, and disappeared again.

Todd fidgeted. "Might this person really be able to help?"

I replied, "We can find out when they get here, can't we? Besides, more contacts can only be a good thing, right?"

Siân didn't look pleased, but I didn't care that I'd ridden roughshod over her somewhat. After all, Todd had asked for our help, and it seemed to me as though Bud was doing just that – getting someone on-side who might be able to do…well, more than nothing, in any case.

Over The Top

When Bud rejoined us, I thought he looked rather sheepish, so I chattered on a bit to give him some cover, while he pottered in the kitchen putting away the dishes we'd used at lunchtime, that had now drained dry.

"Siân was saying that she'd feel much better if she could have a swim, Bud," I called over. "She's found there's a local swimming pool, and thought she'd pop there for an hour or so. Now, as we all know, there's no point me joining her because 'A', I hate the smell of those places, and 'B', I can't swim anyway. Todd doesn't fancy it. So, do you want to go with her?" I hoped I'd managed to imbue my voice with as much of a pleading tone as possible – but only insofar as Bud would spot it, not Siân or Todd.

"Sure – I wouldn't mind a swim myself," replied Bud happily. "That pool at the hotel in Sydney was all well and good, but I couldn't relax by swimming lengths – not big enough. Is this a good-sized pool, do you know, Siân?"

"I looked it up before we got here: there's a twenty-five-meter pool open right now; that should do us. The fifty-meter one won't be open until October. This is Australia, and they like to offer their youth the chance to excel in the water, even if they're in the mountains," replied Siân. "It would be good to go together, thanks, Bud. Could we go quite soon, do you think? I'm seizing up here – no yoga for two days, and no swimming for three. Too long for me to go without helping my body as I know I can, and should."

"I'll grab my swimsuit now," said Bud, heading to our room.

"I'll help him find it," I said, scampering after him…knowing I had no idea where it might be, but needing to talk to him in private.

As Bud hunted through his smalls, I hissed, "Who's coming to stay? And why? And what's going on that you haven't told me?"

Bud held up his swimming shorts, looking triumphant. "Thelma Pruitt. She's the widow of an RCMP officer I knew a little, back in the day. Good man, Dwayne Pruitt – gone too soon. Decorated. Always brave. Died in the line of duty, which was a tragedy. The funeral was…somber, of course, but quite something. As it should have been. Him and Thelma? A sound couple. He'd always laugh about how they met and married; they kept bumping into each other when he was on duty, and he reckoned he'd have to arrest her or marry her one day. They walked down the aisle six months after they first met. A real whirlwind romance. She was devastated when he died, of course, but rallied. Thelma is good. An analyst – data collection stuff, behind the scenes. Started with the RCMP, then moved across to do work for CSIS in British Columbia, and now she's in Ottawa. Over here on what she says is a friendly exchange, which could mean anything; you know I'm not part of any inner circle."

"But why's she coming here?" I pressed.

Bud paused in the middle of rolling a towel around his swimsuit and sighed. Heavily. "To be honest, I've no idea. I told her what was going on – briefly – and she just sorta invited herself. Honestly, she didn't say why…though there could be excellent reasons for that. I know the cell reception she had wasn't good, so we'll find out when she gets here."

"I cannot imagine she's coming just because she wants a free night's digs in the Blue Mountains," I mused.

Bud began to roll again. "Unlikely, I'd have thought. I mentioned Myers, and Todd, then she told me – basically – to shut up, and said she'd come here. A name must have meant something to her."

I pulled a face to signify how bad I thought that sounded, and Bud pulled one back to show me he agreed.

He added, "Todd seems to be mixed up with…well, I choose to believe him when he says he knew nothing about Philp Myers having murdered that girl, but the guy's still a convicted killer, and it sounds like he and Todd were close."

"Myers was convicted, yes, but what if he *was* framed? And maybe by Lennie Orkins, who's now dead. Which could be…convenient."

Bud shook his head as he shoved his goggles into a small backpack. "There's Lowanna Swan's murder and the fire last night: I don't see a connection. However, that doesn't mean we shouldn't be naturally interested in the cause of a fire that killed three people we'd all met. I don't think Thelma would be our person for that, besides, she's rung an alarm in response to the Myers name, so that's going to be a more likely avenue…Thelma and Lowanna, not Louise." Bud chuckled, paused, then added, "Not really a topic for frivolity, is it, eh?"

I agreed.

He continued, "As for how we might be able to get insider information about the local investigation into the possible arson last night? No idea, other than the email I've sent to that old buddy of mine in Toronto. Maybe you could try to come up with something on that front?"

I was equally clueless about how I might do that. "I'll think about it – and, while I'm here alone with Todd, I'll do my best to winkle whatever I can out of him about the Lowanna-Myers case. Or even just about Myers himself."

"Bud?" Siân was calling from outside our door. "You ready?"

Bud kissed me. "Be good," he whispered.

"I always try to be," I replied as I opened the door. "Here he is, Sis – take good care of him, and don't either of you overdo it, okay?"

"Sure," said Bud, as he took Siân's backpack and headed toward the deck.

"Your turn to prepare something for dinner, Cait," said Siân cheerily as she headed off. "Todd's pretty hopeless in the kitchen, but he can take direction well. So don't you two go overdoing it, either."

I shouted after her, "I thought our plan was to eat out – experience the local cuisine," but they'd gone. I ambled into the sitting room, and saw Todd standing on the deck, peering down over the railing. "Penny for them," I said, not stepping forward to join him.

He turned, looking as white as a sheet, and clutching his chest. "Don't do that, Cait. You nearly gave me a heart attack. You know I'm in a nervous state."

I decided to take the bull by the horns: I sat, pulled up a chair beside me, patted it, and said, "So sit down and tell me why you're so scared, Todd. I know you don't want to frighten Siân, but trust me when I tell you I can take it…whatever it is. And I don't want my sister worried either, so I'm unlikely to tell her whatever it is you're holding back. Come on, out with it; I think there's something – if not several things – you haven't told us because Siân's been in the room. Now's the time. Spit it out."

Todd flopped down onto the chair I'd shoved beside him and whimpered, "There was another email. It wasn't just me who got one warning me off, see? My assistant Joyce got one too. And hers was just the same. But…the difference was…she went to see him. Philip."

I sat up, on full alert. "Has something happened to Joyce? You spoke to her yesterday afternoon – have you heard something since then?"

Thankfully, Todd shook his head. "No, nothing's happened to her. Not that I'm aware of. She didn't get her threatening email when I got mine, you see. She got hers well over a year ago, just after she'd got a letter from Philip asking her to visit him."

I nodded. "So that's a pattern – a letter from Philip asking for a visit, then a threatening email, the same thing that happened to you. And did it happen in much the same way? The letter, then about a week later a threatening email?"

"Pretty much. But by the time she got the email, she'd already been to see him. Unlike me. Turns out she was a better friend to him than I was."

I didn't quite know what to say, which isn't like me; in my defense, I was keenly aware that I was still in the process of getting to know Todd, and – since he's married to my sister – I decided I should tread carefully.

I began to wonder if my face was betraying my thoughts more than usual when Todd added, "I know we don't know each other well, Cait – but you're my wife's sister, so of course I trust you. And I'm telling you everything I can about all this, though Siân's always saying that I'm not able to process my thinking about many things half as well as I can wrap my head around topics concerning solid objects like machinery, equipment, and physical processes. I suppose I'm an engineer because my mind works that way – or else the other way around."

I pressed, "But there are things you haven't told me? That's what you're saying?"

Todd shrugged. "Inevitably, I suppose. One thing I haven't mentioned, for example – not because I didn't want to, but because I haven't even thought about it until right now – is that Joyce Trimble and Philip Myers used to be an item. Not sure they ever moved in together, but I got the impression it had been pretty serious. When I joined Philip's outfit, Joyce had already moved to a different company. She'd met someone, and they got married…fast. I know there was talk that she'd married on the rebound. Around the office, on the worksites, you know? I didn't take much notice of it at the time, but now? Well, now I realize she might have been closer to Philip than I'd ever thought, because she was the one he wrote to first, asking her to visit him. Long before he ever asked me. And she actually went. What do you think that means?"

I chuckled. "I'm a psychologist, Todd, not a mind reader. But I'd say it suggests they were close, and certainly that he trusted her…and it sounds likely that she trusted him too. More than that, I can't say."

Todd looked thoughtful, and shoved the tip of his thumb between his teeth. "I couldn't bring myself to do it, Cait. Nothing to do with the threat in the email. I just couldn't stand the thought of looking him in the face again, knowing what he'd done to that poor girl. Do you understand that?"

I nodded. "It's a perfectly normal response – psychologically speaking." I paused and smiled warmly – which I hoped would help my brother-in-law feel a little better. Then I asked, "Did you speak to Joyce about what passed between her and Philip when she visited him?"

Todd looked lost. "I didn't even know about any of this until a few days ago. When I heard that Philip was dead, I had to share that news with someone, and I couldn't tell Siân…not about any of it. So I told Joyce. That's when I learned she'd been to see Philip about a year back. I had to leave Perth with Siân to fly here for the convention that evening, so Joyce and I never took the conversation further – until the phone call you overheard yesterday. And I finally told Siân about all of it after that call, too. Though I didn't want to. Joyce kept saying that Siân deserved to know. But, really, Siân doesn't deserve any of this, Cait. She's done so much to keep this family going – holding it all together when I've been away – and she's dealing with so much pain, with her arthritis, that none of this is fair. I don't want to dump any more pressure on her. But…well, you know."

"My sister's stronger than you think, Todd."

Todd stood and flapped his arms about. "I'm not saying she's not strong – what I'm saying is she's *too* strong. She carries it all, and never complains, and I know she'll just absorb whatever stress I cause, and suck it all up so it doesn't affect anyone else. That's what's not fair, Cait. See? It's not that I think she can't cope, it's that I believe she'll try to cope on everyone's behalf, and end up doing herself no favors at all."

Todd had a point; in that respect, at least, my sister and I were cut from the same cloth. The difference between us was that Siân would always accept what was thrown at her and carry it, making it look as though it weighed nothing at all…whereas I would always try to understand why it had been thrown, and then do my best to work out how I could chuck it back.

Rather than dwell on family traits, I pressed Todd again. "So Joyce got a letter, visited Philip, then got a threatening email…and that's all you know? That's *all* the information you haven't shared with us? Really?"

Todd looked innocent enough, and even screwed up his face to suggest he was thinking hard. "I believe so. But maybe if you asked me specific questions, I'd recall more. I can't remember things like you can, of course; I just wish I had your special memory at times like this, because it would make life so much easier."

I acknowledged his point, but didn't think it worthwhile mentioning that there are many things I wish I could forget that my eidetic memory will not let go of. *Not his problem.*

"Okay," I replied, "let's begin with you telling me everything you recall about the original Lowanna Swan case, before you ever met Philip. You know – just your impressions. Any facts or even rumors you can remember. You'd have been how old when she was killed, for example?"

Todd smiled. "Good idea. Yes, let's keep Philip out of it for now. Right. When did she die? Hmm…I'd have been about fifteen at the time, so living at home in Perth, at school…no, to be honest, I don't have any memories of the case at the time. At all. But what would a fifteen-year-old boy be doing poring over newspapers or watching the news on TV? I was always out doing…something. Or else in…doing something. My room at home was my kingdom, I recall that much. My parents made sure I was as active as possible, though I'll admit I was one of those kids who would rather have never left the house, because that's where all my cool stuff was – I had projects, and little inventions, and hand-built models all over my room. My mother hated it – said it was impossible to keep clean."

Fascinating though the insights into my brother-in-law's teen years were, I was keen to get to his earliest recollections of anything to do with Lowanna Swan, so asked him to fast-forward to those.

"I think the first I heard of her was when I was in the pub. You see, when I started working for Philip, going to the pub at lunchtime was still a part of the work culture. Only a couple of small beers, and maybe a pie, of course, but that was what was normal, so that's what I did. I remember I was keen to be seen to fit in, so even we more geeky types would manage to sip a couple of cold ones just for the sake of looking like we belonged with the rest of the mining people."

"And what was the pub talk about Lowanna?"

Todd finally seemed to relax a little, leaning back in his chair, his eyes roaming across the thousands…millions…of trees in front of us. "It was fascinating, to be honest. See, most of us who work in the business know just how much money is spent on the exploration part of mining: it doesn't matter what it is you're trying to get out of the ground, the first thing you need to work out is where to find it. Did you know that more than a quarter of the entire workforce in Perth is involved in mining and its ancillary services? Over a quarter. And a great number of those people are in research – trying to decide where to dig for whatever it is you want to get to. Every dollar spent on making the X on the map more accurate, can save hundreds of thousands of dollars in wasted effort. So the idea that there'd once been a person who'd been able to look at a map and point to an exact spot where precious opals could be found – and could do that with accuracy time and time again – was, of course, absolutely mesmerising. Even if she was dead before I'd heard of her. Whenever someone spun a yarn about her, most of us would say that it was all a myth…that it couldn't happen. But there was always somebody around who'd worked with someone, who'd been somehow involved with a project that had owed its success to Lowanna Swan. Or so they said. And that was the thing, see? No one I ever met had actually, *definitely* had that experience – not first-hand. But everyone *knew* she could do it, because everyone said they'd met someone, who knew someone, who'd seen it work."

I hadn't really wrapped my head around the entire pointing at a map thing until that moment: as far as I had been concerned, a young woman had been shot in the back and killed, and that was that. Now? Now I wondered about the mythological nature of her abilities. Todd was right, it was fascinating.

"So, could she really do it, or not?" I thought it worth asking.

Todd shook his head. "No idea, to be honest. Like I said, she died when I was fifteen. But I did end up working with a bloke who said he'd been at a find not far from Opalton that had been one of hers. That would have been about five years before she died, so I'd have been around ten at the time. I met him quite early in my career, and he was the only individual I ever met, personally, who claimed to have first-hand experience of one of her finds. But, even then, I'm not sure that he would really have known for certain that the bloke who employed him had actually paid Lowanna Swan to point at the spot on a map where he should dig. I only had his word for that part of it. To be fair to him, I believe that he believed it. But I suppose all I *know* is that he was an experienced opal man; did a fair bit of digging, mainly around Coober Pedy. Good at it, too."

I gave Todd's words some thought. "So a young woman had a skill that might or might not have been real, but — whatever the truth of that — opal miners in general believed she could locate a deposit of opals on a map, and people did, in fact, pay her to do it. Is that right?"

Todd nodded. "And then she was murdered — that's also a fact."

"The motive for Philp Myers killing her that was floated at his trial — and presumably believed by the jury — was that she'd refused to sell her services to him, because he'd been overly amorous on a couple of occasions when they'd met, and that she took a dislike to him for that reason. That was also why her father took her away, into hiding. Siân thinks that might not ring true for the Philip she knew. What about you? You'd have spent a great deal of time with him when he was away from his domestic environment — is there anything about Philip that you can tell me now, that you didn't like to mention in front of Siân? Anything about how he acted toward women when he wasn't with his wife, for example?"

Todd stood and stretched out his back. "I can't say he didn't notice good looking women, but, as far as I was aware, Philip had no interest in any of them. He was faithful to his wife, as far as I know. He and she weren't given to open displays of affection, that's true, but I reckon it was a solid relationship. Her death was a shock: one of those instances of a person being told they've got cancer one day, and being in their coffin within a month. It happened about a year before he got arrested — so at least she never knew anything about all that. She was a nice woman. Not your gushing type, more staid, if you know what I mean. You must have met her at our wedding. Right?"

I nodded. A willowy blonde with bird-like gestures, she'd clung to her husband's arm, and hadn't mixed much. Maybe to be expected for an Australian visiting Wales for the wedding of a man who worked for her spouse – probably grappling with horrific jet lag, and not knowing a soul. In our solitary exchange, over the disappointing canapes, she'd told me she'd never left Australia before that trip – that she'd had to get a passport to be able to travel.

"If Philip wasn't a womanizer when you knew him, do you think he might have been, once upon a time?" All I could do was ask.

"I reckon Joyce Trimble would be more the one to talk to about that. She's a woman, and she knew him before I did."

"Excellent idea, Todd. Can we make that happen?"

"What?"

"Can you phone Joyce and get her to talk to me, please? A video call would be great – because then I could see her when she talks. Read her body language, you know? If you ask Siân, she'll tell you it's my thing."

Todd sighed. "No need to ask, she's often mentioned it. I dare say you know it makes a person feel extremely uncomfortable to believe that their every move is being analyzed, don't you?"

"I don't analyze everyone, all the time, just people whose responses I'm interested in," I lied. I didn't want Todd to feel he had to keep himself in check around me.

"Good. And, yes, I suppose I can ask Joyce if she'll talk to you." He checked his watch. "They're a couple of hours behind us, back in Perth. She should be in the office. But…"

"Yes?"

"Do you reckon talking on a video call is the right thing to do? Anyone could overhear if she's in her…I know, I'll tell her to go into my office to take the call, and to shut the door. It's a good door; all the board members have offices which are soundproofed, because we talk about a lot of stuff we don't want anyone else hearing."

"Industrial espionage?" I was surprised.

"Walls have ears, and just letting word get out about a piece of land we think might offer us the chance to get to something we want could send the price soaring…or mean a competitor gets it before us. And if we're angling for a particular lease? Once those leases are assigned, they're gone for at least twenty-one years. So, yes, we're careful about what we say, and where we say it. The mining business is full of whispers and rumors…my company doesn't want to add to any of that. I'll call Joyce, tell her to get herself into my office and call me back from there. You can use my laptop, if you like. How about that?"

I thought it was a good plan, however, I couldn't help but think that Todd was being just a little too accommodating. Was he getting me to talk to his assistant as a way to get me off his back?

Go West

When Joyce Trimble appeared on the screen of Todd's laptop on the little desk in the bedroom Bud and I were using, I did a double-take; she looked almost exactly like my sister probably would in about ten years' time. She had a long neck, was slim, with piercing blue eyes, well-coiffed, blonde-highlighted, graying hair, and she sat as upright as a mannequin in front of the camera, just the way Siân held herself. It was weird.

I wondered if that was why Siân had been so troubled by the fact that Todd had lied about how much of a debt he felt he owed Joyce. Housewife Siân, and work-wife Joyce? Surely not. I told myself to not allow that thought to percolate, and to make the best use of the time I had with Joyce in Perth, who was clearly feeling none too comfortable about the entire set-up of the call.

I decided to take a leaf from Bud's book, so used calming tones to pacify her before I began my "interrogation".

"Thanks for doing this, Joyce," I opened. "It's nice to meet someone who works with my brother-in-law. He's left the room, by the way, so please speak freely."

"You're welcome, and I shall. Nice to meet you too. You don't look like Siân at all. You're real sisters, are you? Blood?"

Blunt, to the point, not admitting she's feeling pressurized. "Oh yes, Joyce, we're real sisters alright. But, no, we don't look much like each other. Siân got the slim and sporty genes, I got the short, round, lazy ones."

Joyce looked surprised. "Yoga's not a sport though, is it? Nor are activities like knitting while listening to opera, classical music, or BBC radio programs for hours. Todd's talked to me often about what Siân enjoys doing, but he's never mentioned her doing anything sporty."

I felt slighted on my sister's behalf. "She's at the pool right now, and swims almost every day."

"But that's for her back, right? Not really sport. More therapy."

I couldn't believe I was having a sniping match on behalf of my sister with a woman I wanted to interview about a murder. She'd done her best to control the situation, and it had worked. I was annoyed – with myself, as much as her.

"Were you and Philip Myers a couple at one time?" *Take that.*

Unfazed, Joyce replied, "We were. But there was a problem: I loved him, and he loved someone he couldn't have, so it was never going to work out between us. I dropped him when I finally understood what was wrong, and stopped working with him, too. Then I met my husband, and that was that."

"So was that why Philip wrote to you, and why you visited him in prison? Because you had a history." I thought it best to get straight to the point.

Joyce looked thoughtful. "Yes. I think he believed I would do as he asked, and he was right. Not because I still loved him, but because I'd never believed him capable of doing what he'd been convicted of."

"And he knew that?"

"Oh yes. I'd written to him in prison often. I even attended as much of his trial as I could. It was the start of the rift between me and my husband, really. The kids were young, and we didn't have much, but I travelled to the trial in any case. Quite a hike from Perth to Darwin. I stayed for a week, then I had to get back. Saw what I could while I was there."

I was watching every possible move that Joyce made, which, disappointingly, wasn't a great deal, because all I could see were her shoulders and head. Her hands were below the line of sight of the camera, and they can tell me such a lot when I'm assessing body language. I had to be content with her eyes, facial expression, and the changing tilt of her head — all of which are aspects that can be easily controlled by someone who's trying to not give themselves away. Joyce? She was keeping her expression neutral, her eyes staring right at the camera, and her only real "tell" was the way she lifted her chin almost imperceptibly when she spoke about Philip Myers, as opposed to herself, or her family. I decided to try something that might get her façade to crack.

"Obviously I've been talking to Todd about all of this, and I know he's spoken to you. He seems to believe he's in mortal danger. Do you feel your life's at risk, too? After all, he didn't actually visit Philip…whereas you did."

"I visited him over a year ago, and I'm still here, unscathed. Todd can overreact. It's something I've had to speak to him about on many occasions."

Not the slightest chink in her armor. She's either good at acting, or really believes she's in no danger.

"Do you think the deaths of the three members of the S & S Roads Mob here in Katoomba are in any way connected with the death of Lowanna Swan?" I wanted to keep at her, with direct hits.

Joyce shook her head slightly.

At last — a reaction.

Her tone wasn't dismissive, but suggested resignation. "I don't see how it can be. It's terribly sad, of course, but I don't see the links Todd does."

"So what did you and Philip talk about when you saw him?"

Joyce leaned closer to the camera, her expression grim. "He told me he was certain he'd been fitted up. Maintained that he'd never have killed Lowanna. Told me that he and Lowanna were lovers, and that her father hadn't wanted her to abandon him for Philip. He told me that the reason he hadn't said anything to his lawyers about this — so that they could use it to defend him in court – was because he didn't want there to be any talk about Lowanna that might have been less than kind."

I also moved closer to the camera, mirroring Joyce's actions, which is something that can allow a subject to believe you're empathizing with them. "That's interesting. Did you believe Philip?"

Joyce sat back in her chair – *ah, moving away from me, avoiding me* – and smiled, coldly. "I did. Yes, I did. It…it made sense of what I'd always believed, that he couldn't love me because he loved someone else, someone he could never be with. Lowanna was dead, and she was the one he loved. He told me about how they'd met – at a business gathering – and then had contrived to meet again, secretly. They'd fallen in love almost straight away; I could see in his eyes how he'd felt about her. But Lowanna hadn't believed her father would let her out of his control…she'd made too much money for him over the years, and her father had no intention of letting his source of an easy income desert him. Philip told me they were due to meet up to take off together, but she didn't show up. He found out later that she'd been whisked away by her father, but no one knew where he'd taken her. Bereft, Philip continued with his life, until a letter from her reached him when he was visiting Opalton."

"How did she know where he'd be?"

Joyce chuckled. "Opalton is the sort of place where a letter sent to a person without an exact address would find them. Philip's name would have been known in the community, because most opal miners go through the place at some point or another. Lowanna had taken a long shot, and it paid off…eventually. Once again, they planned to meet and escape her father's control, together. She asked Philip to go to her in East Arnhem Land. It's illegal to enter East Arnhem Land without getting written permission from the Yolngu so, if Philip had done that, Lowanna's father might have found out he was on his way to meet her, so Philip talked Bruce Walker into going there to meet with her, on his behalf."

I was all ears. "This is the Bruce Walker who ended up underneath his own piece of roadbuilding equipment out in the Bush a year or so ago? The one Philip helped to set up in business?"

Joyce nodded, then reached an arm out of shot to grab a mug of something steaming, which she sipped. "Poor Bruce. Terrible way to go. And so young. Only my age." She put down the mug and chuckled. "We all think we're too young to die, don't we?"

I agreed. "Did Bruce manage to connect with Lowanna in East Arnhem Land?"

Joyce shrugged. "Philip told me that Bruce did, and that he came back with word of how Lowanna planned to make her escape with the help of a distant cousin, who understood how awful it was to be separated from the man you loved. The plan was that Lowanna and Philip would meet outside East Arnhem Land, in Katherine, and he told me that they did…that it was…well, he said a night of passion, but I won't go into that. They weren't able to actually stay together all night, and the next day when they were supposed to meet up to catch the train, she didn't show up. He looked everywhere for her, but couldn't find her – had no idea where she'd gone. He couldn't exactly advertise the fact he was looking for her, see? She was found dead the next day, a long way outside Katherine, in the Bush. Shot in the back. He had no idea why Lowanna was where they found her. Said it made no sense to him at the time. Philip also told me that he only discovered when he was eventually arrested that the rifle she'd been shot with was, indeed, his – it was a pretty fancy double-barrelled one, with his initials in a bit of gold inlay. Bruce Walker had given that rifle to Lowanna at Philip's request, so she'd have a means of defending herself if she got into trouble. Philip told me he was convinced that her father had followed her to Katherine, had somehow seen them together, then had lured her out into the Bush and had killed her. But he'd never been able to work out how, or why, the rifle had ended up in the waterhole where Lennie Orkins claimed he originally found it, which wasn't in Katherine, nor anywhere near where Lowanna was killed. That's why he'd asked Bruce Walker to take a job with the people Lennie Orkins worked for, to try to get close to him, to find out if someone had put him up to 'rediscovering' the rifle, or if he really had found it in that waterhole, all those years earlier."

I was taken aback. "Hang on – Bruce Walker was working for the S & S Roads Mob at Philip Myers' request, to be able to prove that Lennie Orkins had lied in court?"

Joyce nodded.

"And do you think that's why Bruce ended up dead?"

Joyce looked deeply puzzled. "But he was on his own – miles away from everyone else, at the head of the road. That's what the inquest said."

"You believe that?"

Joyce looked bemused. "Don't you believe anything that anyone ever says?"

I weighed my reply. "I consider it carefully before I make up my mind."

Joyce chuckled wryly. "I bet you're a bundle of laughs at a party. Not."

"Did you happen to see Lennie Orkins giving evidence at Philip's trial? I've not been able to access transcripts, of course, and the press reports about Lennie's evidence were factual, lacking color."

Joyce nodded. "I did, as a matter of fact. He was handled carefully by the prosecution counsel. Direct questions, eliciting short answers. I thought…I thought Lennie wanted to say more than he did. He seemed to be holding himself in check, especially when he was cross-examined."

I considered Lennie's reputation as a spinner of yarns, as well as my own experience of him as a storyteller; I could imagine he'd have preferred to be entertaining the court, rather than responding briefly.

"Did he seem credible to you?" I suspected Joyce was pretty good at sizing people up, and wanted her opinion.

The woman sitting in my brother-in-law's office in Perth seemed to have relaxed, and she nibbled her lip thoughtfully. "At the time, I thought so, yes. Indeed, I was surprised when Philip told me he thought that Lennie Orkins was involved with framing him for Lowanna's murder. When I asked Philip why he believed that, he said it was something to do with a new cellmate of his...something the man had let slip during a conversation they'd been having. But he didn't tell me who the cellmate was, nor what he'd said. Just that he'd asked Bruce to go to work with the S & S Mob to try to find out more."

"Was Bruce still alive when you visited Philip?"

"Oh yes, and Philip was expecting to hear more from him shortly."

"More? What had he heard already?"

"I'm sorry, Philip didn't say." Joyce looked disappointed. "I wish I'd pressed him more about that now, of course."

There was a knock at the door behind me, and Todd stuck his head in. "Sorry to bother you both, but Bud's colleague has just phoned him to say she'll be here in about an hour. He asked me to let you know. And Siân and Bud are on their way back from the pool." Todd waved toward Joyce on the screen, then backed out of the door.

I returned my attention to the woman in Perth.

She said, "You have to go, and so do I. Cait, listen – I loved Philip Myers, but it couldn't work, because I wasn't Lowanna. I didn't know that at the time…I just knew there was 'someone' between us." She cupped her chin, leaning toward the camera. "When he told me about her, when I visited him in prison, I could see how deeply he'd loved her. It all made sense then – she was the one he'd been pining for. That's why he couldn't love me, you see? So, yes, I have no doubt he was telling the truth about that much, at least. And, look, you don't really know me from a hole in the ground, so there's no real reason you should believe what I'm telling you, but ask Todd, he'll speak for me. I truly believe Philip didn't kill that girl – because he loved her."

I toyed with the idea of telling Joyce that I knew of far too many cases where one person loving another had led to murder, but Joyce surprised me by laughing.

"What's funny?"

"Oh, you know, thinking back over the years. What a strange thing young love is; I'd have done anything for Philip, back then. And I wasn't alone. He seemed to attract women who were devoted to him. I know that Cindy, his wife, was utterly besotted with him, of course, but there was a girl back then, when he and I were a couple…no, not a girl, she was a young woman, married, too. But that didn't stop her from hanging around wherever Philip was. Followed him about like a puppy, she did. He told me she'd been doing it for ages – long before we got together – and she'd even turn up when we'd go out on a date. Sometimes she'd show up where we were with her husband in tow, sometimes on her own. He and Philip played pool together a bit. I don't think he had the faintest idea that his wife was hot for Philip. Nice enough woman, I suppose. She even came to visit me in hospital after my car accident, when I had my leg stuck up in the air for weeks. Brought me fruit. And, believe it or not, Philip told me that she even turned up at his door not long after Cindy had died, protesting her love for him and telling him that now they were finally both free, and could be together. Which…I suppose…might mean she wasn't that nice, after all. What was her name? Nina? Tina? No…Trina, that's it. Married to a French bloke…oh yes, that's right, he was Philippe, which I thought was hilarious at the time, given how smitten she was with Philip. Philippe Gagnon, that was his name. I wonder what happened to him. To her, too. But there, I'm rambling now – off down memory lane, and you and I both have to get away."

Todd knocked the door again, this time to tell me that Siân and Bud were back.

Joyce and I exchanged our goodbyes, I expressed my thanks, and she agreed to answer any emails I might send her by way of a follow-up, or to even talk to me again, without Todd needing to act as an intermediary.

I clicked off the call and gave myself a moment to process everything Joyce had told me, which was…a lot.

Did Joyce believe that Philip had loved Lowanna too much to kill her? Yes. But had Philip pulled the wool over her eyes about that for some reason? That was something I couldn't be sure about, and I'd never have a chance to ask Philip for myself, because he'd conveniently died in his cell.

As I made use of the bathroom before joining the others, I had an internal chat with myself about that being one of the main problems with tackling any cold case: so often the people who could tell you exactly what you need to know have gone. And there was no getting around that problem – so I decided to spend a bit of time with my family instead, before the arrival of our unexpected guest.

The Deep End

"Did you enjoy your swim?" I knew the answer before Bud or Siân had a chance to say a word, because they were both glowing, and Siân had grown an inch…at least, she was standing much straighter than she had been before she'd left the house.

"This one's like a fish," said Bud, nodding toward my sister.

"Not really, but I took some lessons a year or so ago to make sure I wasn't doing more harm than good in the water, and the instructor worked on my technique with me. I know for a fact that I swim more efficiently now because of it, which means I'm helping my back, rather than maybe hurting it by bashing up and down the lanes."

Bud chuckled. "I guess I could do with a few of those lessons – then I wouldn't splash as much as I do. And I'd get from one end to the other a heck of a lot quicker, eh?"

"Just as long as you're not damaging anything, that's all," I said.

"Stubbed my toe in the changing room," said Bud. "Same one I dropped the cans on earlier; it's like there's a target on it or something."

"Well, in that case, be sure to keep an eye open," replied Siân, "these things happen in threes, don't they, Cait? According to Grandma Morgan, anyway."

I nodded. "Oh yes, she was quite clear about that; bad things always happen in threes. Though I recall she was strangely silent about the frequency of the occurrence of good things. Maybe they are singular – or maybe they happen in fives, and we were never trusted with that insight, because then we'd have lived in a constant state of happy anticipation, rather than fear."

We shared a sisterly laugh and hugged. "She was a card, wasn't she?" Siân ambled to the fridge to fill her water bottle from the carafe we'd put in there. "She's why I went into nursing, though, so there's that."

"I don't recall you telling me that one of your grandmothers was a nurse, Cait," said Bud, taking the carafe when Siân had finished with it.

"Oh, didn't I? Yes, she nursed TB patients in a place called Garngoch, near Swansea, and must have worked in other hospitals too, I suppose, though I don't recall anyone in the family talking about that. So, she was your inspiration, Siân? Good for her, and good for you."

"If you've all finished," said Todd quite snippily, "I'd like us to have a chat before this person that Bud's invited here turns up." He checked his watch. "Not long now. So – what do we hope she's going to be able to do for us?"

Siân stood understandably mute, I shrugged, and Bud shuffled a bit. He said, "In all honesty, Todd, I've no idea. But she's a good woman with a sharp brain, and if she wanted me to stop talking and just come here, she must have her reasons. Why don't we invite her to explain when she arrives? Meanwhile, Siân and I have some news…on the local front."

"I've hung up my wet cozzie, and I'm feeling lovely and loose, so does anyone fancy a cuppa? I thought I'd put the jug on." Siân was already holding the kettle under the tap. We all nodded. She added, "You go ahead then, Bud – tell them about Winnie."

We dumped ourselves onto sofas as Siân got things sorted in the kitchen, and I asked, "You mean Winnie from last night?"

"Yes, of Winnie's Place – she was at the pool," replied Bud. "Apparently, she loves it there, and she's a fine swimmer, let me tell you that. But, like Siân had a tutor, so does Winnie – her grandson…that young guy who's the volunteer firefighter, who splattered your duck across the table last night, Cait; Timbo. Now if you want to see someone swim, he's the one to watch. I thought last night that he looked well-built, and now I know why that's the case; he's a bit of a specialist when it comes to the butterfly stoke, and his physique suggests he's been at it for years. His grandmother was full of praise for him; said his abilities in the water would come in handy when he's fighting fires – all that muscle tone, endurance, and great lungs."

I raised an eyebrow in my husband's direction. "Thinking of sending him flowers?"

Bud chuckled. "Yeah, right. Like I said, well-built, and a really pleasant manner about him, too. He's only nineteen. Winnie's got him teaching her how to swim underwater; she wants to be better at that before she goes on holiday to Bora Bora, she says – so she can swim with the fish on the sandbanks without using a snorkel."

Todd sat forward, looking irritated. "You said you had news? Are you going to tell us?"

Bud smiled indulgently. "The fire chief suspects arson, that's for sure." Bud shook his head sadly.

"Murder, that's what it was, not just arson," said Siân from behind the kitchen counter. "Timbo didn't say the words, but it's obvious. I hope they find whoever did it and throw the book at them. It's murder. Three men dead. Three. Disgusting."

"Do they have any idea who might have done it? Or how?" Todd sounded as though he expected the answer he got.

"No, nothing yet," replied Bud. "No signs they could find around the house, but the fire had completely wrecked the place."

Siân added, "Timbo hasn't seen too many fires in his short career, though he agreed with the gossip we'd heard around the shops that there've been a suspicious number around these parts in recent weeks. The talk at the fire station is that they might have an arsonist here…a firestarter, he said. Timbo made it clear that isn't something he wanted us to share, because of the chance of the locals panicking, but there's no harm telling you, I'm sure. Anyway, the other fires have all involved small things – abandoned sheds, or rubbish piles, that sort of thing, and he went so far as to tell us he was pleased to finally be 'getting some action' to put his training to good use; but this last one has really knocked the stuffing out of him. I could tell. He said the more experienced professional firefighters kept the younger ones, and the volunteers, away from the house as it burned, and even afterwards…packing them off to work on the surrounding area, making sure the fire didn't spread, you know? I guess they wanted to save them from what must have been a tragic, and horrific, sight. How awful. I hope they've got access to good counsellors. No wonder so many firefighters suffer with mental health problems."

We fell silent as we all grabbed mugs, and Bud brought the pot to the table.

"Anything else?" I asked, hoping there was.

Siân half-chuckled. "Winnie told us that Big Stan and Neal – and Shorty – have been asked to vacate that swish hotel. It seems the state of their suite was more than the housekeeping staff was prepared to put up with, however much they might be paying. So they showed up at Winnie's Place looking for a room. No recollection of having been there last night at all, it seems. Her expression when she told us that she'd sent them packing suggests they didn't have time for a beer. She reckons they'll find somewhere to take them in."

"I dare say they'll be staying for longer than they'd planned," I said. "After all, three of Big Stan's men are dead; they're not going to head back to Sydney any time soon, are they?"

"Why would they stay?" Todd sounded genuinely baffled. "If the men had families, they're not going to come all the way out here, are they? That wouldn't make any sense at all. Won't they transport the…remains…to wherever they'll be buried?"

"They might not be buried at all, Todd, love," said Siân quietly. "You know…given what happened to them."

Todd looked confused, then the penny dropped. "Oh yeah, I see. Well, you know what I mean. Why wouldn't Big Stan and the rest of The Mob just leave? Now. What have they got to hang around for?"

"The local cops might want to talk to them, as part of the arson investigation…if the local cops get involved in that sort of thing here," said Bud. "If they have to bring specialists from somewhere else – somewhere bigger than Katoomba, I mean – then maybe they'll want the ins and outs of the men's backgrounds, and so forth."

Todd begrudgingly accepted that Bud had made a valid point, but didn't look too happy about it.

Siân's tone was thoughtful when she said, "If the professionals around here are thinking this was arson, with an intent to kill, then do we have any theories about why anyone would want to kill Lennie, Ditch, and Dan?"

Todd sniped, "Other than maybe because Lennie framed Philip Myers for murder, and someone's seen fit to kill him because of that?"

Siân tutted. "Yes, other than that. By the way – does anyone know who this Dan Entwistle is? I know we all met Lennie and Ditch – real name Richard – Early, but did I even meet a Dan?"

She looked at Todd, who replied, "Tall bloke. No hair. Lazy right eye."

We all nodded.

"Oh, that Dan," said Bud heavily.

He'd been one of the quieter members of The Mob when they were out and about, but he'd definitely been on the dinner cruise with us; I recalled the comment Big Stan had made about him, which had raised a laugh. I tutted aloud as I felt the pang of a life cut short.

Siân observed, "To think that poor young Ditch tried to drown himself at Manly…and now he's actually dead. Before his life had really started. That Dan didn't look as though he had much going for him in life, but at least he'd lived a longer one than poor young Ditch."

"Dan Entwistle was married with six kids," said Todd quietly. "He might have had a lazy eye, but he was quite active in other ways."

We all admitted that it might be wrong to judge a book by its cover, after all, and I finally understood the joke Big Stan had made at Dan's expense that evening we'd all been enjoying the sunset…and yarns about death. The sad irony struck me sharply.

"Did you get the impression that Timbo might get any inside information about how any investigation into the fire is proceeding…if it's even begun, that is?" I asked.

Bud shook his head. "I think Winnie's more likely to know than Timbo – her cousin is the fire chief."

I tried to not sound too excited when I said, "Excellent," but Siân tutted in any case. I continued, "And did she know anything?"

Siân replied, "No she didn't. I know we want to understand why there was a deadly fire, because it's quite clearly stressing Todd, but I don't think Winnie's going to be sharing any confidences with us – not even if she knows that she and I have a common interest in swimming. We had a nice chat, and that was all. I don't think that's an avenue worth exploring, Cait."

I tried to shrug it off. "Okay," I replied. "So has anyone got any bright ideas about where we go from here? Because I'm out of them."

"Did the chat Todd told me you had with Joyce bring up anything unexpected?" Siân put down her mug of tea and reached into her pocket for something that she popped into her mouth. "Homeopathic," she said as I tried to stop my eyebrow from sliding up to my hairline.

I replied, "She's convinced that Philip Myers didn't kill Lowanna, because he loved her; Joyce told me that Philip and Lowanna were a couple – secretly – and were planning to make a life together. At least, that's what he told Joyce when she visited him in prison, and she definitely believed he was speaking the truth."

Three stunned faces looked at me.

Todd spoke first. "Joyce told you that? Why wouldn't she have told me? She hardly knows you. I trusted her...I do trust her. Why wouldn't she trust me with that information? It makes a world of difference, don't you think? You see? Like I said, Philip wouldn't have killed Lowanna. Lennie Orkins *did* frame him."

"Philip Myers and Lowanna Swan were a couple?" Siân sounded thoughtful. "So, Philip's belief was that the father killed his own daughter to stop her from running off with her lover, then, twenty years later, someone – Lennie Orkins maybe? – framed him for it?"

I nodded.

"You two have more in common than you might think," said Bud quietly. "Your thinking follows similar paths – you know that, right?"

Siân and I smiled. "It's rare," she replied, "but, there again, I don't usually have to think through things like this. Maybe if I did, I'd behave like Cait more often than I do."

Todd's face took on an expression of alarm before he could control it, which I found both mildly insulting and quite amusing.

"Anything else?" Bud pressed me.

I wondered if Todd needed to know exactly how close Joyce and Philip had once been; if she'd not told him herself that she'd loved the man, should I?

I decided to reply, "Joyce told me that Philip had asked Bruce Walker to take a job with the S & S Roads Mob to try to work out if Lennie Orkins was a liar or not. Bruce had communicated with Philip about – something – though she didn't know what. Then Bruce died. I judged that she truly believes Bruce's death to have been accidental."

Todd pounced. "No. See? I told you Bruce didn't just get run over by his own vehicle – that he was murdered too. That's obviously because he was spying on Lennie. I bet you that's what it was. Lennie did it all: he framed Philip, *and* he killed Bruce."

Siân snapped, "You were equally convinced that Lennie himself had been killed in that fire because he did the framing at someone else's request. Now it was all *him*? So why'd he die in a fire last night, Todd?"

Todd stood, his mug shaking in his hand. "Don't be like that, Siân. I'm scared, can't you tell? Whatever's going on, it's not over. You're my wife, you should understand how I feel. Why don't you ever have my back, woman!?"

A massive, shadowy figure appeared on the deck beyond the sliding glass doors.

"Should I say 'Knock, knock'? Or shall I go with 'Ding, ding…end of round one'?"

Surf's Up

"Hey, Thelma, you found us. Great. Come in and meet the gang." Bud was on his feet in a flash, and Thelma Pruitt was in our midst before we knew it.

The large, sturdy woman dumped her large, sturdy backpack in a corner, we were all introduced, and she gratefully accepted a mug of tea as we made sure our new guest was comfortable and settled. The small talk proved challenging – not merely because Thelma had arrived just as we'd all expected Todd to blow his top, but also because none of us really knew why she was there in the first place.

"It's been a few years," said Bud tentatively. "Five or six?"

"Closer to ten, Bud," replied Thelma in a voice with a noticeably sonorous quality; I reckoned she'd make a great narrator of bedtime stories, getting the listener to drop off quickly…though not because she was boring. In fact, the woman had an energy about her that suggested a wound spring.

Bud replied thoughtfully, "Ten years? Maybe. But I have to say they've all been kind to you. You honestly don't look much different than I remember you."

Thelma smiled, then turned to me. "He's quite a guy, isn't he?" She winked. Which made me feel…odd. She returned her attention to my husband. "Being just a little overweight –" *did she glance accusingly at me as she said that?* – "means I fill out a few wrinkles, the hair color's out of a bottle these days, and the only reason I move as well as I do is because I move a great deal. Hence the hiking trip I was on. There are some great hikes around here too, I hear. How about you show me around?"

I felt my toes curl; if someone wants to go for a walk, why don't they just call it a walk? Why do they always have to up the ante by saying they're "off on a hike"?

I said, "There's a path that runs down to the valley just below us, if you fancy a stroll down there." I sounded more mean-spirited than I'd meant to.

"A stroll? In the Bush? I don't think so. Proper footwear is just the start of it, Cait. Trust me, I've done a fair bit of Bush walking since I got here – and I've done all of it in these." She waggled a foot, showing off her well-worn boots, with thick socks poking out of their tops. "And you need the right kit with you, too. Honestly, you can't be too careful in almost any part of Australia; unless you're in a city park – and even sometimes inside those – there really is always something out there that can kill you…even if it's only yourself, because you've not paid enough attention to where you're putting your feet."

"Or your bum," I added somewhat sullenly, recalling what our taxi driver had said when Bud and I had arrived.

Thelma let out a gale of musical laughter. "Exactly, Cait…or your bum." She added, "She's a cracker, Bud, you were right."

I felt my shoulders hunch at the thought that Bud had spoken to this woman about me, whereas I'd not even heard of her until a few hours earlier. A quick glance toward my husband showed me he could tell how uncomfortable I was feeling, and he stepped forward and all but shouted, "How about I show you to your room, Thelma? You might like to freshen up. We've made a plan to go out for dinner – in fact, we'll be going quite soon because we all want an early night." *News to me.* "Nothing fancy – a pub really, with some tables. We ate there last night, then Siân and I ran into the owner earlier today and promised we'd go back for another meal this evening, didn't we, Siân?"

Siân had the good grace to blush slightly when she replied, "Oh heck yes, we did – sorry, I forgot to mention that. Winnie seemed very keen for us to go to her place again tonight."

I said, "Luckily, I haven't spent hours slaving over dinner prep, though it would have been nice to try another place. But I haven't got any objections – my duck was lovely."

"Duck? Hate duck, it's always rubbery," said Thelma. "A nice, juicy lump of meat however? Right up my street."

Todd said, "My roo steak was excellent," as though that were all anyone needed to know.

"In that case," said Thelma, also rising, "it's a quick shower for me, and I'll present myself back here in – what, half an hour?"

We all agreed and headed off to our rooms, shoving our mugs into the sink as we went. I could hear Siân rinsing them off as I followed Bud and Thelma.

When they reached the room we'd all agreed should be hers, I caught her saying, "Sit down, Bud – I need your full attention for a few moments…" before Thelma shut the door. I heard the lock turn.

The woman had been in the house for less than half an hour, and already I felt as though I'd been overwhelmed by a particularly massive wave; she'd picked me up, tossed me about, and had made me feel puffed and powerless. And now she was locked in a room with my husband. Talk about cutting the legs from under a person – Thelma Pruitt could put the surf at Manly to shame.

As we all assembled in the lounge at the appointed time, I still hadn't had a chance to talk to Bud about Thelma; he'd only appeared as I'd left the bathroom, and then he'd dashed in there himself, shutting the door behind him. And the conversation I wanted with him wasn't one that could be shouted over the noise of the shower.

Todd had changed from a pair of beige shorts topped with a navy golf shirt, to a pair of navy shorts topped with a beige golf shirt, whereas Siân presented herself in yet another floral frock

– beige, with lemon flowers. I'd started to wonder about their clothing choices days earlier, but realized it wasn't my place to comment. I was still nursing the sting of my sister blithely telling me that my cunning plan to best the fashion police by wearing horizontal stripes in fuchsia and orange wasn't working, and that I still looked "big". She even made those nasty rabbit-ear shapes with her fingers when she said "big". Sisters, eh?

Bud looked pink-faced and fresh when he made us a quartet; he still had a bit of shaving foam behind one ear, which I wiped off, then we all waited for Thelma, who pushed her thirty-minute deadline way past its breaking point. The atmosphere grew tense.

Finally, Bud got up and said, "I'll just check she's finding everything she needs," and headed toward Thelma's room. Again.

"Maybe I'll try the duck tonight," said Siân. "You said it was good, Cait."

I nodded. "Not at all rubbery," was about the best I could muster.

"Here we are," said Bud emerging into the room triumphantly with Thelma at his shoulder. "Ready for the off. We should all fit into the SUV we've rented, if we don't mind things being a bit cozy in the back. Thelma's own rental wouldn't accommodate all of us."

"I thought we'd be walking," was Thelma's surprised response.

I noticed she'd replaced her hiking boots with sturdy walking shoes, above which sprouted her muscular calves – she didn't seem to have any ankles. Her khaki capris looked voluminous, mainly due to their many well-stuffed pockets; I wondered if they allowed her to carry "the right kit" necessary for going to a pub on Katoomba's main street.

"It's a bit far for me," said Siân. "I have a condition that makes walking difficult, Thelma, especially if the ground isn't level, which it certainly isn't around here; walking down a hill can be a problem for me, let alone walking up one. Even if you lot want to walk, I'll still drive myself."

I said, "I'll definitely come with you, Sis," before I realized that might rob me of a chance to be alone with Thelma and Bud, to talk "business".

"I think we should all go in the car," said Todd glumly. I had no idea why he was so down – he was the one who'd asked me and Bud for help, and that was why Thelma was with us.

The tension within our group was annoying me, so I decided to be my true self and said, "Before we go – to a place where we won't be able to talk because it will be public – can we please address the elephant in the room? Thelma – it's lovely to meet you, and I'm glad you're here, but when Bud said he'd talk to someone about the whole Lowanna Swan and Philip Myers case, you said you'd rather come here than speak about it on the phone. So could we please talk about it now?"

Bud studied his toes wriggling in his flip flops, while Thelma's eyes slid around the room. I didn't find either reaction to be encouraging.

I pressed, "Bud? Anything?"

Bud sighed. "Okay, let's all sit for a moment, shall we? Thelma, Cait's right – this isn't going to work. We need to thrash through a few things before we go out. I'll leave the talking to you, because you know where to draw the lines."

I nodded my thanks to my husband, and patted the cushion beside me on the sofa, where he took a seat.

Thelma perched on a stool beside the kitchen counter, looking down at the four of us – which I suspected was exactly how she wanted things.

I watched her closely, intending to read her every move; she still had that air of pent-up energy about her, and I could tell she was focusing on maintaining her professional detachment as she spoke.

She began, "I'll do what I can, Bud. Yes, Philip Myers. The first thing I can tell you, in confidence for the moment, is that he did not die a natural death in prison. There was initially a belief it was suicide, but that's now been almost completely ruled out. Philip Myers was probably killed. I cannot share the details. There's an ongoing investigation, of course, about which I can say nothing. But the likelihood that he was murdered has raised…certain flags. All of them red."

Siân replied curtly, "Thanks for that, Thelma – I'm sure we'll all appreciate being kept in the picture about any developments on that front, even if it is awful to think of poor Philip being killed. But what I really want to know, to be honest, is what any of this has got to do with you in the first place?" Siân had asked a question that had been rattling around in my head since Bud had told me Thelma was coming to stay. "You're just visiting Australia from Canada, aren't you? So…what's the connection?"

"Good question." Thelma beamed at Siân as though she were an intern who'd asked what her prospects might be.

"Obvious one, really," grumbled Todd. Siân shot him a withering look.

Mz. Secret-Service-Jolly-Hockey-Sticks loomed over us and continued, "I'm here because I happened to be quite close to you, geographically speaking, when word came through that one Bud Anderson was looking for a bit of help in the area." She beamed at Bud, who smiled back – a bit pathetically, I thought. "The other factor? I'd already been briefed on the Myers case for an altogether different reason. Explanation? Without going into too many details – because I can't – over the past dozen years, several Canadian organizations with mining interests have purchased companies that once belonged to Philip Myers. That's not so unusual – both our countries have a significant involvement with many types of mining, and minerals are globally traded, as one might imagine. When Bud and I were put in touch today, via mutual contacts, I'd already been re-briefed. The fact that you, Todd, have been named as Myers' next of kin made me decide to come here to talk to you all face to face, though I'll admit it's Todd who's my main focus."

My brother-in-law sat more upright. "Because he named me as next of kin in the prison's paperwork, you mean? But that was so long ago, when he was first convicted. We were...still close back then, and he had no one else, so it made sense. Until they got in touch with me last week, I didn't realize it was an arrangement that had been in place right up to his death. So *that's* the problem? That's why you're here?"

Thelma nodded. "That's part of it. But I'm really here because I've also been informed that Myers made you his sole heir, Todd, which means you'll have to deal with a great number of matters that might be more substantial, and delicate, than you're used to handling."

Todd's face fell as Thelma spoke. Siân looked at me, her mouth open, then at Thelma. She said, "You know what was in Philip's will? Already?"

Thelma shifted on her stool. "His lawyers made his will available to the authorities almost immediately he died. Word was passed, and your name came across my...well, not my desk, because I was out in the national park at the time, rather than at my office in Canberra, but you know what I mean. You see, even though Philip Myers was in prison, convicted of murder, he still owned companies that hold a variety of mineral leases. His companies, under his direction from prison via his legal representatives, have continued to meet the criteria set down in law needed to retain those rights. However – as you must know,

Todd – rights leases in Australia are granted with a lifespan of twenty-one years, with a possible renewal for a further twenty-one, and some are coming up to their deadlines. With Philip now deceased, there's every chance they will be seen as ripe for transfer. And that's where the rest of the world, including Canada, comes in. There are people who want to get their hands on those leases, and they want to exploit them to a much greater extent than Myers' lawyers have been doing. Now the decisions about releasing said leases, or seeking to retain them, them will be yours, Todd, and that might put you in a dangerous position."

Things Look Down

No one responded to Thelma. I stared hard at Bud – who still seemed to be finding his toenails fascinating – while Siân and Todd held each other's hands and looked confused.

"I thought Philip had sold everything," said Siân. "That's what you told me, Todd, isn't it? Liquidated everything to cover his legal fees. Donkey's years ago, you said."

Todd scratched his head, made contact with the sticking plaster there, and absent-mindedly rearranged his sparse hair. "I thought he did. And I had no idea that him telling Corrective Services that I was his next of kin meant that I'd inherit *anything* from him – let alone *everything*. You're sure about this, Thelma?"

"As sure as spring comes in September," she replied blithely.

"Is it…I mean will we be…is there a lot of money involved?" Siân shifted on the sofa.

Thelma replied thoughtfully, "Cash? Not really. But assets, yes. Worth a great deal, if they were to be realized. Which is where the decision-making will come into play."

Bud volunteered, "Thelma was telling me that some of the places where Philip's companies hold mineral rights leases are in areas now identified as being of great significance for lithium mining. Apparently almost one quarter of the world's known lithium is in Western Australia. Canada? We're coming along strong, and want to be involved in the global picture. Thelma – tell them about the Canadian interest."

We all returned our focus to Thelma. She studied her thumbnail with the same intensity Bud had been giving his feet. "It's hard for me to be specific, because there are…various interests in play. But, yes, of course Canada wants in on the global lithium scene. Accessing resources within other countries could help us do that – even while we work on developing our own output. Mining organizations are truly global, these days, you see. Minerals without borders you might say – especially when it comes to the explosion in demand for lithium, which is needed for the production of batteries for electric vehicles. And Australia has no objections to international exploitation of its resources…which are all state owned and which, of course, produce income in terms of taxes and royalties."

I took her words on board. "Alice Cadwallader and her Chilean ancestry," I said.

Siân's mouth formed an O. "What a coincidence," she said. "The woman who owned the castle in Wales where you two got married had a link to lithium too, didn't she? Well, her family did. What a small world. Now here it is again. It's as though it's following you two about – stuck to your clothes, so to speak."

Thelma took us all aback when she commented, "Your Welsh accent's surprisingly strong for someone who's lived in Australia for – what – about twenty years now? Right, Siân?"

"It's been getting stronger since her sister turned up," said Todd, not sounding as though this were a compliment.

"Cait's has been, too," said Bud, smiling. "You two together? Talking faster and with stronger accents every day. It's charming."

Charming? Who are you, and what have you done with my husband? was what I thought; "Thanks, it's nice to natter, right, Sis?" was what I said. Then I added, "But let's not get off topic here, Thelma –" I was sure that was what she was trying to do – "this doesn't sound as though it has anything to do with the murder of Lowanna Swan almost thirty-five years ago, nor of Philip Myers' conviction for that murder decades later. So why exactly are you here?" I wasn't going to let her get away with it.

Thelma sat up even straighter, if that were possible. "When Bud and I spoke, he mentioned that Todd believed Philip had been framed for Lowanna Swan's murder. He also said Todd had been suggesting that Lennie Orkins was involved with any such arrangement, and Todd was frightened that Lennie's death might mean he was also in danger."

Todd leaned in. "I do. I was. I am. What can you tell me about it? Am I...are me and my family...in *peril?*" His voice had lifted half an octave, and he was clutching Siân's hand so hard that she had to shake him off.

Thelma looked grim, as did Bud. I didn't think I was going to like what was coming.

Thelma stood up and arched her back. "I can't give you any details, and I hope you'll understand that. What I can tell you is this: just over a year ago, Philip Myers sent a letter to...a person in the Australian government, who discussed the contents of said letter with...a representative of the Canadian government. We're more than joint members of the Commonwealth – we're partners in many endeavors, so this was not as unusual as you might think. Certain...enquiries...were carried out as a result of information contained in that letter, which were then elaborated upon during subsequent interviews between certain government representatives and Philip Myers."

Siân sighed loudly. "For goodness' sake, Thelma – we're not watching some sort of true crime documentary where they drag out three facts over a whole hour, are we? Can't you just say what you know, or think, and don't worry yourself about all of the subterfuge? To be honest, none of us cares who's who. I certainly don't. I just care about my family. There – I've said it."

I wanted to cheer my sister, but satisfied myself with a wink, which I could tell she'd caught out of the corner of her eye.

Thelma cleared her throat. "Very well. Briefly then: there might be a case to argue that Philip Myers was indeed framed for the murder of Lowanna Swan – by a person or persons unknown. Likely with the knowledge and participation of Lennie Orkins – possibly on behalf of one, or more, consortia where the belief was that Myers' conviction would allow them to achieve their goal of acquiring the leases he held to certain areas of mineral deposits."

"And some of the people in the consortia in question are Canadian?" I asked.

"Some of the companies are," replied Thelma. "The amounts of money we're talking about cannot be summoned by individuals."

I felt both my eyebrows sprint for my hairline. "Big numbers?"

"Massive."

"So high stakes?"

"The highest."

Todd, Siân, and Bud watched me and Thelma as though we were two tennis pros lobbing a ball across the net.

I dared, "If they were prepared to frame Philip more than a dozen years ago, and have, presumably, spent that dozen years trying to gain access to the leases they want by legal means, do you think they finally decided they'd waited too long, and killed him, to remove the control over the leases from his hands?"

Thelma dragged her nails along the right side of her jaw. "That's the thinking, in certain circles. It was only officially confirmed late yesterday that his death was possibly not a suicide. Then the news came in about the death by fire – probably arson – of Lennie Orkins, the man whose discovery of Philip Myers' rifle was, ultimately, what tipped the scales to send Myers to prison. When Bud subsequently called a contact of his in Canada, and it was discovered – by those who care – that he was here, in Katoomba, with his brother-in-law – who's now the legal owner of all the companies holding the leases in question – I was contacted. Todd, you're about to become a very important person, to many organizations around the world. My presence here was thought to be…judicious."

I replied carefully, "In that case, are your people, or any of those with whom you are connected here in Australia, able to offer any protection to my sister, my brother-in-law, and their children?"

Siân's face lost all its color, and it was her turn to grasp Todd's hand.

Thelma appeared to whistle, silently. "That's not seen as a budget-friendly use of resources," she eventually replied. She nodded at Bud. "I owe him, and this is me paying him back. You need to understand your situation – and you need to act to protect yourselves...though I will add that I honestly do not think that any of you are in immediate danger. I believe that all the interested parties will use Philip Myers' death as an opportunity to reset – to return to seeking the leases they are after by legal means. And we need to discuss how you should manage any such approaches, Todd."

Bud spoke gravely, "Thelma tells me that news about Todd being Philip's heir will not be made public until it's absolutely necessary, but...but these things do have a habit of getting out more quickly than you'd hope. There'll be all sorts of people clamoring for news about who'll be making decisions about the lease deals from now on, and they can't be held at bay for more than a few days...or maybe a week. So you've got that much time to wrap your head around all this, Todd, because your life – and yours, too, Siân...and those of your children – will change forever, once the news is out."

Siân leaned forward and held her head in her hands. "Oh no...all I can think of is kidnappings, and threats, and the kids always being in danger because someone wants to use them to get to Todd. It's like finding you're living inside some horrible thriller...where your family's torn apart, and there's a baddie with a gun around every corner. With all due respect, I don't think we need you, Thelma – we need...Liam Neeson, at least."

Thelma puffed out her cheeks. "Yeahnah. That's the response I'd hoped we could avoid. You're not in any immediate danger, I said that. And I've come here to help you to avoid it down the line, I've said that too. Now? Now I suggest we all let this sink in for a while – and maybe over a slab of meat at that pub you talked about? I was hell-bent on getting here as fast as I could so missed lunch, and right now I reckon I could eat one of these old shoes of mine, with a bit of tomato sauce on it. Can we please go eat?"

As if on cue, both her stomach and mine rumbled at the same moment.

"Snap!" We shared a genuine laugh…though it didn't really ease the tension in the room.

"If you think I'm going to be able to go out, or even drive, after what you've just told us, then you're mad," said Siân, raking her hand through her hair. "Besides, what if someone knows who we are? Where we are? They could be looking for us now. Todd, I'm off to phone Beccie and Mattie right this minute, and I want us to go home to them as soon as we can make that happen."

Thelma's face straightened in a flash. "No worries about them, Siân; that's something I've managed to get an Australian colleague to convince a few of the local Perth cops to take care of. Watching brief, nothing intrusive. Neither your children nor the families they're staying with will have any idea there's anything going on."

Siân almost collapsed she was so relieved. "Thank you," she said, tears starting to flow.

Todd gathered her into his arms. "Thanks for that, Thelma. But…how do you even know where Mattie and Beccie are staying?"

Thelma stroked her jawline. Again. "The Australian government might have had good reason to check your incoming and outgoing calls for the past little while, Todd. Since Philip Myers died, and the closeness of your relationship came to light. You too, Siân. Purely to ensure that no one's been putting any undue pressure on you, you know?"

"Bloody government," mumbled Todd as he held Siân close.

"Shush, love," said a slightly calmer Siân, "for once they might be able to help. Our tax dollars at work – for us." She gathered herself a little more and added, "So you don't think anyone knows we're here?" Her eyes pleaded with Thelma.

"Other than the people who do, in fact, know you're here, no…I don't believe so. Nor do I think the word's even out, yet, that you 'matter'. It's a good thing they kept back the news about Myers' death for as long as they did; even that's only being released today, and there'll be no mention of the cause, which is – officially – undetermined. No one wanted it coming out while that conference was on in Sydney; the news about his death would have been around the world in a few moments, and the rumor mill in the mining industry about who'd be taking the reins would have started churning out suggestions right away. So, in a nutshell, that's why I'm it, folks. Here to brief you. But – again – can we please eat before we get to work? I don't care what it is – let's order in, if you want – but I need protein, or I might not make it to bedtime."

Bud stood. "Siân, you're the one on the insurance documents for the rental vehicle, so if you could manage to drive us to dinner, that would be good; I think the best thing for us all is to be out and about – where we won't even be tempted to talk about any of this. We need to let it all sink in, as Thelma said. It's a lot to process. And I say we stick to our plan to go to Winnie's Place, where we'll hardly be noticed; we've already spent time with the woman herself. Twice. Agreed?"

We all agreed. Eventually.

G'day, Again

Knowing there was parking behind Winnie's Place made our arrival for the second time a good deal simpler, and we even sat at the same table we'd had the night before. It was almost surreal: we were greeted with friendly "G'days" by both Jonesy and Frank Tipton, who were occupying the same bar stools they'd been perched upon the previous evening. Winnie even left her spot behind the bar to come over to hug Siân and Bud – an action that was clearly not the norm for her, if the response among the regulars was anything to go by.

We all ordered beer, with a sparkling water for Siân, and were soon being handed menus by Timbo, who vibrated with good health and solicitousness as he hovered at our table.

It was as though Bud and Siân's attendance at the local swimming pool had created some sort of invisible bond between them all, which struck me as a bit weird, but quite touching. It was clear that word of the aquatic adventures were being whispered about at the bar, and everyone eventually turned, in their own time, to give us a closer look.

"Why are they all staring at us?" Todd was sweating through his golf shirt, despite the fact we were sitting beneath a ceiling fan. He did his best to not stare back, but failed. "They're talking about us, too," he said more than nervously.

"The woman who runs the place, and our server, are telling them that Siân and Bud were at the pool earlier today, and are saying very nice things about Siân's backstroke technique, if you must know," said Thelma.

I was impressed. "You read lips?" I asked. "Something you learned…for work?"

Thelma winked. "Could do it long before I ever needed it there, but I got some good, professional help at work, yes."

"Is it difficult to lipread Australians, especially with all the 'Strine' they use – you know, the Australian slang words?" I asked. "They don't seem to move their mouths much when they speak."

"Yeahnah. You get used to it. You Welsh are easy to read; you make great use of your mouths, wonderfully clear pronunciation. Thank you." She smiled.

"You're welcome, though I'm not sure that's why we do it."

"I'm having a roo steak." Siân surprised us all.

"Not the tofu…or the fish, or even duck?" Todd sounded startled by his wife's choice.

"I'm so hungry I could eat a horse, then chase the jockey," she replied, with a straight face.

Thelma slapped her thigh and let out her characteristic musical gale of laughter. "That's how I feel too. Will all of us women be having the roo, Cait?"

"Why not?"

When Timbo returned to take our orders, he was greeted with "Roo steaks all around," and merely had to inquire how we wanted them cooked. Siân was the only one who insisted on her meat being very well done.

"I can't stand the sight of the blood," said Siân when Timbo had headed back to the bar, "so I won't look when you're eating yours, Todd."

Todd replied sharply, "I've told you before it's not blood, love. It's the myoglobin that makes it look red, not blood. All the blood's been drained out; there isn't any left." He took a glug of beer when he'd finished instructing my sister, and the rest of us followed suit, possibly to cover our embarrassment.

I wondered if Todd had managed to put everyone off the idea of their meal as much as he had me; Bud's face didn't suggest that was the case, nor Thelma's, but I reckoned Siân was reassessing her choice.

She surprised me when she replied, "I worked in operating theaters for years, you know, Todd. Blood is something with which I'm quite familiar. And I do, indeed, know the difference between the way it pumps out of a living human being, and the red stuff that lies on the plate when you eat meat – but I was speaking for effect. If you really want to know why I don't like the look of what comes out of undercooked meat it's exactly because of my experiences over the years – too many memories, of too many patients. I don't have my sister's eidetic memory, but there are still things I wish I could forget, but can't. Now just let it lie, will you?"

I was a bit cross with my sister for mentioning my abilities, but then reasoned that Bud had probably told Thelma all about my so-called photographic memory, and even maybe about the way that it works not just for what I've seen, but for all my senses. I glanced at him, but he seemed completely absorbed by something happening in the street beyond the leaded windows.

"I think we might have company before too long," he said quietly.

I followed his gaze and spotted Big Stan and his son heading toward the front door.

"I hope they're more sober now than they were last night," I muttered.

"At least with them in the place none of us will be even tempted to talk about what's on all our minds, eh?" Bud forced a smile, which we returned – all with equal effort, it seemed.

"Who's this now?" Thelma turned as the pair entered the pub. "Oh, them," she added. "Let's hope they're not trouble."

Winnie called from behind the bar, "You two sober tonight?"

Big Stan walked across the pub, took off his hat and almost swept the floor with it as he bowed – first to Winnie, then to the men seated in front of him, then to all of us, "My most sincere apologies for last night. You were all very accommodating. We'd had a bit. Well, alright then, we was rotten…had the wobbly boots on, good and proper. Didn't mean to be yobbos, but I reckon we might have been. Lovely Miss Winnie —" Big Stan smiled at Winnie in such a way that he almost appeared good looking — "how about you give everyone here a nice big cold one, on me and me son. Best way we know to say sorry."

He reached forward, handed Winnie some cash, then leaned in and spoke softly to her. She nodded. Big Stan and Neal grinned at us and headed toward our table.

We invited the men to join us, introduced Thelma, and they pulled chairs across to our table, causing us all to shuffle around. It was a sung fit.

"Were we raging last night?" Big Stan looked pretty sober now, and sorrowful.

"That's Strine for 'partying'," said Siân, translating the Australian slang, "and yes, you were having your own party, it seemed."

"Apologies for that — especially to you ladies," said Neal, matching his father's shame-faced expression. "Wine's sneaky. Creeps up on you. Can't judge it like beer. Sipping it all arvo, we were. It got the better of me. Dad had to wake me up for the evening session." He laughed heartily. "'Wake up, son, I'm thirsty. Time to get back to the boozer,' were his exact words…I think."

As if on cue, Timbo arrived with two bottles of beer and two menus. We explained to the father and son that Timbo had been one of the firefighters who'd tackled the blaze the previous night, and they thanked him heartily for the bravery displayed by him and his colleagues. They accepted their beers, but waved off the menus.

"Two steaks, as thick and rare as you can make 'em, mate. Beef, not roo. The roo you city folks get isn't anything like the real thing. We'll be right with that." Big Stan shoved a wad of notes into Timbo's hand. "Cheers," he added, raising his bottle to the rest of us, then drinking almost half of it in one go. "And keep these coming, mate," he called at Timbo's back. The server waved an arm, and returned to his post behind the bar.

I didn't know what Big Stan had meant about the type of kangaroo the restaurant would be serving, as opposed to the type he and his son were used to, but I suspected it had something to do with living for so much of the year in the Bush and Outback. However, the exact nature of "Bush Tucker" wasn't something I really wanted to think about for too long.

"All the rellies tonight, plus one, eh? And where does the lovely Thelma come from?" It was clear that Big Stan could be quite a charmer when he wanted to be; he took Thelma's hand and fake-kissed it.

"Rellies are relatives," whispered Siân to Bud.

"Yes, it's a full family turnout, and Thelma's an old friend of mine from Canada," said Bud. "She happened to be in the area, so we took the chance to have a bit of a reunion. Haven't seen each other in years, and here we are now, in this place. It's a small world, at times."

"If you say so," replied Neal.

The young man had none of the verve for life I'd seen him display previously, which I judged was probably because he'd just lost a lifelong friend. I decided I didn't want to be the one to bring up the topic of the fire, and yet I had so many questions; I wondered if Big Stan and Neal might know more than us – the victims of the fire all having worked for Big Stan's company.

"It's a terrible thing," said Big Stan, cradling his bottle in his massive, leathery hand. "There we were, raging around town here last night while those poor men…I know there was nothing any of us could have done, but I feel bad about it. Had to talk to all the families today."

Neal put his hand on his father's shoulder, only to have it shrugged away. "It's been a bad day," said the young man quietly. I knew he didn't mean because of his over-indulgence the night before. "To mates who can't be with us," he said, and raised his bottle to his father.

"Yeah, to them who's gone," replied Big Stan, and polished off his drink. He immediately turned toward the bar and waggled his empty bottle in the air, then pointed at Neal and himself. "Any of yous want another?" We all declined. "Just two, mate," he shouted. Timbo waved back, and headed toward our table with replacement bottles.

"It must be a blow for you both," said Thelma. "I guess you knew all the victims well."

I'd wondered who would decide how the conversation would go; I wasn't surprised it was Thelma. I supposed that if anyone was going to pry, she was as good a person as any – it being her job.

"Me and Ditch have been joined at the hip since we was ankle biters," said Neal heavily. "I...I can't believe he won't walk through that door in five minutes, saying he lost us. Always trailing behind, he was, right, Dad?"

Big Stan nodded. "A bit slow in some ways. Sharp as a knife in others. Bit of a galah, to be honest, but harmless," he said.

"I understand you and Ditch were in kindergarten together, Neal. Do you both know his entire family?" I expected that maybe Big Stan would at least know of Ditch's parents, the two boys having been friends since they were not much more than toddlers.

"His father blew through before he even started kindie," said Neal, "and his mother never went with another bloke after that. Just her and him. She'll be...she'll be real crook over this."

"We'll take care of her, son. She'll be apples," said Big Stan. I had no doubt that he meant he'd look after her financially speaking; he was a man who appeared to believe that a wad of cash could solve all problems.

"I don't know about that, Dad. She always was a battler, but this? Did it all for Ditch, she did. And now he's gone."

"Any idea how it started, yet? The fire, I mean. It was a real tragedy. I heard about it from this lot," said Thelma, looking as innocent as only someone from the secret service could.

Big Stan shrugged. "No one's telling us nothing. All over us like bities this morning, they was. Now? I phoned the coppers to ask, but will they tell me more than what's been on the news? Nah."

"Buckley's chance of hearing anything from that lot, I reckon," added Neal.

Bud stared at Siân, who offered, "It means fat chance." Bud nodded his thanks for her help. I suspected my sister might have to kick her translation service into overdrive during the evening. Of course, having watched hundreds of hours of *Blue Heelers*, I could have translated all the Strine for my husband had he but asked – but it was nice for him and my sister to have something to connect them, I thought.

"Didn't you say they suspected it was arson, Bud?" Thelma clearly had an agenda. "When you and Siân were at the swimming pool this afternoon – that was the gossip, right?"

Big Stan and Neal stared hard at Bud across their full bottles.

Bud nodded, taking Thelma's lead. "That was the talk, yes. Though I don't know if that's because of any evidence they've found, or just because gossip loves a vacuum."

"Yeahnah, can't be," said Neal wiping his mouth with the back of his hand. "Who'd want to burn down a perfectly good house? And with people in it? They must have known people were in there. That lot wouldn't have been quiet. None of us ever are – too used to shouting to each other in the Bush to be quiet anywhere else. But what I don't understand was why they was all in there anyways. Lennie wasn't staying there – he had a room at the same place as us."

I noticed Todd becoming more tense; the implications of Neal's comment wasn't lost on any of us.

"You mean Lennie Orkins shouldn't really have been there at all?" I spoke first.

Neal and Big Stan shrugged. "No reason not to be," said the father. "He was with us for a bit in the arvo, then he went off on his own. Said he wanted to get his sunnies. Never came back. Might have decided to take a slab down to the other blokes."

"Sunglasses, and a carton of beers," said Siân automatically.

"How unfortunate for him," said Thelma. "So the two other men had rented that house just for themselves?"

Neal shook his head. "Ditch had a room in a pub along the way here, not far from the place where we are…was. It was Dan who had the house, with five of the others, who weren't there at the time. They were eating at a place where they heard the tucker was decent. Except for Shorty, who was with us, when it happened. They was lucky. The others…you know."

I was rapidly reassessing my thoughts about the fire: had whoever had set it known who was there, and who wasn't? I cast my mind back to the dinner cruise and the yarns that had been spun: Ditch had claimed to know about an unsuspected murder, and he was at the house when it had burned down, but only by chance, it seemed; Lennie had his connection to the Myers case, but had also not been a resident at the house, though he'd been a victim of the fire; Shorty, with his story of "Carver" Richards in Alice Springs, had not been involved in the fire, though he was one of the men who'd rented the house – and then there was Dan Entwistle, who'd not been one of the yarners on the dinner cruise, but had died, nonetheless. Maybe Lennie hadn't been the intended victim after all? I decided to take my chance to find out more about the victim I'd paid very little attention to so far.

"Todd was telling us that Dan Entwistle had six children," I opened. "You said you'd spoken to all the families today – how did they seem to be faring?"

Big Stan gazed at the inch of amber liquid in his bottle as though it might be the last remaining beer on the face of the earth. "Not good. I spoke to the wife's sister. They had to get the doc in for the wife, so the sister was there, looking after the kids. Dan was a good worker…and a decent father, I heard. I know we'll miss him, and I dare say they will, too. Another family we'll see to, as we can. That's a lot of mouths to feed. Quiet bloke. Head down. Get the job done. Get back to the family. Steady."

"Yeah, quiet bloke," added Neal. "You hardly ever knew he was there. Read books a lot. *Books*." His tone might have been the same if he'd been telling us that Dan Entwistle had always walked on his hands, juggling koalas with his feet.

"Close to anyone in particular on your crew?" I pressed.

Neal chuckled. "He took Ditch under his wing like he was a baby chook. Me and Ditch were friends, yeah, but Dan was like a dad to him. Ditch never had one, and Dan had a lot of practice."

"Why was he called Ditch?" Siân leaned forward as she spoke.

Neal laughed. "His mother named him Richard, but he couldn't say his name – it always came out as Ditch when he was a young fella, so that's what he was called."

"Given his actions on the beach in Manly, Ditch might have gone to the house to have a bit of a chat with Dan, if they were close," I suggested.

Thelma gave me a sideways look, and I wondered if maybe Bud hadn't told her about Ditch walking into the sea, fully clothed, a few days earlier. I decided it wasn't the right moment to explain.

Timbo hovered with two fresh beers as Neal and his father polished off their dregs. I wondered how many more bottles they'd manage to tuck away that evening, and what the repercussions might be.

"Ditch was good when we came up here on the train, wasn't he, Dad?"

Big Stan smiled. "Yeah, he was right by then. But maybe he wanted to share a couple of cold ones with Dan, like Cait said. They were close. Tight."

"Had Dan been with you long?" I didn't want to lose a chance to gather information.

"Gotta be about thirty years, off and on, I'd say," replied Big Stan. "We didn't always have enough work for him, so he'd do a bit with other crews, or working other jobs. We always used him when we could. He was one of the early ones we worked with. Knew the value of sweat did Dan. Like I said, he'll be missed. Hard to replace."

"And Shorty?" I thought it best if I kept going. "Has he been with you just as long?"

"Lennie brought Shorty on, didn't he, Dad?" Neal spoke, and Big Stan nodded. "Lennie and him went back. Back to when Lennie was doing a bit of fossicking."

Both Bud and I glanced at Siân who said, "Prospecting for gold, or generally hunting about for precious things. I think I should have given you two a book to read before you came here."

Neal laughed, "Can't talk Strine, eh? Sorry, Siân, love, you're in for a busy night. I'll do me best to remember. I did pretty well at that fancy convention. Talked proper nearly all the time. Hard work, mind. Don't mix with people from O.S. a lot…" He paused, grinned lopsidedly, and added, "That's 'overseas' for you lot." He slapped Bud on the back. "You'll be right, won't you, Oscar. See? I do remember bits of last night. It's not all a blur. Though I reckon we should have stopped and had some proper tucker for our tea, instead of just drinking it."

"Speaking of which," said Todd, "where's our food?"

"Exactly," said Thelma.

"Here comes Timbo now," replied Bud.

Within moments we had the right steak in front of the right person, and I for one was salivating. We didn't stand on ceremony, so when Big Stan encouraged us all to "Bog in," all conversation stopped for at least the next five minutes or so, as *mmm*s and *ah*s replaced actual vocabulary.

Everyone praised the cook, and I did my best to not gobble down the meal; I forced myself to take small mouthfuls of the mashed potatoes, which I was convinced must contain at least a pound of butter, then to eat a few of the glistening green beans, before allowing myself to sink back into the luscious arms of my Skippy Steak, as Bud laughingly insisted upon calling it. It was well worth the effort, because I was still eating when Big Stan and Neal had cleared their plates, as had Thelma, and Bud. Todd picked his way around the edge of his meat, and Siân? She was going to need a doggy bag.

Bud led the conversation as it picked up, with me still chewing away, and he followed the path I'd been taking before the food arrived. "Lennie was quite the yarn-teller, wasn't he? Was that something he did a lot when you were away for weeks on end, building roads through the Bush?"

Big Stan polished off his eighth beer and began another. "He did, and we're going to be stumped without him. Can't beat a good yarn after you've had your tucker of a night. You know it's a wonderful life we get to live out there. This place? It's so different from where we work. This is all green, even if it is dry right now. Our places? When we cut a road through the Bush we make a scar that's so red it's like a gash in the flesh of the earth. And the dust? You can't even imagine it. All wear masks now, don't we, son? Not like back in the old days. We're out there where the country goes on forever, all around you…just us and whatever else manages to cling to life out there. So, yeah, when we're done for the day, it's good to have someone like Lennie who can yarn, and take you out of yourself. Help you forget what you're missing back home, and yet remember why you're out there doing what you are."

"And no one's going to be able to cook like him, are they, Dad?" Neal turned to us, his eyes glowing. "Lennie made this Mongolian roo-tail stew that was the best thing I've ever tasted. Never told anyone the recipe. He said he'd take it to his grave. And…he did. To Lennie's Mongolian roo-tail stew." He raised his bottle, as did his father. The rest of us joined in rather half-heartedly.

Todd piped up with, "Do you think he really found that rifle in the waterhole all those years ago?"

Big Stan and Neal looked puzzled. "Course he did – where else would it have come from?" Big Stan looked sideways at Todd, then at me. "Is he not the trusting type? Or is he asking that because it was his old boss that got done for killing someone with it?"

I didn't want to be drawn, but said quietly, "Todd worked for Philip Myers a long time ago. The man's been in prison for a dozen years or more, as I understand it. I would think that any closeness Todd had once felt for him would have melted away by now, wouldn't you agree, Todd?"

I could see a vein pulse in Todd's neck as he downed the last drops of what I knew to be his fifth beer, and wondered how he'd respond. I suspected Siân did too, because I saw her press her hand onto his thigh as she changed the conversation – and with what I knew to be a lie. "I'm sorry to spoil the party, and I know we've only just finished our food, but I've just realized I've forgotten to bring my meds with me – the ones I have to take within half an hour of eating. I'm going to have to get back to the house. Of course I'm happy to drive everyone, but – if you'd rather stay – maybe just Todd and I could go now, and you could walk back when you're ready?"

I could hear in my sister's voice that she was desperate to get her husband out of the place, but I didn't want to lose the chance to learn more about Big Stan's Mob, and the men who'd died.

"We should all go," said Thelma abruptly, rising immediately. "I'll pay at the bar."

"All done," said Big Stan. "Sorted it before we'd even ordered. Wanted to apologize for last night. And it was good to talk with yous about the men we lost."

"What's happened to the men who were fortunate enough to escape?" I had to know before we all split up.

"All of them except Shorty have gone back to the smoke…to Sydney," replied Neal. "Everything they had with them was lost in the fire, so Dad sent them back to the city to get kitted out again, best they can. Shorty stayed on because…well, he was too shaken to travel, he said. We got him a room next to us, at a place here in town. He'll travel back with us. We're right back to it when we fly home, see? Can't miss too much time. Important to be at the conference and keep all the clients sweet, but it's back to the Bush for us in a few days. Clients might say nice things when you're feeding them and paying for the beer they're pouring down their throats, but they still want us to hit our deadlines, right, Dad?"

"Too right, son," replied Big Stan. "But we'll hang on here until as late as we can tomorrow, in case there's any news."

Winnie had obviously spotted we were planning to leave, and came across to our table, beaming. "How was it? All good?"

"Best steak I've had in a long time," said Big Stan, standing to shake her by the hand.

"I heard you asking about the fire," Winnie added. "They know it's arson, of course, and now they think they've found the cause."

Big Stan looked confused. "How d'you know that? Is this the place where all the news gets gathered?"

"That, and I'm the fire chief's cousin," said Winnie proudly.

"What did they use?" Thelma sounded a bit too keen to my ears, and I hoped no one else picked up on her tone.

Winnie sounded grim. "A candle in a bucket of kindling. Candle burned down, the kindling caught, the whole house went up. But my cousin said it was odd – the blokes who died must have seen the bucket, because of where they found it; it looked like it had been in the corner of the upstairs sitting room. So that's the question, now, really: why didn't they do anything to stop it from happening?"

"Why indeed," said Thelma.

Siân stood, and we all made a move to leave. Just as we were saying our goodbyes, I heard Big Stan say to Thelma, "Have we met before? You seem…familiar."

"No," she replied. "I'd remember you. You're one of those unforgettable rogue types."

Big Stan roared with laughter. The last we saw of him and his son, Timbo was heading toward them with two more beers and Winnie was wagging a finger at them.

Big Noise

Once we reached our rental vehicle, Siân opened the door and got in, while Thelma hung back. I saw her tug at Bud's sleeve. She whispered, "Stay with me?"

Determined to not be left out, I said, "I think I should try to walk off at least a couple of ounces of that massive steak. Fancy walking me home, Bud?"

Bud's lips creased to a thin line, and I could tell he'd worked out that I'd overheard Thelma. "Tell you what," he said, "if Siân and Todd are okay with it, why don't they drive back, and we three will follow on foot? Winnie reckoned it was only about a twenty-minute walk – so you guys wouldn't be alone for long. You okay with that?"

My sister and brother-in-law agreed they'd feel safe enough being alone for that amount of time, so off they went, leaving the three of us in the darkness behind the pub, with a good walk ahead of us. The evening was chilly, and I was glad I'd brought a jacket; Thelma shivered as we set out at a brisk pace. I feared she was fit enough to keep it up for some time and suspected I'd fall behind at some point, so decided to get the conversation going in the direction I wanted.

We turned off the main street almost immediately, and headed down a slope toward a residential area that I knew would take us in the right direction: we'd been driven around it by our taxi driver.

"It's notable that Lennie Orkins wasn't staying at the house that went up in flames," I opened. "It might mean he wasn't the arsonist's intended target."

"We don't know who the target was, or even if the arson was intended to kill anyone," replied Thelma. "Could be part of this pattern of unexplained fires they've been having here, and…you know…something went badly wrong."

Bud deferred to his sometime colleague. "Thelma's right, we don't know enough about it to be sure," he replied.

I snapped, "A flaming bucket in the sitting room? Really?" It was out before I could stop it. I ignored Bud's glance, took a breath, and considered my next comment carefully. "Look, I think Neal made a good point: none of the members of The Mob ever whisper. We've seen and heard them, Bud – they all tend to be a bit rowdy, and shout to each other even when they're just chatting in a bar. I think that anyone setting a fire would have been in no doubt there were people in that house. And then there's Winnie's information about the location of the seat of the fire. If the three men who died could have seen there was a bucket with a candle in it in the room with them, why on earth would they not have extinguished it before the fire got going? It makes no sense. Unless they were already incapacitated in some way."

"Hold your horses," said Thelma, pausing at a corner. "I think you're getting a bit ahead of yourself there, Cait. Like I said back at the house – and, no, I wasn't holding anything back because I didn't want to scare your sister and her husband – we have no idea if this fire was targeting anyone specific. In fact, it could be a completely isolated case. Though I accept that the idea that three men wouldn't notice a bucket catching fire in a room they were sitting in is a bit of a stretch – so I agree with your analysis of that aspect."

We all walked on; luckily for us the street was deserted. A dog barked in the distance, and the birdsong was negligible.

"Okay, no civilians here, so let's thrash it out," said Bud. "First of all, I should tell you that Thelma's fully briefed as far as you're concerned, Cait. But I haven't told you anything about Thelma, sorry." He threw one of his special, crinkly-eyed smiles at me. "That's largely because there's not much I'm allowed to tell you about her, and then there's the fact I wanted to check with her when she got here about exactly what I could and couldn't say. Thelma – you're up."

I didn't look at Thelma as we walked, instead, I enjoyed my surroundings. The lovely Victorian homes we were passing had well-tended front gardens, and gingerbread trimmings sporting a variety of paint colors. Illuminated by the streetlamps, they each had their own unique style, and I even snatched glimpses of lives through glowing windows. No one seemed to close their curtains; I saw occupants dining, watching TV, and, in one case, playing the clarinet. A melody floated out as we walked past, and I listened as Thelma filled me in.

"Bud and I only worked closely together a couple of times," she said, in a voice that wasn't dissimilar to the receding woodwind notes. "Once in Europe, once in Canada. I can't say more than that. Usually, I'm in the background. I supply intel and others act on it, but – sometimes – I'm needed on the spot during an operation. When we were involved in a large undertaking in Canada, Bud got me out of a tricky situation. For which I shall always be grateful. On this occasion, I got a call from a superior in Ottawa regarding Bud's original inquiry about Myers. I was put in touch with Bud because I was in the nearby national park, which is a coincidence that's not lost on me. And, yes, there are some particularly nasty things that go on in the world of international mining, and I think your brother-in-law and his whole family are about to discover they're in the crosshairs of a campaign that's being waged to gain control of Australia's remaining areas of likely lithium production. Has this got anything to do with the death of Lowanna Swan? No idea. But it's believed that it's connected to the death of Philip Myers. And no, before you think it, I am not giving a greater priority to the death of an old white guy over a young Aboriginal woman…it really is just that a murder thirty-five years ago is not something I've been fully briefed on, whereas I have been asked to act regarding Philip Myers' death, because of the Canadian interests in the mining angle. You can ask me whatever you want, and I'll answer, if I can. And I'll be able to access intel you wouldn't."

I slowed to a stop, and thanked Thelma for her candor. "The first thing I would ask you to do, then, is get me the full court transcripts of Philip Myers' trial, please. I've read all the press coverage I can find, but know I'm missing a lot of insights."

Thelma nodded. "I can do that."

"Thanks. Then I'd like access to background checks into Lennie Orkins, Dan Entwistle, Richard 'Ditch' Early, plus Stan Swan and his son Neal. And there's a bloke called 'Shorty' – I'd be interested in finding out more about him, too. He's…always on the fringe of things, and there's something about him that makes me think he's…oh, I don't know. Maybe it's because he's a bit shifty that I think there's something there. Shifty Shorty – that must be it."

We began to walk again as Thelma replied, "All in hand already, except the Shorty guy. I'll look into that. No other name known?"

"Not a clue," replied Bud. "Also, we need up to date information from the local fire and police services – and any specialist arson investigation involved," he added, "and we'd like to know exactly what was communicated to various parties by Philip Myers about his suspicions regarding those who were seeking to gain control of the mineral rights leases held by his companies, and what the names of those companies are."

"Sorry, Bud, can't do that last couple of things. Off the table. That's all 'need to know'. And you don't. I can't tell you about the specific consortia involved. To be honest, giving you that list wouldn't mean anything to you, in any case, because – with respect – it's just a list of company names, all designed to create a façade to allow those who run them to remain anonymous."

"If the names wouldn't mean anything to us, then there can't be any harm in us knowing them, can there?" I produced my best and sweetest smile, which made Thelma burst out laughing.

When she finally stopped, she said, "Sure, the list…why not? But on a totally confidential basis, of course, and just the names of the consortia, nothing else…like where they're based – which is usually somewhere offshore with conveniently opaque company registration requirements. Anything else?"

"I just want us to be clear about what we're considering here," I said. "So many people are already dead, and I do want to play a role in ensuring they get justice, but – to be honest – my main concern has now shifted to ensuring the safety of my sister and her family. However, considering what you've told us since your arrival, Thelma, I believe – in order to do that – we need to work out if Philip Myers' death is connected to these consortia, and, if so, whether that means my sister and her family are in danger, or about to become so, once it's known that Todd has inherited Philip's holdings. Of course, if any of the consortia *are* discovered to be behind Philip's death in prison, then the question arises: did *they* play a part in getting him convicted in the first place? And does that mean they used Lennie Orkins as their cat's paw to achieve that? And I'd also, ultimately, like to consider the following question: if Philip Myers *was* framed for the murder of Lowanna Swan, then who really killed her? I have no idea if that last question links back to the immediate safety of my sister and her family, but I have to be honest with you and tell you right now that I don't think I'll be happy until I know."

Thelma and Bud both nodded, though a sideways glance toward Thelma suggested that she thought I might be asking for the moon.

Bud squeezed my arm, supportively, and added, "Any chance of getting your hands on the records of the *original* investigation into Lowanna Swan's death, Thelma?"

"I'll do my best, though I'd be pushing the limits of my brief."

"Her father's death too, as well as the deaths of Bruce Walker, and Little Stan, Big Stan Swan's deceased business partner – though I don't know his full name," I added. "Plus, I think Joyce Trimble has more to tell us."

"Joyce Trimble?" Thelma's voice betrayed her surprise. "What's she got to do with all this?"

I relayed the highlights of the conversation I'd had with Joyce, but left out the personal dynamics between her and Philip, believing those were of a sufficiently private nature for me to keep them quiet for the moment.

Thelma mused, "She could know something more, I agree, though I'm surprised the briefing I received didn't mention that she'd been to visit Myers. Corrective Services must have known about that. To be fair to them, however, I have requested full details of everyone who's been to see Myers over the years…so maybe they didn't mention just one of his visitors when they knew they'd be letting me know about all of them. I suggest that you and Bud speak to her again while I work on gathering the intel you've asked for. By the way, I've also requested anything we can get about S & S Roads, because there seem to be a lot of connections to that company, wouldn't you agree?"

Bud and I did. We'd reached the point where we needed to turn sharply onto the street that led down toward our rental property. It was unlit. As our eyes grew accustomed to the darkness, I concentrated on my footing, while I tried to enjoy the sounds of the night, which were more noticeable now, and still exotic to my ears. I could hear bats, which we have at home – though not of the same size as the local ones which looked more like flying cats than anything else – and yet everything else was alien; the strange calls of birds, and that oddly familiar, yet unexpected, scent of eucalyptus again. And…smoke.

It seemed that all three of us smelled it at much the same time, and we all became fully alert. Bud started running first, and Thelma kept pace with him. I did my best. As we rounded a bend in the road we could see flames, and I reckoned they were just about in line with where our rented house was located.

"I'm calling it in," said Thelma, pausing to dial on her phone. "Don't do anything stupid, Bud."

But Bud was already out of sight. He'd disappeared in the direction of the driveway and all I could do was jog along as fast as I could to try to catch up.

Up In Smoke

By the time I reached the bottom of the steps that led up to the deck around the house, Bud had gone – around to the back, I guessed. I hauled myself up, using the banister, and was grateful that I couldn't see any fire close to the structure itself. Indeed, it seemed as though the smell of smoke was less noticeable now that I was at the house itself. *Maybe the wind's blowing it away?*

Indeed, all the flames we'd seen when we were further along the street seemed to have disappeared…which puzzled me. It wasn't until I got to the back deck that I realized why: yes, there was a fire, and a pretty big one at that, but it was across the valley on the hillside opposite the rear of the house.

Bud was bent double, his hands on his thighs as he caught his breath, and Siân was patting him on the back. Todd was almost hopping about in a state of high anxiety.

"I phoned it in as soon as I saw it," he said, nodding across the valley. "We spotted it when we got here. Looks like it's a couple of miles away, but it's big. The wind's blowing it up the hillside, see? No idea if that area's inhabited and didn't even know what over there is called, but the person I spoke to knew it and said there were teams on their way. Only a few cabins over there, they said – not rentals like this one, but old places, derelict. Said it's in hand."

He looked at me as I gasped for air, then his gaze shifted to Thelma who'd rounded the deck behind me, pink in the face.

Finally, the penny dropped. "You didn't think it was here, did you?" Todd looked horrified. "You really think we're in that much danger?"

Thelma replied, panting, "No, I didn't, but these two were concerned, obviously."

I'd have laughed if I'd had the breath to do it.

A few moments later we were all in the sitting room, with the sliding doors closed against the smell of the smoke outside, which had become more noticeable. Todd was still trying to calm Siân.

She was in tears. "No matter what you say, I want to get back home to the kids as fast as we can. If you lot are scared that we're in danger, then I want to be with them – to know they're alright. I just spoke to them both – and, no, I didn't give anything away, Thelma – but I want to hold them, see? To know I'm doing everything for them that a mother can. So what are you going to do to make sure we're all kept safe?"

I know what's coming when my sister sticks out her chin, but Thelma didn't; there was no way Siân was going to shift her opinions, and now she was challenging Thelma, I suspected we were in for a long evening.

Thelma stood. "What I'm going to do is what I do best – I'm going to gather information. We've discussed what that should be, and I need to start now, because there's a lot of it."

"Shouldn't there be police here to watch over us, or something like that?" Todd was bleating, which didn't go down well, not even with Siân who probably agreed with what he was saying.

I sighed. "Would it make you happier if someone was 'on guard' all night? Because, if so, I volunteer for the first shift. You go to bed, and I'll stay up – I can't possibly think of lying down, I'm too full. And all that running's just jiggled my food about inside me something rotten."

"But it's too early to go to bed," whined Todd.

"Well let's sit here and talk about what's on all our minds, then," said Bud, very sensibly, I thought. "I've found that just chatting can bring important facts to light…Cait knows that too, don't you?"

I nodded. "Don't worry, Todd, we won't point shiny lights at you and pepper you with questions…well, okay, there might be lots of questions, but no bright lights, I promise. Let's all just try to keep calm, and talk about old times – as naturally as we can. You never know what might come up."

"I'll leave you to that," said Thelma, and made herself scare.

"Fancy a cuppa?" Siân seemed determined to force-feed us tea, so we all agreed; I was glad that no one suggested beers, because I was still so full that one more beer might have made me go pop.

We turned off a few lamps and settled into the peace of the sitting room with mugs of tea; it all felt surprisingly cozy and normal, considering the circumstances.

I did my best to try to think of a way to gather more information without making it feel as though the representatives of the Spanish Inquisition had made a house call, so I opened with: "You had lovely weather for your wedding day, didn't you? Hard to believe that's nearly twenty years ago, now. How do you remember it, Siân?"

My sister rolled her eyes at me. "Nice try, Cait. You mean, 'Tell me everything you can remember about Philip Myers', don't you? Well, I was focused on other things that day, so I won't be of much use. And, like I told you, I hardly knew him. So it's over to you for this one, Todd."

Todd looked up from his mug with the glum expression I was getting weary of seeing. "What? Our wedding? Yes, it was sunny – and dry, thank goodness. It was the first time I'd been to Wales, and I was more nervous about impressing your parents than I was about the wedding itself. I'd only met them for the first time a few days earlier, and I thought your father had taken an instant dislike to me. Your mother was quite something that day, wasn't she, Siân? I know they'd organized everything on our behalf, because you and your mum made the arrangements together on the phone while you were still here in Australia and she was on the spot in Wales, but I wouldn't have wanted to be those caterers. She watched them like a hawk. I remember her telling off one of the servers pouring the wine, saying they were giving people too much, too often."

We laughed at the shared memory, then I was surprised when Todd put down his tea and said, "Back in a minute," and headed off toward his room.

"No – I don't know why he went," said Siân when I raised an eyebrow.

Returning with his laptop and an external disk drive, Todd faffed about for a few moments then turned the screen to face the three of us. "Here you are, Bud, now you can see Philip Myers for yourself."

We all leaned forward and peered: wedding photos popped up, and I was looking at my sister, my late parents, and myself, about twenty years earlier.

"Look at you," said Bud, reaching for my hand and giving it a squeeze. "Very fancy."

I was, indeed, looking very fancy; Siân had insisted upon me being her one and only bridesmaid, and had further insisted that I wore her choice of dress, which I had absolutely hated. I know it's a tradition for brides to select hideous frocks for their bridesmaids just so they look comparatively much better – well, that's what I've always believed, in any case – and Siân had not disappointed. My get-up had been a poor color choice for me – a winey-purple – and the shape? Well, let's just say that gathered waistlines and poufy sleeves have never done anyone any favors, and they especially didn't suit me. And she'd made me wear my hair curled on top of my head. I looked like a series of balls balanced on top of each other. And my make-up? Good grief, I looked as though it had been slathered on with a trowel.

"You look fantastic," said Bud quietly, then added, "and you're a picture of loveliness, Siân."

She was: taller than me, half my girth, swathed in a fitted creamy dress, with long, ethereal blonde curls and a smile that could melt your heart. One hundred percent bride.

Mum was also wearing a shade of purple, but it had suited her, and her headwear – a cross between a proper hat and a fascinator – looked like it had been designed after a night on the town shared by a mad milliner and a florist. Dad's gray, pinstriped waistcoat pulled at the buttons, but his face? Glowing with happiness. I wondered if he'd been thinking, "One down, one to go," at the time, though was pretty sure that neither he nor Mum had ever expected me to marry.

At least I knew that I wouldn't have to look at any photos of my boyfriend at the time, Angus: I'd told him I was going to the wedding on my own, and he hadn't argued. I'd been glad of the break from the stress of living with an addict, even if just for a long weekend. As I looked more closely at the photos of me, seeing past the heavy eye make-up and the blusher that made me look like a clown, I could see the circles and bags beneath my eyes. Maybe that was why the woman Siân had booked to come to the hotel to do our hair and faces had used every bottle and palette in her bag on me; she'd been trying to make me look less drawn and exhausted.

Todd scrolled through photographs – those taken by the hired photographer first. Rows of people carefully positioned, all with frozen smiles; the train on Siân's dress perfectly placed. Todd? He'd been much plumper in those days, with a great deal more hair. I wondered how he felt looking at these images of himself. A glance at his face told me...uncomfortable.

"Philip wasn't in any of the formal pictures," he said, "even though he was the only person I really knew there." He shrugged. "Never liked having his photo taken. But I've got more here – the snaps your father took, Siân. Remember? He had that new camera."

I certainly remembered Dad and his blessed camera; he'd splashed out on a fancy digital model, and had spent the entire day popping up all over the place snapping away, delighted that he didn't have to change rolls of film.

"I edited them down a bit after he gave them to us," added Todd, which I could imagine he must have needed to – Dad's reputation for lopping body parts off his subjects was well known within our family.

After we'd been subjected to dozens of shots of people's elbows and backsides – mine especially, it seemed – Todd said, "Here's one of Philip."

And there he was, the man convicted of shooting Lowanna Swan, twice, in the back. Tall, with a shock of white-blond hair that was long, even for the day's fashion. His navy suit was immaculate, putting Todd's appearance on his big day to shame. Myers was slim, trim, tanned, and his crisp white shirt remained wrinkle-free, his tie still properly tied, even though the photo of him had been taken at the so-called "disco" that had taken place after the reception proper.

The shot showed him dancing with his wife, who was almost a mirror image of him, her svelte, leggy figure hugged by a sheath of hyacinth blue. They seemed to glow among the others on the dance floor. Their smiles were intimate, reserved for each other.

"She was dead a few years later, Cindy, poor dab. Pancreatic cancer. It's vicious." Siân sounded as though she were far away, momentarily living in a different time. "I might not have really known her, but that's a cruel disease for anyone to have – though they're making leaps and bounds in its treatment nowadays. Too late for too many."

Todd looked away from the screen, concern showing in his eyes as he gazed at my sister.

Siân added, "On that happy note, I'll just pop to the loo. You lot can talk about Philip while I'm gone."

Bud took his cue nicely. "Now that I've seen him, I suppose it helps a bit. At least I can picture him…how old would he have been here, Todd?"

Todd considered his reply. "Mid-forties? Still looks good for his age, doesn't he? Never changed, really. I always wondered if prison might have taken the shine off a bit."

"Not quite a surfer dude, but not far off," said Bud. "I dare say I'd have labeled him Australian if I didn't know it. And his wife? A beautiful woman. Very sad."

"Cindy didn't die of the cancer," said Todd, surprising us both. "Philip said she took the diagnosis, and prognosis – which wasn't good – remarkably well. But she got up one morning, did her hair and make-up, put on a posh frock, crushed a load of tablets into a favorite cocktail, then drank it down. He found her laid out like she was asleep on their bed when he got home, the next day. He'd come in to do a few final bits and pieces so he could get away to spend what he believed would be their last few weeks or months together, then went out and got himself well and truly lashed…drunk. Got home the next morning, and there she was. He was lost without her. The business took a bit of a nosedive for a while after that. He was just getting his act together when they arrested him."

Bud and I managed to exchange a glance without Todd noticing; it was his turn to visit the land of past times, dewy eyed, then his head snapped up and he said, pointedly, "No question but she did it herself. There was an inquest, of course."

I wondered why he sounded so vehement.

Siân rejoined us. "That Thelma's got quite the voice, hasn't she? It carries, even when she's on the phone. Mezzo, or alto, if she sang, I should think. Lovely and round. Like Mum."

Todd was smiling at Siân when he said, "I'd never heard your mother sing before our wedding, of course, and I couldn't believe the sound that came out of her little body. Amazing, singing those hymns. But no one said anything – as though it was to be expected."

"It was," replied Siân. "Mum and Dad knew most of the people at the church service, and she was renowned for her voice. Dad on the piano, her singing 'We'll gather lilacs' and so forth, at home. I think that's why I wanted a lilac theme for our wedding, to be honest – all those years believing that lilacs and romance were synonymous."

Todd laughed. "And me in that lilac tie. Tasteful." I was pleased to see my sister and brother-in-law share a genuinely loving exchange, for once.

Thelma's arrival snapped us all back to reality. "I hear they're thinking that fire over on the opposite side of the valley is another case of arson. Dangerous. Though not as tragic as the fire that killed those three men, of course. No loss of life involved this time. They reckon they should get it knocked down by morning, if the wind doesn't change."

Bud observed, "Cait and I are only too familiar with wildfires, living where we do. Our part of British Columbia is supposed to be the wet west coast, but it's been so dry of late. Huge fires, thousands of hectares, some of them. Let's hope these guys are good at their job, and that the wind cooperates. Arson again, eh? Maybe that casts a fresh light on the tragedy that claimed those lives."

"Exactly," said Thelma as she wandered to the kitchen. "Fancy a cuppa, anyone? I'll fill the jug if you like."

Siân was up in an instant. "I'll do it, you get back to work." She smiled sheepishly. "Sorry, I didn't mean that to sound the way it did. I hope you know what I mean; we're really very grateful, Thelma."

"Cheers," said Thelma, who had already filled the kettle. "I'll do this, then back off. You were all talking family stuff when I interrupted – I'll let you lot get back to that." She glanced at Todd's laptop screen as she crossed the room, which was showing the photo of Philip and his wife, and stopped in her tracks, staring. "When was that taken?"

I was surprised by her accusatory tone, as was Todd, judging by the look on his face. He replied, "At our wedding, just short of twenty years ago."

Thelma shook her head. "Cindy was a skinny thing, wasn't she?" She stomped off.

Following Thema's bizarrely catty comment, we all returned our attention to Todd's photos, and continued to chat about family memories. I was glad that Bud was having the chance to see the pictures, because I have very few family photographs – my eidetic memory means I really don't need them, and who wants even more things on bookshelves to gather dust?

Once the wedding photos were finished, Todd passed the laptop to Siân so she could hunt about for more pictures to show Bud, and they huddled over it, with her telling him what he was seeing, while Todd and I made tea.

I volunteered to take Thelma's to her room, largely because I wanted to get the woman on her own; I couldn't decide if she'd been purposely avoiding being alone with me since she'd arrived, or if that was just the way things had worked out. Either way, I knew this was my chance.

I knocked on the door to her room. "Just a second," she called. I heard the lock being opened, then she pulled the door open a crack, clearly with the intention of not allowing me to enter. I made an instant decision and "tripped", making sure the tea I splashed mainly caught her sleeve – I knew it was hot and didn't want to scald her…I just wanted to get myself through the door.

"I'm so sorry," I gushed, stepping forward. I opened the door wide when she leapt backwards, popped the mug onto the chest of drawers, and rushed into her bathroom to grab a towel. "Here, let me help." I fussed about, dabbing her here and there, as I took in everything I could about her room, noting it so I could recall it later.

Thelma pushed me off, and grabbed the towel from my hand. She was muttering oaths under her breath, and became pink with anger, which I thought was a pretty strong reaction to what was, after all, just a small "accident".

I moved to retrieve the mug and she all but barred my way. I responded with a pathetic, "I'm so sorry, I'll make you another cup," at which point she handed me the mug.

"I'll come and get it in ten minutes. Now let me get back to work," she snapped.

I took the mug and backed out of the room, wearing my most apologetic expression. "I'll give you a shout when it's ready," I said, just as she locked the door again.

I made my way back to the sitting room to make another cuppa, delighted that I'd been able to gain access to Thelma's inner sanctum – but puzzled by some of the things I'd seen there.

Hot And Heavy

The effects of a large dinner, and an incredibly tense day, were starting to take their toll on Siân and Todd; my sister kept standing to stretch and had lost all interest in scrolling through photos, while my brother-in-law had begin to pick the sides of his fingernails, which was annoying.

When Thelma came to collect her tea she announced, "I've got a whole bunch of stuff about the mining situation ready to go. I don't think I'm going to get much more before tomorrow on any other topics, so does anyone want to use my laptop to read through what I've got so far?"

Bud glanced at me, and I nodded. "That would be helpful. One more mug of tea should keep me going for a few hours. I'll take it, thanks." I hoped the tea would do the trick.

"I'll stay up with you, for a bit of company," said Bud, "but why don't the rest of you head off? It's been a long day, and maybe you'll sleep better knowing that Cait and I are still sitting in here. We'll keep our ears open for anything…unusual."

"Noses too," said Siân. "Though that sounds daft, you know what I mean. And not for that fire over there – but for any signs of anything not right around this place. Okay?"

I hugged my sister. "Don't panic, we're on it."

She chuckled in my arms. "Thanks, Sis."

"You're welcome. Now get some sleep – your back needs it, as does the rest of you."

Finally alone in the lounge, both Bud and I took a few moments out on the deck to give the night air a good sniff; yes, there was still smoke in the atmosphere, as well as the tang of eucalyptus, but there was sweeter air too, fresher – a breeze taking the smoke away from us.

"I hope that doesn't mean they'll have a tougher time fighting that fire," said Bud. "Tell you what, you get started with that stuff on Thelma's laptop, and I'll just pop down below, to the empty apartment beneath us, to give it a quick once-over. I'll feel better once I've done that."

I didn't dare peer over the edge of the deck, not even in the darkness, but I didn't fancy the idea of my husband padding around on his own.

"I could do with stretching my legs a bit – I'll come with you. But we need light down there; let's see if there are any useful switches, eh? As everyone keeps telling us, there are some creatures around that can be dangerous, and we don't want to go treading on anything that might bite back."

"Agreed."

The owner of the rental house had been thoughtful enough to label the light switches, and list items that could be found around the place; we flicked on the outdoor lamps for the lower deck, and excavated a couple of good, solid flashlights from a cupboard, then headed off. We had to go all the way around the house, then down the steps at the front, before being able to get to the lower deck, which ran around that level in the same way ours did above it. The lights mounted on the walls of the bottom apartment were taking their own sweet time warming up, so everything was a bit dim, and I was glad of the ability to point a beam of light into dark corners.

"Is that a stick, or a snake?" I asked, stopping abruptly. Bud grabbed my arm, and I hovered, with one foot in mid air.

We stared at the brown wiggly thing until we were certain it was just a stick, then continued. The back deck was, as we'd hoped and expected, deserted; there wasn't even any furniture there. Just one floor down from our lovely perch above, the air was noticeably more cloying and humid – though the general dryness in the area hadn't suggested any humidity at all would be possible. The breeze rustled in the trees, making them feel much closer in the darkness than they had done up above, and I felt hemmed in by my surroundings, which was odd, given that we were most definitely outdoors.

Unlike ours above, this deck didn't completely surround the lower level – beyond the back of the house, it stopped short on the far side at a balustrade that allowed enough room for a chair, but nothing else; spots suggested something had been there for long enough to leave rust marks on the wooden planks. "Maybe Frank Tipton only renewed the upper deck," I commented. "This one looks to be in much worse shape than ours, and those marks seem old."

"Whatever the case, everything appears to be fine down here," said Bud, sounding confident. "Glad we had a look, though."

As we turned, I threw the beam of my flashlight above us, toward the deck around the upper level. It was clear that ours reached a good five or six feet further out into the valley than the lower one, and I realized that the entire body of the house was also smaller on the lower level than on ours. "A good way to make use of a smaller footprint," I noted as we made our way back toward the front of the property.

"More rooms upstairs means more heads in beds," said Bud knowledgably. "That's what they call it on the rental websites I was checking – heads in beds. A big deal for the owner of a rental property."

I was, once again, delighted by my husband's magpie mind, and found myself weirdly relieved to be making our way back up the steps to our higher level, the air freshened markedly as we did so.

"I'd find it too claustrophobic to be staying down there; the way our upper deck overhangs the lower one seems to trap the air, doesn't it?" I said, "At least we catch whatever breeze is available up here. You wouldn't think one floor would make such a difference, would you?"

"True," said Bud.

We clicked off our flashlights, and turned off the wall lamps below us, then Bud made yet more tea for me, while I settled myself at the dining table to begin to work through the information Thelma had corralled into a specific folder on her laptop. It was one of those solid, roughty-toughty models, nothing like the one I had at home, the main selling features of which were its wafer-thin dimensions and the fact it was as light as a feather; this one was solidly built, and weighed about the same as a brick.

"I wouldn't have fancied carting this thing about in a backpack while hiking around a national park," I said as I positioned it on the table and fiddled with a chair. "Thelma's well-built, and has muscular legs, but this would weigh anyone down. I wonder why on earth she has it with her."

"Just as well she did, for our sakes," said Bud, placing a mug of tea on a coaster a good arm's-length away from the laptop.

"True. Oh look, everything except this one folder is locked. Thelma's not taking any chances, is she? Is this laptop stuffed full of 'Top Secret' documents do you think?"

Bud smiled. "If it is, she's showing great faith in us by letting us use it at all. I dare say that whatever we're not supposed to see isn't just locked off, but encrypted, too. So what's in the folder you can open?"

Bud peered over my shoulder as I clicked, and I could see his lips move as he read the titles of the documents listed. He drew back with a sigh. "Good luck with that lot, then. All looks like legal gobbledegook, to me. I hate stuff like that. Never my forte. I know I was forced to read it at certain points during my career, but not my…mug of tea." He winked at me, shoved his mug in my face, then headed toward the sofa.

I settled myself, and opened the first document. It was as dull as Bud had suggested it might be, and the legalese wasn't at all appealing, though it was pretty straightforward, to be honest. I plowed through it, and the next, and worked my way down the list. I allowed my reading speed to build until I was going at full tilt, skimming, encoding, and locking it all away in my memory banks. By the time I sat back and reached for my tea it was stone cold, and Bud was snoring gently on the sofa, his head lolling back, his mouth wide open. I checked my watch – I'd been at it for almost two hours…how had that happened?

I didn't want to disturb my husband, but at least dared to sit back in the creaky chair to sip my tea; my mouth was dry, and even cold tea was better than nothing. The house was silent. I couldn't even hear any night birds in the darkness beyond the closed windows and doors. The only illumination in the place came from the pendant above the dining table where I was sitting, so I stretched my neck in my little pool of light, and allowed the tea to do its job rehydrating my tongue. I tend to have my mouth open when I'm concentrating, and my poor tongue dries out until I can barely make spit.

I felt I'd increased my knowledge about Australian mining, and the laws connected to it, exponentially – not difficult, given how little I'd known about it all to start with. But what was deeply frustrating was that I really couldn't see how any of that knowledge helped me, or my sister and her family, at all; Thelma's summary had been just as enlightening, though I supposed I was grateful that she'd allowed me the opportunity to develop my understanding to such an extent that at least I now knew that to be the case. Yes, Todd was going to be in a bit of a pickle, and he'd have a lot of decisions to make, some of them very soon, since a few of Philip Myers' lease-rights were about to expire, unless they were renegotiated with the government pretty quickly.

I'd worked through Australian law, the details of the companies Todd was now taking over, where their leases were, and how they'd been maintained, as well as information about the consortia Thelma had mentioned.

That particular information had been most disappointing, considering it was the most "secret" thing she'd let me see. As she'd warned me, it was no more than a list of names – and weird ones at that. Some seemed to be made-up words, that possibly comprised bits of other words to make a whole that was – almost – pronounceable. Kejoka was one, Kathewagapru another, and Paulinamast made me think of a boat called Paulina sailing across the ocean. Others hinted at grandiose plans – Pegasus, Thor International, and the ominous Megamining being prime examples. But she'd been right – nothing leaped out at me. I wondered why I'd had to work so hard to persuade her to let me see them.

I took the chance to mentally consolidate what I'd read, then stretched, making my chair creak so loudly that Bud truffled into wakefulness. He clamped his mouth shut, wiped his eyes, then stared at me. "Did I drop off?" I nodded. "Sorry – pretty poor watchdog, me, eh?"

"Not a peep from anyone," I said, whispering. I stood and arched my aching back. "All done. Not much there, except to confirm what Thelma told us."

Bud looked as disappointed as I felt.

"Maybe what she can find out for us about people, as opposed to legal stuff and companies, will be a bit more enlightening," he said quietly. "Why don't you go to bed? I'll just freshen myself up, first, then I'll stay awake – maybe if I grab a book? That should do it."

I didn't argue.

As I lay in bed beneath the cozy covers, I felt uncomfortable; psychologically uncomfortable, not physically. I couldn't help but feel that I was looking at the whole mish-mash of confusion surrounding the situation with Siân and Todd through a lens that was smudged and foggy. I sat up and tried beating my pillow into a position where it would cradle my head, rather than just sitting beneath it in a lump.

I felt as though Lowanna Swan was a distant figure, getting further away from me every hour, and that didn't feel…right. I analyzed why I felt that way: prior to Thelma's arrival I'd been focussed on Philip Myers and his role as the killer of the girl who could show a paying client where to locate opals, and the tragic deaths of three men I'd come to know, even if only slightly. Since Thelma's arrival? The focus had shifted to legal dealings, international consortia, and the mining of lithium. And that felt…wrong.

I wondered what it was exactly that my gut was trying to tell me, and whether I should trust my gut in any case. As a psychologist I know very well that "gut instincts" are anything but – they're feelings we have that arise from knowledge we really do possess, even if we've perceived cues to build that knowledge completely subconsciously. What had I perceived that was making me feel a bit like a sheep being herded into a pen I didn't fancy the look of?

I cast my mind back to what I'd managed to see when I'd "accidentally" spilt tea over Thelma. Her room had been generally neat. Her large backpack had been standing open in the corner, seemingly empty, but still rigidly upright; I wondered just how stout a backpack would have to be to be able to do that.

Her laptop had been open on her desk and on the screen had been…

I closed my eyes to the point where everything goes fuzzy and began to hum, which – for some reason – helps me recollect more accurately.

I can see the screen of Thelma's laptop and it's got a picture of one of those old-fashioned mine entrances on it; it could be something from an old Western film – a rectangular, door-shaped entryway surrounded by a wooden frame, with a hand-painted sign warning those who enter that there can be falling rocks, so they must wear a hardhat. There are pickaxes and shovels set to one side of the entryway, and there's a suggestion of illumination within the dark interior – so there must be power inside. *Light bulbs?* What else can I see? There's a portion of another sign in the top right-hand corner of the screen, but all I can see are the bottom bits of what might be letters. Not much help…they're really no more than dabs of paint: seven short ones, a long one, four more short ones, something that was pretty definitely the bottom of a capital letter G, five more short ones, and a semi-circle – *possibly the bottom of an O?* Could be anything. Ah, and there's a leather hat on the ground – battered and dusty, with sweat stains around the base of the crown. It looks large, when compared with the head of the shovel beside it.

What else do I recall of her room? The curtains are open, but it's a dim room – the light's being filtered by the trees outside. She has no lamps turned on, so I believe she's been at the laptop, working. Her phone is face up beside the laptop, and its screen is illuminated with…a photograph of a kangaroo? Yes, that's what it is.

She has a lot of papers on her bed – they are spread out, but not in what looks like an organized manner – some are lying in open folders. Can I read anything there? No, it's all too far away to make any sense of it. *Shame.* There's a toilet bag open on the bedside table nearest the door. Deodorant, a bar of soap, a box of something with a woman's head on it – *hair dye? Really?* – and medicated talcum powder. And there's an amber plastic pill container beside the lamp. No, no chance of reading that either, but the pills inside it are large capsules, two-toned.

At the foot of the bed, on the floor, lies one more open folder – *has it fallen off the bed?* – and I can see a photograph printed on a sheet of paper, poking out from beneath the cardboard covering. It's a picture of a…a rifle. An old-looking one, with the light catching a flash of metal on the stock. *Is it Philip Myers' rifle – the one that got him convicted?* There's no reason why Thelma shouldn't have such a photo, but why hasn't she passed it to me? And why didn't she say she had it? There's no printer in her room – she must have brought the paperwork with her. *All that stuff? In her backpack? On a hiking trip? Really?*

I opened my eyes to see Bud standing at the foot of our bed. "You know you hum quite loudly when you do that, right? I came to check on you. What have you been recalling?"

I told him what I'd seen in Thelma's room. "What do you make of it?" I asked.

Even in the gloom of our room I could tell that Bud was puzzled. "I don't know. Like you say, no reason why she shouldn't have a picture of Myers' rifle; it was evidence in the case against him – the case we know she's been briefed on – but why not say so? She came right here, she said, directly from her vacation trip; why have paperwork with her…or even her laptop…at all?"

"Is she…is she 'handling' us, Bud?" I couldn't help but ask. "I feel she's forcing us to look at her right hand when we should be giving our attention to her left; misdirecting our attention. All that stuff she gave me to read about mining and regulations? More or less a complete waste of my time. Is she giving me busy work to keep me away from what I can't help but think is at the heart of all this trouble – the death of the girl Lowanna? At least, that's how I felt until Thelma shoved all this lease and consortia stuff under our noses. See? Misdirection. Or am I not seeing things clearly?"

Bud perched on the end of the bed. "I don't know. I don't...I don't want to believe that's the case."

"You reckon she's trustworthy?" I had to ask, though I'd been taking it for granted that he did.

"Sure...at least, I found her reliable when I worked closely with her."

"Twice. Ten years ago," I said quietly.

Bud stood and I could hear him raking his hand through his hair – I had no idea it made such a noise until he did it in the still of the night, in the dark, like that. "People who do what she does are constantly assessed – it's not a 'one and done' thing – you know, Cait? It's not like, 'We checked your background once and we'll just believe every word you say from now on'. There are all sorts of reasons why some people in her line of work might go off the rails, and there are safeguards against it, of course. So, no, I don't think she'd have been the go-to person for the folks I spoke to in Ottawa unless she still has their confidence. Is she trustworthy? I would say that our government believes so, Cait, and I dare say the Aussies would have made their own checks before allowing her to take up any sort of liaison position between the two countries. If not someone so carefully vetted, by two governments, then who can we trust?"

I shrugged. Unsure if my husband could see me do it, I added, "Who knows?"

Bud reached for my shoulder, making me jump. "I trust you, Wife."

"And I trust you, Husband," I replied. "And I trust my sister, though I think Todd's a bit...unpredictable. It's not that I don't trust him, it's just that I think he's most likely to act in his own interests."

"Don't we all?"

I considered my reply. "You've put yourself in harm's way to do your duty for your country, Bud. That's not putting yourself first, is it? I believe there are people who don't always put themselves first, but truly do put the greater good ahead of their personal interests. First responders do it all the time. Just think about those firefighters, like young Timbo from Winnie's Place, who run toward danger all the time to help others. Now that's where I think you and Todd would differ; I honestly don't get the impression he'd do anything for the greater good. My sister? Yes. If there was someone she felt she could help, and she believed she could do so without endangering her children or her husband, she'd help them – putting her personal safety to one side. Not that I think she'd take a stupid risk – though we're not necessarily good at judging risks when there's an emergency."

"Thelma's definitely put herself in harm's way for the greater good," said Bud quietly. "She chose to support her colleagues in the field to a much greater extent than her job description demanded. She put the team's needs before her own. Nearly died because of it, too."

I took my chance. "What happened? I won't let on that I know."

Bud sighed. "Without sensitive details? She accompanied a small group whose brief was unexpectedly shifted from 'watch' to 'intervene'. She could have stayed back, in safety, but we all knew that her intel could help us as we entered…a delicate situation. She knew the people we were after almost like they were her family – she'd been watching them, and gathering intel on them, for months…knew their habits, their likely responses to our arrival. She could have viewed the feed from our cameras in a safe place, but chose to be on the spot to be better able to communicate what our responses should be. She got…hit. In the shoulder. Someone had to haul her out."

"You?"

"Yes, me. But one of our targets had been off-site when we'd gone in, and he spotted us as he was returning to the…location. I…got her out of that situation too."

"She owes you a great deal," I said softly, grateful that Bud was able to tell me about this operation, and that he'd survived it. Just the idea of it gave me chills.

"I really would have done the same for anyone," he said quietly. "But, yeah, she seemed to believe I'd gone out on a limb for her. She…she was very kind, after that. Always there for me, whenever I needed back-up, feeding me intel before I'd even asked for it on occasion. But, to be honest, I guess I was a bit relieved when they moved her from BC to Ottawa. Jen had started to get a bit…not jealous exactly, because she knew our marriage was as strong as it could be…so she knew there was nothing going on between me and Thelma – who was a widow by then. But…but Thelma was always first to show up whenever Jen invited her over to any sort of get-together, and last to leave. Always hovering around, that kind thing. But Jen knew…she knew we were us, and always would be. Until we weren't, of course. Until that…dreadful human being…killed her."

Whenever Bud talks about his late wife, I always try to allow him time to do it without me talking over him; sometimes the greatest gift I can give him is my silence.

Eventually he added, "And now we're us, Cait; this life…this time…is ours, and I'm so fortunate to have you with me."

"I'm sorry, Bud." I was. "And I'm grateful, too." I was. "Do you think Thelma really was at the Gardens of Stone national park? Or did she somehow want to insert herself into this situation because of you being involved?"

I could hear Bud's intake of breath. "Okay, let's think this through logically – all subjectiveness aside: I called Ottawa, they said 'someone' would be in touch with me, and Thelma was the one who emailed me, then called. I can't see why she'd even be in Australia unless she was over in Canberra on official business. That's something I can actually check on, and she'd know it, so wouldn't…couldn't…lie about it. As for where she was, exactly, when whoever it was got in touch with her? Cellphones mean you can be anywhere at all when you take a call, within reason, and, unless someone really wants to find out where your phone is, that's good cover. But, you see, unless someone from within government circles really had contacted her about all this, then how would she have known about it at all? I used…well, not exactly high-clearance lines of communication, but certainly not the sort of email addresses or phone numbers it's easy for anyone to monitor unless they put some real – and illegal – effort into it. And I don't think that's realistic, or likely. On balance, I'd say it went the way she said it did: someone looked into who I was when my request for help came through, noticed that she and I had worked together in the past, got in touch with her. She must have been relatively close when all that happened, because of how relatively quickly she arrived here. Her story stacks up."

"And yet the presence of her laptop, and a pile of paperwork related to all this, don't suggest she was on a carefree hiking vacation in a nearby national park, wouldn't you agree?"

Bud "Hmmm-ed" in the darkness, then said, "How about we see if she comes through with what we've asked her to dig up for us in the morning? I accept there's little she could do to get her hands on all the background that we requested this evening; yes, the people who could release it are always at work, but those who have to agree to it being released aren't necessarily always accessible. Maybe we hold off judging her until then? After all, if she gets us what we need, that's what matters, right?"

I agreed, though not truly happily.

Bud kissed my head and suggested I got some sleep. "It's almost four in the morning…try for a few hours at least?"

I promised I'd do my best.

Slow Start

Bud took the unilateral decision to let me sleep in a bit, so, when I finally stumbled into the kitchen, everyone was out on the deck having almost finished eating.

Siân immediately suggested about fifteen breakfast options to me, and I had to tell her at least half a dozen times to stop fussing.

"You're faffing over me like Mum used to," was the only thing that finally got her to sit down and shut up.

I nibbled on toast, which turned out to be annoyingly full of seeds; I assumed Siân had chosen the bread and that it was supposed to be good for me. I inhaled two mugs of coffee, which was fantastic. The smell of smoke had gone completely, and the air was cool with a hint of moisture in it, which I suspected would be a relief for the locals. There were dark clouds above us, too. "Looks like it might rain," I noted.

"Forecast said it would by lunchtime," said Todd brightly. "And they said there's only one team needed up at that fire, now, tackling hot spots, which is excellent news, wouldn't you agree?"

We all did. Thelma stood to leave. "I'll take this coffee with me – things to do. How d'you get on with that intel last night, Cait? Helpful?"

I yawned and nodded. "Thanks. Lots of it." I didn't want to ask her why she'd, basically, wasted my time. "I'm ready for anything else you can throw at me, as soon as you can," I added as brightly as I could manage.

"Hopefully people will get back to me soon," she said, and headed off, a mug in one hand, her chunky laptop under her arm.

"Plans for today?" Bud beamed, though I could see he needed sleep.

"Todd's going to look into getting us a flight back home later today," said Siân, "aren't you, Todd?"

Todd nodded. "Yes, I am. Though it might be difficult."

Siân plopped an apple core she'd been nibbling onto her plate. "I can think of at least four airlines that fly from Sydney to Perth, Todd – and we don't even have to fly direct. I wouldn't mind changing in Melbourne if it meant we could get home tonight – at least we'd be on our way. If we leave here in the next hour or so we can be home to pick up the kids and all sleep in our own beds tonight. That's what I want. If you can't make it happen, I'll sort it out myself. And don't even think of saying we can't afford it – we can. That's what credit cards are for."

Todd half-smiled. "It's not that – it's because Thelma said it might be best if we stayed here, at least until tomorrow, like we planned."

"Why?" I was truly curious.

"Because someone she believes can help us is coming here to talk to us," replied Todd, his tone wavering between wanting to sound hopeful about the visit, and yet worried about what it might mean.

Bud and I shared a furtive glance, but it didn't escape my sister's eagle-eye.

She snapped, "You two – what's going on? You know something, don't you?"

Bud and I both shrugged silently, both equally aware that our conversation might easily be overheard by Thelma in her room, just along the deck.

"Nothing at all," I said. "I just wondered who'd be coming, but I can tell that Bud knows nothing about it. That's what that look was about."

Siân picked up a banana and began to peel it. She said huffily, "Well why don't you look into times of flights, Todd? And ask Thelma why this person who's coming is so important that we have to wait here to meet them. Couldn't we just have a video call with them from our own home, when we get back there?" She dropped her banana and stood. "Hang on, why am I asking you to do that? I can do it for myself. I'll be right back."

She stomped into the kitchen, with Todd stumbling after her.

Bud and I exchanged an exaggerated shrug.

"Did you sleep at all?" I said loudly, then whispered to Bud that he should give me a long, loud, and boring answer while I crept along the deck to be close enough to Thelma's window that I could hear whatever might pass between her and Siân.

He batted the air at me as I passed him, seeming to think he could stop me, but I just waved my arms to get him to keep banging on about how much tea he'd drunk, and how many chapters he'd read of his book.

I leaned against the wall beside Thelma's window which was, thankfully, open, and I heard Siân knock at the door. I even heard Thelma sigh heavily when Siân's muffled voice called, "Can I have a word, please, Thelma."

Thelma's "Just a minute," made me jump; she must have been right beside the window when she replied. *Had she been listening to us chat on the deck?*

I heard the noise of her unlocking her door. "Come on in. Excuse the mess."

Siân said, "No worries. And it's tidy, really. Anyway, Todd said you want us to stay here until tomorrow, because someone's coming to see us? Who's coming? And why do we have to see them here? Can't they come to see us in Perth instead? Then we could fly home today."

Thelma replied, "They're coming from Canberra. Can't get here until the morning."

I heard my sister's thoughtful reply. "Canberra? Are we that important? Are *they* that important?"

"Yes, they are. And once you've all had a sit-down, you'll be better prepared to get on with the rest of your lives. You need to be here to meet with them. I'm not asking you to stay longer than you'd planned, just to not leave early."

"You don't have kids, do you?" Siân's tone was dismissive. "No, you don't need to answer that one, because it's obvious. If you did, you'd know that me being here when I want to be with my children is torture. I cannot believe for one minute that all this twaddle you're on about is going to put us in danger – that's all just so that you secret service lot have a chance to feel important."

Thelma's usually mellifluous tone had acquired a harder edge when she replied, "You seem to forget that someone might have just killed the man who used to own all those mineral leases, Siân. Now your husband controls them. Do you want to take that chance?"

I didn't like the tone Thelma was using, but I needn't have worried; Siân gave as good as she'd got.

"Now you listen to me, Thelma bloody Pruitt." Siân's voice had dropped half an octave, which I knew meant trouble; it gave me chills. "Alright then, we'll stay. But you tell whoever is on their way that they'd better get here and get this over with so we can leave early in the morning. We are out of here first thing, got it? No one will stand between me and my children. And don't you go using that tone with me, either. Think you're going to frighten me with that? You have no idea, do you? I'm Welsh, see? We can come out singing or swinging, and trust me when I tell you that you'll prefer it to be singing. You? A data cruncher, that's what you are. A possible murder? Connected to some old mineral leases? Philip Myers might have been killed in jail for any number of reasons we can't even guess. He might have owed someone a packet of ciggies, for all we know. He was convicted of murdering a young Aboriginal girl…people in jail get killed all the time, or don't you watch the news? Oh no, I forgot, you're only over here from Canada for a bit, aren't you? Don't any Canadian killers get murdered in prison? Or are even the prisoners there too polite for that?"

Thelma didn't respond at first, then her tone was noticeably conciliatory when she replied, "I'll put in a call to my contact. Find out his ETA. I'll let you know."

Siân snapped, "No need to let me know – I'll stand here while you phone him."

I jumped when I realized that Bud was beside me. "Are you hearing this?" I mouthed.

He nodded, and rolled his eyes, mouthing, "Siân's bonkers."

I thumped him, making sure my eyes told him that I loved him, but that he was talking about my sister and only I could say such things…which is quite a lot to squeeze into one look, but I managed it, I think.

Thelma was suddenly right beside the window, and speaking calmly, and quietly. "When will you be here? Yes, they want to know. Need to get away. Yes…I told them that. Nope. Okay." I heard a sigh. Speaking more loudly – to Siân, I guessed – Thelma added, "He can't get here any earlier than about eight o'clock in the morning. You are one of his priorities, but he has others that mean he cannot get away sooner. He'll be traveling overnight to get here."

I checked my watch – it was half past eight. About twenty-four hours, then.

Siân seemed placated. "Right. Good. Come on, Todd, let's check on those flight times tomorrow."

I heard the door close, also heard Thelma lock it, then I heard her voice, once again close to the window, and once again using hushed tones. "They're getting edgy, I told you they would. And Bud's wife? She's sniffing around like she thinks something's up.

Yes, see you at the Three Sisters lookout point, at nine tonight. Don't be late, but do be careful. Bye."

Bud and I stared at each other, not even breathing, and I – for one – felt scared. Thelma's tone had more than alarmed me.

Not Happy Campers

I dragged Bud back to the table on the deck, then whispered, "Right – that's not good. You need to check in with your Ottawa lot; I don't care what you think about how often people are security cleared, go and check on Thelma, now. Go up the road to do it – somewhere she can't possibly overhear you. She's up to something. A secret meeting – here – with someone who's not due to 'arrive' until tomorrow? Why? And when you've done that, also try to find out if there is a real eye being kept on Mattie and Beccie. I…I'm wondering now if Thelma told the truth about that."

Bud looked shaken. "Yeah, okay. I'll give it some thought, make some calls. I'll be as quick as I can, but as long as it takes. Take care, right? Don't…*do* anything." He kissed me, then left, looking visibly disconcerted.

I decided the best thing I could do was…push my luck. I made my way to Thelma's room and knocked on the door. When Thelma opened it a crack, I waggled my hands. "Look, no tea," I said, grinning in what I hoped was a winning way. "I just wanted to see if you had anything for me yet – I'm kicking my heels, a bit."

Thelma turned away. "I need my laptop myself." She sighed. "Okay then, I guess you can use Todd's laptop to open these documents. They're sensitive, but not secret, strictly speaking – but not for public consumption. Got it?"

I took the thumb drive she was offering me, nodded, and mugged a salute. "Is everything here?"

Thelma shook her head. "Nothing from Corrective Services yet – though whatever they send will have to be vetted before it gets to me, and is likely to be redacted. Nor have I been able to get anything about the inquest into Bruce Walker's death yet, but

I'm expecting it. Also, nothing yet on the deceased partner of Stan Swan – whose name was Stanley Hayes, by the way – and I've been promised full background on S & S Roads soon, though it's not here yet. I can't email anything to you – all too sensitive for that – but I have more thumb drives, so I'll pass stuff over on those when I have it. This should keep you going for a while."

She shut the door without further ado. I stood outside Siân and Todd's room and said loudly, "Can I use your laptop again, please, Todd? It's to help with…everything."

Siân stuck her head out of the bathroom, and Todd appeared from behind the door of their wardrobe. "It's on the bed," he said. "Feel free. The password is Siân's birthdate."

I winked at Siân, dared a quick whisper, "I promise we're doing all we can to help," grabbed the laptop, and made my way back to the indoor dining table, where I wouldn't have to battle glare on the screen.

Once again – for the second time in less that twenty-four hours – I settled my mind to take in a mass of information, and I knew speed was of the essence.

It was a slog, but not quite as bad as the previous night, because this was all information I actually wanted to be reading. Having built up my reading speed, I pounded through the files Thelma had given me.

I was horrified by the almost complete absence of effort that had gone into the original so-called investigation of Lowanna Swan's death, and the seemingly unquestioning acceptance of her father's presumed suicide. The rapidity with which charges had been brought against Philip Myers once the rifle showed up was breathtaking, and his trial had been conducted by two opposing counsels who had, apparently, each been addicted to overly dramatic speeches, it seemed. I had already known it had been an unusually long trial, but now I understood why – the transcript was massive, and contained a huge amount of testimony given by a seemingly endless list of witnesses the prosecution had called against Myers. I paid particular attention to the evidence given by Lennie Orkins, which was, as Joyce Trimble had suggested, relatively brief, and factual.

I waded through the testimonies given by the dozens of members of Lowanna's extended family, and friends, who'd been called to the stand. In the main, they all supported the story her father had originally given, as part of the brief investigation into her death, about Philip Myers having made unwanted advances toward her. It made for interesting reading, though their evidence became increasingly predictable the more often I read slightly different versions of the same tale, often using common phrases. There was also an impressive list of fifteen people who were called to state that they had seen Philip Myers in the vicinity of the area where Lowanna Swan had been killed, within days of her time of death.

The appendices covering details of the physical evidence submitted at the trial contained within them the exact photograph I'd seen peeping out of the folder on the floor in Thelma's bedroom, which didn't surprise me, but did confirm that she could have shared at least that much with me when I'd first asked for it, rather than holding back information – *and maybe pretending it had just arrived?*

I told myself I couldn't get sidetracked, that I needed to focus – I could try to work out why Thelma was acting the way she was when I had more information, more insights.

I whizzed through the background notes on the three members of the S & S Roads crew who had died. I was saddened, but not exactly shocked, to discover that young Ditch had been treated as an in-patient following a suicide attempt about six months earlier; first, to allow for his wounds to heal where he'd opened veins in his arms – which might have explained why I'd never seen him without sleeves, even on the warm day we'd all traveled to Manly – and then for counselling and treatment, following a diagnosis of clinical depression.

Dan Entwistle's file was all but empty; he'd received one speeding ticket on a local road in his hometown one Christmas, and that was about it – other than the fact he was a devoted member of his nearest Catholic church, and had a background as a locally-famous boy soprano.

Siân frightened the life out of me by plonking a mug of tea beside me. "Todd's got us on a flight that leaves Sydney around half-two tomorrow afternoon, a couple of hours earlier than the one we'd planned on taking, so that's something. Will you and Bud come back to the city with us in the car now that we'll be leaving a few hours early? Or will you stay on here, then get the train…taking your own luggage, of course?"

I stared at her. "Perfectly reasonable question – don't know the answer. I must read all this – it's important. Don't like the idea of the luggage on the train though, to be honest. Is Bud back?"

She shrugged. "I don't even know where he's gone, but no, he's not here, and you've been sitting there muttering for an hour. Is this normal for you?"

I wanted to say so much to my sister, but restricted myself. "He had stuff to do, and I need to do this. Please let me get on – I've only got a few bits left to read, then I can think."

Siân looked huffy, but I ignored her and returned my attention to the laptop. I opened the documents pertaining to the investigation into the fire that had just killed three men, and was surprised that there was little written information. There looked to be, however, a great number of photographs. I steeled myself, and opened the folder. The charred remains of a house stood stark in the sunlight. The skeleton of a home I could imagine had once looked like the one I was sitting in remained, but only in part; the top floor had essentially completely collapsed onto the bottom floor, and both were a tangle of charred planks and bits of furniture, only some of which was recognizable: chair legs, a metal tabletop, a couple of televisions, and a jumble of what had once been steel-framed deck furniture, and the steel roof panels were heaped on top of blackened, broken timbers. Two fridges, two cookers, and two microwaves were huddled at one end of the mass of debris, and I also spotted a few toilets – blackened and broken. Everything glistened wet in the bright sunshine, though it was obvious that the trees that had escaped the fire were casting deep shadows; the photographer had done a good job of taking shots from different angles to give the most complete views possible.

I gritted my teeth when there were shots of the human remains *in situ*; two bodies to the right, quite close to what appeared to have once been a sofa with metal springs, one to the left, away from the other pair. I paused when I saw a shot of someone in fire-fighting gear pointing to a blackened bucket, lying on its side at the corner of the edge of the perimeter of the skeleton of the burned house – which I assumed was the bucket Winnie had told us had been determined as the seat of the fire. I enlarged the photo as far as I could, until the pixels blurred in the image. Yes, a normal, household, galvanized metal bucket.

I shut the laptop, and closed my eyes. Yes, an eidetic memory is all well and good, but I'd never be able to forget the sight of those poor men…they'd be with me forever. I felt the anger grow inside me – they shouldn't be dead – so why were they? I stood, and stretched.

"Has Thelma brought in anything else for me?" I asked Siân, whose head popped up from her phone.

"Not a sausage."

"Okay, thanks. And no Bud yet?"

"Nope."

I pulled my phone from my pocket and texted Bud.

You OK? Where are you?

He replied almost immediately.

Am fine. Come meet me. Tell no one. Come to Three Sisters lookout. See you there – ASAP

I looked across the sitting room at my sister, who was chatting to one of her kids on the phone, then at Todd who was chatting to – presumably – the other kid on his phone, out on the deck.

"Just going to stretch my legs after all that sitting down," I said quietly as I wandered along the deck to leave, past Todd. He nodded. I didn't believe Thelma had seen me through her window, and didn't think Siân or Todd would even really notice or care where I'd gone.

I cantered to the end of the road where it swept upward and took the turning to the right that headed in the general direction of the Three Sisters lookout. As I approached the roundabout and public viewing area, I could see throngs of tourists milling about, some making their way to or from the heads of the hiking trails. Others were beetling toward the public loos, while quite a few seemed intent upon getting into the shop, rather than enjoying the view. The sun was hotter than I'd expected, even though there was a slight haze.

I searched the crowds for Bud's face, then spotted him lounging in what appeared to be a most carefree manner against a tree, with Big Stan and Neal beside him. I waved, he waved back and beckoned me to join him.

"Look who I ran into," he said loudly, and cheerily, as I approached.

"G'day, Cait," said Big Stan, grinning in his usual warm and jolly manner. He smothered me with an all-encompassing bear hug, then laughed aloud at my surprised expression when he released me.

"Lovely to see you too," I said. I nodded at his son. "Neal – how are you today?"

"G'day, Cait," said Neal, still not back to being his ebullient self. "Can't complain, thanks."

His father chuckled wryly, then said, "No bugger would listen if you did."

"You're both out doing a bit of sightseeing?" That was my assumption.

"Yeah – hanging about until we can get something out of them coppers is like waiting for water to boil," replied Big Stan. "Thought we'd at least see this before we leave. Got an appointment at the cop shop first thing tomorrow, so we'll hang about for one more night. Something to tell the wife about when I get home, not that I'll be there for long before we're back off to the Bush again."

"Have you taken lots of photos of the views to show her?" I asked, hoping Big Stan and Neal might wander off so I could talk to Bud about Thelma.

"Not yet, we've only just got here – and we bumped into…Oscar," said Neal with his lopsided grin. He nudged Bud playfully. Bud nearly fell over.

"We could take some photos of you both, with the Three Sisters behind you, if you like," I volunteered.

Big Stan looked at me as though I'd offered to buy him a lifetime supply of beer. "Cheers, Cait, that would be ripper. Come on, son, let's see what all the fuss is about." He grabbed Neal's arm, and the pair ambled toward the semi-circular metal balustrade that ran around the edge of the lookout. As we followed I whispered to Bud, "Anything? Is Thelma to be trusted?"

Bud grinned as the two men looked back to see where we were and hissed, "Later, Cait – this isn't the time or the place."

He added, more loudly, "That's a great spot, guys. Let me have your phones – open them up and I'll take the photos."

Both men pulled out their phones, fiddled about with them and handed them to Bud. We all hung about for a couple of moments so they could get into a good spot against the railing, where Bud could get them and the massive outcrops of rock in the distance into the frame. He handed me one of the phones while he bobbed about, trying to avoid getting passers-by in the shot, and I looked down, wondering whose phone I had. It was a bit dented, and I suspected it was Neal's, because it was sleek, and well used – the one Bud was holding was an older model. The screen went black, so I immediately touched it to keep the camera function active, but instead I got the screensaver: it was a picture of Neal as a small boy – it had to be him, with that lopsided smile, Big Stan – though a younger, more muscular version of him, and another man – shorter and wider than Big Stan, who I suspected must be Little Stan, who I now knew to be named Stan Hayes. They were posing in a dusty, red landscape, and were surrounded by discarded shovels, buckets, and pickaxes. Behind them was the edge of an entryway to what was obviously a mine – one that looked almost exactly like one I'd seen before, on Thelma's laptop. I squinted at it, but truly couldn't be certain if I was looking at the same place. Did all mine entrances look similar? I really didn't know.

Bud stepped toward me, and we swapped phones; he fiddled about with the one I'd handed him, but couldn't make the camera function work, so Big Stan stepped forward to reset the camera. *Right – his phone, not his son's, then.* I needed to come up with a way to get him to tell me about that photograph. I dared to try to reset the phone I was holding to check the screen saver on that one, too. Neal's showed what had to be a recent photo of him holding a massive fish; he was looking particularly pleased with himself. Interestingly, the name of the boat he was standing in front of was familiar to me: Kejoka. That was the name of one of the consortia on the list Thelma had given me. I was immediately on high alert: surely such a strange word wouldn't occur twice unless there was a connection? Or was "Kejoka" some Australian word or placename I'd never heard of, but more common than I'd imagined?

With the photographic session concluded, I nodded at Neal's phone as I handed it back to him. "That's a big fish. Did you catch it yourself?" He nodded, beaming. "Is that your boat in the photo, too? It looks fancy." I lied, because all I could see was a nondescript white slab with a name emblazoned upon it.

He didn't even glance at his phone before pocketing it. "Yeahnah. The boat belongs to a mate of Dad's. Used to be Little Stan's but now it's someone else's. We still get to use it, sometimes, out of Broome."

"Funny name," I dared.

Neal looked puzzled.

I added, "The name of the boat. It says 'Kejoka'. Is that an Aboriginal word? Or a place? Does it mean something?"

Neal's brow furrowed momentarily, then he brightened. "Oh yeah – that's right. I remember Dad telling me that Little Stan made it up: 'KE' for Keith, 'JO' for…well, Jo, and 'KA' for Karen. His father, sister, and mother. Good, eh? Doesn't mean the same to the bloke who owns it now, of course. Maybe he'll change it. Who knows?"

I agreed, even as I wondered if there was any chance that Little Stan Hayes had played a part in naming a consortium set up to develop mineral mines…presumably before his fatal heart attack a year earlier.

Neal and I wandered to another part of the lookout area, and I decided to press my advantage. "I saw that your father had a smashing photo of you as a little boy on his phone's screen. Do you remember it being taken?"

The young man paused. "I know the photo you mean, but, no I don't remember when it was taken. I remember the place itself, but not the time…the occasion. But I've seen that photo so often I feel like I do – does that make sense?"

I told him it made perfect sense, then added, "Where was it taken? It looked hot and dusty. Was that an old mine you were visiting?"

Neal laughed. "One of the mines the two Stans had when I was a young fella. When they weren't building roads for other people, they were doing their own bits of fossicking, or even working a proper mine. That was a proper one. Worked it for years, so I believe, but didn't get much out of it. My mother said it would be the death of one of them, or both of them. In the end they gave up on it."

I didn't even have to fake being interested when I asked, "So what happens to a mine like that? Does it just sit there with no one doing anything to it forever?"

Neal answered absently, "You can sell on the rights to exploit it, if you can find someone who wants to buy them. Not easy, of course, because why would anyone want a mine with nothing in it? But it happens all the time. People think they can do a better job than those who've been working it before them – and sometimes it pays off. I know an old bloke who'd sunk half a million dollars into his opal mine, and maybe got about fifty thousand dollars' worth of stones out of it. And even that took him twenty years. In the end he couldn't make enough to keep his equipment in working order, so he walked away. Sold the rights on for a fair sum, then the bloke who bought it off him dug up a couple of hundred thousand dollars' worth of stones a few weeks later. That's the way it goes. But I don't know what Dad and Uncle Stan did with that mine. Dad never talks about it."

"What don't I talk about, son?" Big Stan loomed over me, blotting out the sun with the silhouette of his massive hat, on his massive head.

"That old opal mine you and Little Stan used to work, Dad. The one in that photo on your phone. You never talk about it. Did you sell it on?"

"Nah, it was a dud. Little Stan found it for us, out in open mining territory, just had to buy a claim, he said. I dare say someone else has given it a go. No idea. We did our best and got a few decent pieces out, but it's a mug's game, opal. Just for them who's got the time, and the luck. Best left to tourists who want to do a bit of noodling or specking."

I had to try, so I asked, "So you were never tempted to use the services of Lowanna, the girl with the opal fingers, back in your youth? Try to find a massive deposit of precious opals somewhere? You and she shared a name – Swan. I wondered if you were related."

"The girl with the opal fingers was a Swan?" Neal sounded surprised. "I never knew that. Was she one of our Mob, Dad?"

"There's a lot of Swans about, son," said Big Stan, his voice dropping to no more than a growl. "Not all connected…except by the things that connect us all, of course. And her services were always beyond our means. Her father insisted on being paid in gold, and he charged a lot. Back then? Me and Little Stan was just starting out. Had a bit of luck, you know, but not because of her. All our own efforts. Had a good spot out in Lightning Ridge for a few years. That got us set up right."

Neal looked puzzled. "That photo's not in Lightning Ridge. Not enough mullock heaps. I might not remember much about the place in that photo, but I know there weren't the mullock heaps there that you get at Lightning Ridge. That's Coober Pedy, surely? 'Tunnel into the side of the land when you can, not straight down into it, son,' you said. It was your 'Coober Baby'.

You always said that when you talked about it. 'My other kid', you said."

"That's right," replied his father. "The photo on my phone is Coober Pedy. The old place, before that one…before you came along…was Lightning Ridge."

For someone who'd just said that hunting for opals was a mug's game, it seemed to me that Big Stan had spent rather a lot of time doing it.

Neal seemed mollified, and immediately lost interest in the topic, gazing beyond his father's shoulder. "Hey – look at that, Dad, wonder if there's anyone out there in those millions of trees. Cooee!"

Neal called across the yawning valley that lay beyond us, his voice carrying for what must have been miles. In the far distance an unknown person returned his call, which made the tourists standing close by laugh, and try their own luck. It was weird – despite their best efforts, no one else's voice carried quite the way Neal's had done.

"All those years being out in the Bush," said Neal proudly.

"You're your mother's son," said Big Stan quietly. "She could make a call you'd hear wherever you was…out getting into trouble, usually…when you was a young fella. You and Ditch would come running back for tucker. Him always behind you by a mile. Never could run, could he, poor kid? Like a lame Joey, always."

Neal's face fell. "I miss him," he said quietly. "Nothing's the same without him. It's like I'm missing my shadow. You don't even really notice it's there till it's gone and something's…not right."

"Other than walking into the sea in Manly, had he ever tried to kill himself before?" Bud startled all of us with his directness. It was an unusual approach for my husband, and I, of course, knew the answer to Bud's question, so I waited for the response of the two Swan men with great interest.

Big Stan shuffled, his shoulders hunching. "He had an...accident a while back. Needed a bit of help. But he seemed right after a bit of a break, didn't he, son?"

Neal didn't look up as he replied, "Not right, exactly. Not really crook, I suppose, but sort of...less. Was never really the same after that Bruce Walker bloke got killed, was he?"

"Who was that? Did another friend of Ditch's die?" I did my best to look innocent as I asked.

"He was a bloke who'd just joined us, so, no, Ditch didn't know him well," replied Big Stan. "Walker was off at the head of the road. Bad accident with some of the equipment. All alone, so no one to help him. Young Ditch took it real bad. No idea why. He didn't know the bloke any better than the rest of us did. Not with us more than a month before he was dead. Held up the job for a week." He paused, looked me in the eye and added, "That sounds bad. Hard. Didn't mean it to. But time is money in our business, and that week cost us a bit. You're right, son, Ditch was crook after that. Never seemed to be...himself."

My mind was racing; it sounded as though my initial assumptions had been right: Ditch *had* been deeply affected by the death of Bruce Walker. But he was a man Ditch had barely known, so wasn't it unlikely that his death itself was the trigger? Or... An idea formed itself at the back of my brain.

I asked, "What exactly did Ditch do for you? His specific job? He told me he was an equipment specialist."

Neal's lopsided grin broke out like the sunshine. "Equipment specialist? Yeahnah – though maybe you could say that. He did drones."

"Drones?" Bud sounded confused, though I cheered internally; it made perfect sense, to me.

I jumped in. "To get a better look at the lie of the land where you're going to build a road than you're able to get from satellite imagery, right?"

Big Stan looked impressed. "Yeah. You can't get the detail you need from satellites, though we get a good idea of what's coming. For all that he was a bit slow in some ways, Ditch was good with the controls for the drones. Those little boxes, with joysticks, you know? He'd send a drone ahead with a camera so we could see what we'd be facing. The clients like videos of the whole thing when we've finished a job, too; like proof of work, they can see exactly how straight the road is, how we've done a good job."

I dared, "And I bet they were Ditch's passion, too, his drones."

Once again Neal's genuine affability shone through. "You could say that. Ditch liked to tinker, always aiming to be the best 'flyer' he could be. Not that there's much that gets in your way out in the Bush, but he liked to treat every tree and shrub as a challenge, and get down as low as he could. He'd practice for hours while we…well, you know, got on with the job of making the road."

I adopted a thoughtful expression when I asked, "Don't drones bother the wildlife, making all that whirring noise? I should imagine the poor kangaroos and koalas are terrified."

Big Stan and Neal started to laugh, and ended up holding each other up; every time they made eye contact with each other, they broke out again. People around us stared, then some began to look quite concerned when Big Stan began to cough – and didn't seem to be able to stop.

A young woman offered him a can of something fizzy, which Big Stan took and managed to sip as he finally regained his composure. Once he was able to breathe, he pushed some cash into his son's hand, and told him to find the young woman who'd helped him and give it to her.

"How about we stroll over to the shop and that little café," suggested Bud. "I wouldn't mind a coffee – or even a beer, if they have any. How about you?"

Big Stan bucked up. "Don't mind if I do," he said, still spluttering. "Give Neal a shout, and get him to follow us over?"

I volunteered to do that, and Bud and Big Stan headed off.

Coming Up For Air

By the time Neal and I arrived at the coffee shop, it was clear that no beer was available, because Bud and Big Stan had four mugs in front of them.

"Sorry about all that coughing," apologized Big Stan upon my arrival at the table. "It's just my way. But, like I was saying to Bud here, it was your fault really, talking about roos like they're frightened little creatures. And koalas? Believe me when I tell you they take some shifting. Laziest creatures on the face of the planet, them. Roos? They'd take you down as soon as look at you. If there's a mob of them coming at you, you'd better get out of their way. You were asking if Ditch's little drone frightened them? Maybe for a minute or two. The stupid things bounce around the place until they realize they don't know what's really going on, then they ignore it. Koalas couldn't give a stuff. But you saying that? Sorry, I know you're just visiting, but – as you saw – we thought that was funny."

"So the drones Ditch used were quite loud then?" I needed to know.

Neal answered my question as he looked at the coffee in front of him with some suspicion. "Ditch did his best to make them run quiet. You talking about the roos like that? Ditch is an Aussie through and through…was…and yet he had a stupid soft spot for roos. Didn't even like to eat Lennie's Mongolian roo tail stew, and when you're living on Bush tucker, if you won't eat roo you can miss a lot of meals. But one thing he did – he tried to make the drones run quiet. Mind you, when we come through with our equipment, then all bets are off, because we have to slice through the Bush like it's not there, and that makes a real racket, so I never knew why he bothered. Just a Ditch thing.

There was lots of them." He stared into his coffee as though it held the answer to every question in the universe.

"Enough about Ditch," said Big Stan, which disappointed me. "We'd better head back to town after this coffee, get packed up."

"I thought you said you weren't leaving until tomorrow," Bud noted.

Big Stan nodded. "Right. But we'll have to go through Ditch's hotel room first, though Shorty's volunteered to sort through Lennie's stuff. He's taken this real bad, Shorty. Worse than I thought he would, to be honest. Though, of course, he was close to Lennie, who brought him to work for us…and he and Dan went way back, too. So I dare say he's got good reason to be as jumpy and long-faced as he is. Ha! Roos, again. Anyway, once we've gathered everything up, we'll take it all back to Sydney with us tomorrow morning and we'll meet up with the others there. We're flying back home tomorrow arvo. One more try to get something out of them coppers, face-to-face, before we go, then we'll have to do it all by phone. You haven't heard anything, have you? And what about that other fire last night? Did you hear about that?"

I didn't know what to say about the fire that had killed their colleagues, so focused on the more recent one. "We could see it from our rental, up on the opposite hillside," I replied. "It looked big, but we think they've managed to put it out."

Neal nodded. "Yeah, that was on the news. But did you hear about what happened up there?"

Bud and I shook our heads.

Neal said, "They said on the news that they reckon it was another in a series of what they're saying have been some nasty arson attacks, though someone else said they thought it was one gang trying to get rid of another gang's meth lab. But the fire chief hereabouts knocked that idea down. Dad and I was talking;

that might be what happened to the house our blokes was staying in. You said you never know where you're going to run into that sort of drug stuff, didn't you, Dad? Dad's good at getting everyone tested on The Mob – won't have any druggie business when we're on a job, will you? Not unless the doc's told a bloke he has to take something. Right?"

Big Stan sat a little more upright. "Not with all that equipment about, I don't. It costs a fortune – I won't have anyone operating anything if they might be as high as a kite. Random testing, that's the way to do it. Take care of it myself, I do – you can buy kits, you know?"

Bud and I did, in fact, know, but both feigned amazement. I asked, "How do you cope with the drinking? I know you're all away from the job now, so it's to be expected you'd indulge a bit." I congratulated myself that I'd managed to refer to their massive intake of alcohol so lightly. "Do you have a zero tolerance for booze as well?"

The look that passed between Big Stan and his son suggested I'd lost my mind.

Big Stan grinned and said, "Not going to work, if I want anyone to join the crew, Cait. But we all know our limits."

"Will there be…services, or memorials for your colleagues when you get home?" I didn't want the men to leave – I wanted to ask so much more.

"That'll be for the families to decide," said Big Stan. "If we're around, we'll go – but they'll all understand that we've got to get back to it; contracts have timetables attached, and they won't wait. It's the life."

"Time is money," said Bud, sagely, echoing Big Stan's earlier sentiment. "And we should probably be getting back, Cait – even though we're on vacation, and our time is our own…though I do have one question for you guys, before we leave, if you don't mind."

"Ask away," said Neal, grinning.

Bud said, "At dinner last night, you asked my chum Thelma if you two had ever met before, Big Stan. Why was that?"

Big Stan's grin was as wide as his son's, but without the lopsided charm. "Talked about that after you'd gone, didn't we?" Neal nodded. "She reminded me of someone I used to know a little, a long time back. Not the way she looked as much as how she sounded. The girl…young woman…she reminded me of was married to a bloke I knew a bit back in Darwin, a long time ago – before this one was even born. That one? She was as skinny as a rake, dishwater blonde, pasty…mooned about the place. But what a voice – like that Thelma. Can't remember her name, but her voice made an impression. Your Thelma's a much more…definite person, more substantial, in every way."

I understood what Big Stan meant about Thelma being "substantial" – she wasn't as round as me, though taller, and she had a commanding presence.

"Thanks," said Bud. "It's funny how things like that give a person a bit of déjà vu, isn't it?"

I turned over what Big Stan had said as Bud began to rise from his seat, ready to leave. I was just about to follow suit, when Big Stan added, "Before we say our final g'days, I must say it's been good to run into you today. We was talking about you this morning, to Winnie, you know?"

We nodded, and Bud sat down again, though I could feel the increasing tension in his movements, which concerned me.

Neal added, "She said about how your sister Siân, and you, Oscar –" he paused and winked dramatically – "was at the pool with her and that Timbo bloke the other day. How Siân's a good swimmer, you know? And that set Dad and me talking about folks who can't swim being good at drowning, and we remembered something…odd. We can't explain it. Maybe you can – 'cause you're quick, you are, Cait. Right, mate?" Another wink in Bud's direction.

I said, "Go on then, try me. Though I have to warn you, if it's anything to do with swimming I might disappoint you, because I can't swim; my sister's the family fish."

Neal did the lopsided smile thing, and said, "Yeah, that's it, see? Me and Dad was talking about a time when I'd just started working with him. We was all mucking about down at the beach one day – just us blokes, so, you know, not really swimming, more splashing in the surf, really…"

Big Stan butted in. "It's that yarn Lennie was telling us, the one about finding that rifle, see? He's told it before, and like all good yarners he always fancied it up a bit, depending on who he's telling. That's what good yarners do. Play to the audience. Anyways, the basics never changed, really, and that's the thing…the penny never dropped before. That day we was all in the sea, but *he* didn't go in. I never thought anything of it, until Neal and I was talking this morning. And he said that Shorty had told him that Lennie had said to him at the time, that he didn't feel confident in the water."

It was Neal's turn to butt in. "We were talking about swimming, and about Ditch walking into the sea like that the other day, and I mentioned to Dad about how good it was that he made sure I got swimming lessons when I was a little 'un and I'd been saying that Ditch really was a good swimmer, and that maybe he really did fancy a swim that day…"

Big Stan waved at his son. "Not the point, son. The point is this…well, you tell them what you remembered Shorty telling you. Go on…get on with it."

Neal tutted, and said, "Shorty likes to talk…jabbers on for hours, he does, and he told me that Lennie said that day at the beach that he preferred to be on the land, or in a boat, because he wasn't good in the sea, not a strong enough swimmer. And, like Dad said, we realized when we was talking about it that made no sense. If Lennie wasn't a strong swimmer, why would he have gone diving down to the bottom of a waterhole when he was a kid? You'd have to be good in the water to do that, wouldn't you?"

Big Stan added, "And that's where he's always said he found that rifle – at the bottom of a waterhole – that bit of the story's never changed. So – what do you reckon about that?"

I was speechless. Which takes some doing.

Bud said nothing, either, so Neal filled the silence. "And then we both talked about what that meant. If he never found the rifle like he said he did, how did his grandfather have it in his house when he died? And we wondered…what if Lennie's grandfather was mates with that Philp Myers, and hid the rifle for him all those years, so Myers could get away with murder? What do you think of that idea?"

Charming though Neal's grin was, I didn't want to encourage the line of thinking being proposed by the father and son sitting across from me.

"That's an interesting question. What do you think, Bud? Do you think that Lennie's grandfather might have been mixed up in Lowanna Swan's death somehow?" I dared.

"But why would Lennie say he'd found the rifle in a waterhole if he'd really found it at his grandfather's house?" Bud sounded sensible.

"It makes a better yarn?" Neal sounded unsure of himself.

I didn't want to push things, but it seemed I didn't have to, because Neal added, "But, no – see, thinking about it, Lennie went and gave evidence at the Myers trial, didn't he? Actually swore on the Bible that he was telling the truth. That's not the same as having a yarn over a few beers. That's different. That's proper lying. Why would he do that?"

"Never a big one for the white man's law, or religion, was Lennie," observed Big Stan quietly.

I was torn; I didn't want us to have a massive discussion that could spiral out of control, and Bud and I hadn't received any background insights into Big Stan or Neal that had helped us reach any conclusions about their possible involvement in the Lowanna-Myers case, so we'd not had any sort of conversation about the extent to which we might be able to trust them, or should suspect them.

Bud surprised me when he said, "Do you think Lennie might have played a part in framing Philip Myers for murder?"

I wanted to kick him; he hadn't seen the list of names of consortia trying to get their hands on Philip's mineral leases, so didn't know about the "Kejoka" connection to what we now knew had once been Little Stan Hayes's boat. Maybe the Swan men were mixed up in this somehow, because maybe Little Stan had been? But there was no putting the genie back in the bottle – the men opposite me were staring at Bud as though he'd just accused Lennie of choosing milk over beer.

Big Stan spoke first. "Lennie? Frame Philip Myers? But why would he? What would be the point of that?"

"He wouldn't," said Neal, with conviction.

"They didn't even know each other," added Big Stan. "I knew Myers, from way back…Lennie wasn't the sort of bloke he'd have mixed with."

I pounced. "You knew Philip Myers?"

Big Stan nodded. "One opal miner to another, that sort of thing. Me and Little Stan had a couple of holes in the ground over the years, like I said. Myers knew his opals. That sort of thing. Passing the time over a few beers now and again if we ran into him in Opalton, or Coober Pedy. That's all."

I gave the matter some thought, then said, "Lennie told me he'd worked in every sort of mine there is. He and Myers might have crossed paths, somewhere, at some point, like you did. They might have had a falling out – something might have happened that meant Lennie wanted to hurt Philip, get back at him for some reason."

Big Stan looked at me as though I were a bit dim. "But the rifle really did belong to Philip Myers – he never denied that, because he couldn't. It had his initials on it, and the bloke who made the fancy gold bits on it for him went to court to say so. So where would Lennie have found Myers' rifle if not in a waterhole? Or in his grandfather's house… if he couldn't swim real good?"

"Someone might have given it to him, and told him what to do with it, and he saw that as a way of getting Philp Myers into trouble," said Bud.

Big Stan shrugged morosely. Neal stared at his coffee as though it might be hydrochloric acid.

"Maybe someone gave Lennie the rifle and they had something on him, so he had to play his part…which he might have thought would end when he handed it into the cops." Bud's tone suggested this was something he'd just thought of, rather than it being a gambit, which I knew – Bud being Bud – it had to be.

Neal pushed away his undrunk coffee. "That sounds more like Lennie," he said, sounding sage. "Lennie might have got himself into trouble, so he might have had to do what he was told to do, just to get out of it, somehow." He appeared to give the matter some thought, then added excitedly, "What if Lennie was in trouble with the boys in blue and they gave him the rifle…to, you know 'hand in' to them? Maybe they found it during an illegal search of…somewhere…and had to come up with a way of getting it accepted in court. Lennie might have been in trouble with the law, and they made him do it, then let him off…whatever it was."

Big Stan stared at his son. "You could have a point. Coppers can't be trusted. Yeah, you might be right. Lennie was pretty good at getting himself into all sorts of scrapes."

I was a bit taken aback that, between them, Big Stan and Neal had come up with an explanation that might actually hold water…and it wasn't something that had occurred to me – nor Bud, if the look on his face was anything to go by. I was still wrapping my brain around the ideas the Swans had come up with, when my phone rang in my pocket.

I excused myself and stepped away from the table. It was Siân.

"Have you two got any intention of coming back to the house at some point?" She sounded cross, verging on the incandescent. "You both just disappeared without saying a word. Thelma's on the warpath, and I can't even tell her where you are. So, where are you?"

I didn't dare mention we were having coffee with the Swans, because I didn't fancy the idea of the phone disintegrating in my hand as she screamed into it.

"Sorry, we got a bit caught up in something – nothing dangerous, and we're both fine. We'll be back very soon. Bye." I clicked off before she could say anything I'd regret hearing.

I rejoined the men. "It was my sister, Siân. She's a bit…anxious…about us getting back," I said to Bud. I added, "Sorry," to Neal and Big Stan.

"No worries," said Big Stan, rising. "Like I said, we need to get up to town and get those rooms sorted out. We'll give Shorty a call, see how he's got on with Lennie's stuff. It'll be a tough go having to sort through Ditch's gear, but it's got to be done. Can't just leave it where it is. Mustn't take too much of your time." He shoved a leathery hand across the table toward Bud. "Good to have met you. I reckon this is the final goodbye, now. We've had a couple of false ones, haven't we?"

He pulled me in for a suffocating hug, and Neal followed suit, having also shaken Bud by the hand. I caught my breath, and reckoned my husband had got off lightly.

"We'll raise a couple of cold ones to you back in Sydney tomorrow," said Neal as the pair headed for the door. He mugged raising a drink and chuckled as he said, "To Cait and Oscar!" Then they were gone.

Once we were alone, Bud asked, "Is Siân okay?"

"Having kittens," I replied. "We'd better get back. Can we walk as we talk? What was it that you wanted to tell me?"

We exited the coffee shop, and strode out across the roundabout area, keeping an eye open for vehicles, and tourists who were looking in one direction as they walked in another, which was exactly what a lot of them were doing…but, there again, there really was such a lot to see.

Once we'd cleared the throngs, Bud slipped his arm around my waist and pulled me close.

"Oh, that's very forward of you, Mr. Anderson." I beamed.

He whispered, "This is not something I want anyone else to hear. So stay close."

"Typical – I think it's a *cwtch*, but really it's something that's Top Secret?"

Bud actually hushed me. "Don't use those words," he hissed.

My heart sank even as my pulse raced. "Right-o, out with it. What have you found out?"

We paused at the turning to the road on which our rental house stood. If anyone had seen us at that moment, we would have looked as though we were sharing a particularly loving embrace, nose to nose, our arms around each other, and whispering sweet nothings, with smiling faces.

"Thelma Pruitt was told to take a leave of absence just after the news about Philip Myers' death came in. She's not on vacation, but on 'special leave'. Yes, she's in Australia on behalf of the Canadian government as a liaison, but no, she shouldn't be here, with us, now. Turns out she should be at her government-owned apartment in Canberra, where she's supposed to be waiting to be questioned about having accessed some sensitive data she had no business seeing. Of course, no one would tell me the nature of that data."

I squeezed my husband, tight. "She's gone rogue?"

He hugged me, and whispered, "I think 'rogue' might be a bit of a strong term, but she's certainly not here under the auspices of the government...though they now know exactly where she is, and are acting accordingly. It seems my original message to Ottawa was passed through to Canberra, but it's still awaiting action there – which, to be honest, isn't a surprise. Me and my requests would be a low priority item. I don't know how she did it, but Thelma must have somehow intercepted the communication about my request, and got in touch with me directly. Which is...puzzling, and worrying."

My tummy flipped, but it wasn't because of Bud's embrace. "And she's with my sister and Todd, alone, right now? And there's someone she was talking to on the phone who's coming here to join her, who might have nothing to do with the government at all? Which was what she implied." I pulled back from Bud a little as I hissed at him, just to be sure he could see the horror in my eyes, despite the smile on my face.

"Shall we head back, Wife?" He kissed me, then we swung our hands in the most pseudo-carefree manner as we jogged toward the house where I hoped my sister and brother-in-law were still blissfully unaware that the woman in the place with them might pose a significant threat to their safety.

Delving Deep

I was absolutely delighted to find Siân and Todd sitting on the deck at The Overlook with everything appearing to be perfectly normal, allowing for my sister's expected anxiety about getting away to be with their children.

"Thelma not about?" I asked as casually as possible.

"In her room. But she gave me this for you, for whenever you got back from wherever it is you've been," snapped my sister as she handed me another thumb drive.

As I took it, I wondered how Thelma was able to give me information she must have gathered through official channels, while she was on "special leave", and under investigation. Surely any privileges she had regarding access to such files would have been cut off under the circumstances? Unfortunately, I was going to have to get Bud on his own to be able to ask him about the niceties of that situation, and I felt it was more important to check what was on the thumb drive itself, rather than worry about how the information had ended up there.

"Okay if I use your laptop again, Todd?" I didn't think he'd object.

Waving an arm toward the sitting room he said, "It's where you left it."

I lost no time plugging in the thumb drive, and opened it to find the background information regarding S & S Roads and the Swans, as well as Stan Hayes, aka Little Stan.

I dug into that first, because I was intrigued by the man I'd never met – and who'd once owned a boat named Kejoka. The file on the man was surprisingly large, and I wondered why so much data had been pulled together about him, so I opened it with enthusiasm.

One of seven children born to a father who'd earned his living as a peripatetic sheep shearer and a woman whose maiden name had been O'Malley – *the generally-held suspicion of Irish blood suggested by Todd had been based upon truth, after all* – Stanley Hayes had managed to get himself into trouble with the law on several occasions before he'd even turned sixteen. The file mentioned several run-ins with the police, though the one official charge made against him earned a non-custodial sentence. There seemed to be a definite inability on the part of the young Stan Hayes to differentiate between what was his to use – bicycles, cars, and personal property – and things that rightfully belonged to another person. What was also interesting was the fact that the single criminal charge mentioned another person – Stanley Swan – as also being involved; it was felt that Stan Hayes, at fifteen, had unduly influenced the thirteen-year-old Swan boy.

I calculated that Big Stan Swan could only have been twenty-one years old when he and Little Stan Hayes had established S & S Roads, and the file about the company itself was within Stan Hayes' file, which helped to explain its size.

I settled more comfortably into my seat as I read about how the company had grown slowly, then quickly, in terms of turnover, and their investment in capital equipment had been substantial. I was amazed at the most recent figures: Big Stan Swan certainly flashed the cash around, and now I knew why – he was rolling in it. Neither he nor his son spent a great deal on how they presented themselves to the world, but S & S Roads was a highly profitable firm, and I assumed it was now all Stan Swan's – to be passed down to Neal one day, no doubt.

Stan Hayes had never married, nor had any children, and his will was included in the file, which was an unexpected bonus. He had, indeed, left more or less everything to Stan Swan, his "business partner and lifelong friend", though it specifically mentioned his boat, Kejoka, which was to be given as "a gift, whole and with all its contents, which are also to be his" to Ryan McCready, of Broome, "in memory of special times". I assumed this was the same man Todd had told me had given the moving eulogy at Stan Hayes' memorial.

I Googled Ryan McCready of Broome, and found only one mention on social media; I couldn't be certain it was the same person, until I noticed a familiar boat in the background of one of the man's photographs, which were all set to "public". In what was a recent picture, Ryan appeared to be a contemporary of Stan Hayes in terms of age, and was clearly someone who enjoyed a close-to-nature lifestyle, thanks to a camper van he owned; he seemed to always be hiking, or boating, or fishing, or hiking, or swimming, or...hiking. He never ever seemed to be indoors, and wore practical, yompy clothing appropriate for every activity. And he played the guitar – often beside a campfire, it seemed; photos of a collection of guitars suggested there'd be little room in the camper van for the man himself.

I returned to Hayes' will, which, fortunately, contained some information about why Stan Hayes valued Stan Swan's friendship so much: Stan Swan had "rescued" the smaller, though older, ten-year-old Stan Hayes from a beating he was receiving at the hands of a group of youths, and their connection had grown from there. There was also a mention of Hayes' gratitude for Swan never having "judged" him for being who he was, which gave me pause. I flicked to a few photos of Stan Hayes: one a studio portrait which suggested it hailed from about thirty years ago; another of him on stage where he appeared to be giving a presentation much more recently, silver-haired and looking dapper, much trimmer than in the earlier shot, where he'd looked pudgy, and a little haggard (perhaps taken the day after a heavy night before?). Yes, he had a bit of a waxy appearance, I thought. There was no mention of a company called Kejoka, specifically, in the will, though there was a mention of "a gift of my personal papers" as being bequeathed to his sister, Jo-Anne Ramirez, nee Hayes.

I Googled the name and was amazed by just how many Jo-Anne Ramirezes there were. I discounted almost all of them, and eventually homed in on one whose avatar was a cat, with all the settings on "private", which didn't help much.

I went back to the Hayes file, but found I'd reached the end, except for the details of the man's death: cardiac arrest – which is pretty much what we all die of – with an instantaneous popping of clogs on stage, in front of lots of witnesses. No obituaries except for in the mining trade publications, where he was spoken of as the life and soul of the party, but a true professional as well.

I moved to Big Stan's file next: once I realized that the file about S & S Roads had been copied within it, there was little left to read. There was nothing to contradict what Todd had told me about Stan Swan's background, and he didn't even have the legal blot on his copy book that his good friend Hayes had borne. A couple of mentions were made of him having been kept under lock and key overnight as a result of inebriation during his youth, but nothing at all in the past fifteen years or so. There was a newspaper obituary for Stan's wife, Neal's mother, Arabella, where she was spoken of most highly by the local Salvation Army captain, which surprised me a bit. I hadn't got the impression that the Salvation Army had played any sort of role in Stan's life, nor in Neal's upbringing. I read on, and the clipping mentioned that Arabella Swan had come to see the values of the movement as meaningful toward what had turned out to be the sudden end of her life, at the age of forty-five.

The file on Neal Swan was almost non-existent: school achievement for track and field – discus throwing, of all things – and that was it. Nothing else. No big revelations.

I felt...deflated, but knew I had to press on.

Next, I turned my attention to the records from Corrections Service, Australia, detailing Philip Myers' time under their control. I scrolled through the list of visitors, which was short, especially considering it covered a period of more than twelve years. There were no names with fat black lines scrawled through them. *Maybe the names of government representatives who'd visited Myers had been removed from the list by other government representatives before anyone else was allowed to see it?* I identified Myers' surprising number of legal representatives, and noted both Bruce Walker's and Joyce Trimble's names, appearing just about a year ago. Otherwise, the man had received no visits at all, which spoke volumes.

Beyond the list of visitors, I read that Myers had worked in the prison kitchen and library over the years, and I also noted that he'd been admitted to the prison hospital about ten years before his eventual death to be treated for a "wound". He'd had seven cellmates over his prison term; not long before Joyce had visited Philip, he'd been given a new one – the one she'd mentioned, in all likelihood. When I saw that the name of his new "roommate" was Richard Richards, my tummy churned. Could that be Ricky "Carver" Richards, the man Shorty had witnessed stabbing someone to death in Alice Springs, a few years ago? The one the yarn-loving Shorty had claimed to not really be friends with?

I sat back and let my mind sort out the facts: Lennie, Shorty, "Carver", Philip, Bruce, Lennie again…and Ditch. Yes, that made sense. But Dan? Hmm…maybe. Was I actually getting somewhere? But what about the real why? And how did Thelma fit in – if she did?

As if my thoughts had conjured her, Thelma Pruitt stomped into the sitting room. "Any use, those files?"

Yes, her voice was certainly distinctive. Could I imagine her forty years earlier as a scrawny, dishwater blonde? That was a challenge. And…that would mean she was Australian, not Canadian, in any case, which made absolutely no sense at all. I pushed away the distracting thoughts, and forced a smile.

"Great, thanks – they must value you, to give you all this stuff as fast as they have. My thanks to the whole team – whoever they are." I didn't think it wise to push it further, but did my best to be my most grateful, normal self.

"Sure. You're welcome. I'll pass it on," she said. "I'm putting the jug on – want anything?"

Her comment made me feel as though I'd been electrocuted.

I had to talk to Bud – right away.

Hell, Or High Water

I forced myself to sound carefree when I said, "Wouldn't mind a cuppa, thanks Thelma. By the way, Siân said someone's coming here to talk to her and Todd in the morning. Any idea of their ETA?" As I spoke, I kicked myself for having used the same term she'd used herself when talking about…whomever it was she'd been whispering to on the phone. I hoped it didn't matter.

Thelma replied evenly, "First thing tomorrow. I know Siân's keen to get away, but I believe this is an important connection to be made, for Todd's sake."

I didn't respond, but made my best attempt at a casual saunter toward the deck where I lunged at my husband and nibbled his ear, which bemused Siân, Todd, and even Bud, in equal measure.

Bud played along; I knew neither he nor I cared what my sister and her husband might think of us, so we giggled and joshed around playfully like a couple of love-struck teens, then I said, "Just popping inside to have a shower, then to change into something a bit cooler – it's humid today. Come and help me pick something out, in about ten minutes, will you please, Husband dear?"

"But of course, Wife," mugged Bud, and I scampered off to our room.

I shut the door, closed the window, sat propped up on the pillows on the bed, and closed my eyes. The ability to use the technique of wakeful dreaming is something I've worked hard to harness over the years; it's where I allow my mind to float free, unencumbered by the associations and assumptions of my everyday life, so that I can allow what I know, and that of which I might only be subconsciously aware, to create connections and tell a story I might not be able to grasp if I just sit and think hard about a situation. It helps if I can be physically comfortable when I do it, and I have to close my eyes to the point where everything goes fuzzy, or else shut them totally. I hoped it would work for me again…

I'm swinging in a hammock, on a dusty red planet that has four moons and a wind-blasted landscape. There's a flock of white parrots in the sky, red stains on their wings, and beaks. I can hear the sound of metal striking stone as if beside me, but I am alone. A mountain of white powder glitters on the horizon, and I know that it is lithium, but, as I float toward it, I can see that the mountain is now made of opals…glowing red in the light of the multiple moons – no…they are dripping with blood.

A moan like a woodwind instrument carries on the wind, and I turn to see a frail figure, who I know is Lowanna Swan. She's crying, and pointing at the mountain of opals. Her heart is visibly beating beneath her white shift, then it breaks open through her dress, and black opals pour out of it. A man with snowy hair is suddenly beside her, catching the opals as they fall with his massive leather hat, then she evaporates like mist and he is rolling the opals on the red soil, trying to bury them…to hide them from me. He turns, looking terrified, as a massive boat approaches, hovering above the earth. Its sails are filled with wind, and it's moving fast. KEJOKA is painted on its side in letters two feet tall, and in it I see two men carrying pickaxes, one man large, one small, both laughing, with tiny fish shooting from their mouths as they do so.

Bud is clinging to the anchor chain, which is bouncing along the ground as the boat passes me. "Cait…it's all of them…" he calls. "Look for the smoke." The boat, the men, and Bud, are all gone, but I can see a billowing wall of smoke coming toward me, fire spitting in its wake.

Ditch Early is running ahead of the smoke carrying a flaming bucket; he's struggling to keep going, having difficulties because he seems very drunk…he keeps tripping, falling down, then getting up and running again. He's calling, "Daddy…Daddy, why did you do it?" The sound is pitiful.

As the smoke and fire get closer, I can see that Shorty is also running toward me. I can't move, my feet have sunk into the red soil, so I reach out to him and beg him to free me.

"I wanna tell you a story," he shouts in the voice of Max Bygraves, over and over again, as he passes by, ignoring me. Then Joyce Trimble pops up on the horizon, wearing a hat that is the Sydney Opera House, and with two broken legs. She's carrying a bunch of maps rolled up in each outstretched hand. "I told you the truth," she says, then blows me a kiss, and the maps fly away, like birds, their wings catching fire as they fly. Their cries sound like a clarinet on the wind.

I opened my eyes and was surprised to see Bud standing at the foot of the bed, smiling.

"Any luck sorting it all out?" Despite his smile, he looked concerned, and tired.

I leaped up. "Yes, and no. I have questions – and I hope you can get me some answers. You're in touch with the people in Canberra directly now, right?" Bud nodded. "Good, then maybe they'll give you the information I need. Fast. And I need to talk to Joyce Trimble again. Can you go and tell – sorry, *ask* – Todd to lend me his laptop, and bring it to me, here, please? I'll write up a list of questions for you to ask various people, though I'm not sure who. But I know you'll know."

Bud nodded, and turned to leave, but I added, "When you said that 'people' know where Thelma is now, does that mean that…*someone*…is coming here to pick her up?"

"Yep. Security detail from Canberra. They'll be as discreet as we need them to be. Or not. You know."

"Good. When?"

Bud checked his watch. "They're coming by road. A couple of hours from now, I'd say. By early evening, at latest."

"Good, so before her secret meeting at nine?"

"For sure. They'll apprehend her contact, no problem, they said. The photos you gave me to send to them gave them all they needed. But listen, Siân's not doing well, Cait. Very twitchy."

I didn't know what to do for the best. "Don't say anything specific to her, because I don't want Thelma to see a change in Siân's anxiety levels, but try to keep her as calm as you can, please. And Bud?"

He smiled his crinkly smile. "Yes?"

"Can you track down the Swan men and Shorty? Winnie at the pub might know where they're staying. Get them over here this evening – an invitation to a farewell dinner? Offer lots of free beer – that should help convince them. And if you ask Todd and Siân to organize the refreshments, that might keep them busy, too…something to take their minds off the fact they're just, basically, hanging about, worrying about things. Okay – I'll get going with that list of questions for you. Thanks. I love you."

"Love you most," said my husband warmly as he left.

I sat up, grabbed a pen and paper – and my reading cheats – and used my best handwriting, instead of the scrawl Bud often accuses me of having; it was critical that he asked exactly the right questions, so I could get the answers I needed.

> 1) Most up to date info about cause of death, <u>and toxicology work</u>, for Ditch, Dan, and Lennie. TOP OF LIST AND MOST IMPORTANT, HUSBAND!!!
>
> 2) Ask Frank Tipton, from Winnie's Place, if the house that burned down and this one we're in are *exactly* the

same design as each other. If not, exactly how did they differ?

3) Phone records for Dan, Ditch, and Lennie – Ditch is the priority – while here in Katoomba.

4) Get as much info as you can about Ryan McCready, of Broome, who inherited Stan Hayes' boat, the Kejoka. I will keep going with my online trawl about him, but I'm interested in anything that's not available to the public. ANYTHING!!

5) Records of the inquest into the death of Philip Myers' wife, Cindy, approximately fourteen years ago. Specifically interested in cause and time of death.

6) Transcript of the trial of Richard "Carver" Richards (I will find what I can online about any reporting of the trial, but the actual records might help).

I made a few other notes, and signed off with lots of kisses, because I knew I was asking a lot of my husband, but had no doubt he'd be more than equal to the task. When he returned, carrying the laptop, he scanned the list, tutted – with a smile on his face, thank goodness – then headed out again, after giving me an indulgent kiss on the top of my head.

As soon as I was alone, I had a business-like five minutes on a video call with Joyce Trimble, who was very helpful…and more than a little curious about my line of questioning.

I sent Bud a text with an additional request for research I wouldn't be able to access on my own, then I started a deep dive, trying to find information about one Philippe Gagnon, who'd lived near Darwin, about thirty-five years earlier. The chat I'd just had with Joyce had made him my prime target, and I just hoped the man's life had left some sort of trail in the public record.

Jewels In The Dirt

The next few hours passed in a blur of activity for pretty much everyone. Siân and Todd threw themselves into creating dinner for a surprisingly large group; I was delighted to hear that pizzas were going to play a significant role in those plans. Bud had headed out of the house again; I suspected he was making good use of his telephone manner and thumb-typing skills where he couldn't possibly be overheard or interrupted. Thelma remained in her room; I couldn't be sure what she was doing, but at least I felt more comfortable knowing where she was. I used all my powers to cast my research-and-read net as far as possible, and pushed my speed-reading ability to its limits, focusing on encoding everything I read as I went.

Bud sent me texts and emails as he got the answers to the questions I'd asked, some of which were lengthy and really helpful, though a couple were incredibly brief: **lithium and alcohol, all 3 victims** and **exact same floor plan** were two of them. He also confirmed that Big Stan, Neal, and Shorty would arrive at The Overlook by seven o'clock, and that the "people from Canberra" – which sounded delightfully mysterious – would certainly be on-site by six, which was good, because I wanted them to be tucked away on the deck surrounding the apartment below us before the evening got going; Bud was handling how that could be achieved without alerting Thelma to their presence. A text finally zipped through from him saying: **Ryan & SH? Lightning Ridge.**

I managed to stop my sister and brother-in-law from incessantly asking questions by quietly telling them that Bud and I were doing everything we could to create a situation where they'd be as safe as possible both overnight and when they left

Katoomba in the morning, though Siân didn't make that easy for me.

By the time Bud entered our room to freshen up with about fifteen minutes to go before our "guests" arrived, I was as ready as I was ever going to be. He had an inkling about what was going to happen, but neither of us could be certain of how the dynamics of the evening would develop.

"I hope this works out safely for everyone," said Bud as he headed into the bathroom after I'd left it.

"Me too, of course, but it's good to know you're here when I need you, and that the 'people from Canberra' are already just below us. You're in charge of making sure that all the windows and doors stay open the whole time, so they can hear what's going on, even if someone's moved indoors, okay? Otherwise, we both have to engineer things so that everyone's out on the deck at all times. Agreed?"

Bud gave me a muffled, "Sure," from the bathroom.

I stuck my head inside and said more quietly, "Have your people from Canberra been fully briefed?"

Bud was brushing his teeth, so all I got was a foamy smile, though he told me with his eyes that he'd done everything I'd asked. I left him to rinse.

When I entered the main area of the house the smells were wonderful; Siân had been busy producing pizzas, and there were bowls of fruit, and even plates of cookies, which she'd made as a surprise. I wasn't sure how she'd managed to magic up all the necessary ingredients, but didn't have time to inquire.

Bud emerged from our room and offered to hang about at the front steps to the house to welcome our guests and show them the way in, and Thelma finally put in an appearance – her eyes widening at the sight of all the food.

"Who's all that for?" I hadn't told her what was happening; in my defense, she hadn't asked.

"We're having a sort of 'farewell' get-together with the remaining members of the S & S Roads Mob," I replied as lightly as I could, "and Siân's famous for her pizzas, so this should be a real treat."

"I did a couple with your favorites of extra pepperoni and mushrooms, Sis," called Siân, who was hovering, happily pink-cheeked, behind the kitchen counter, "and it's not all down to me, Todd's been brilliant."

I was thrilled to see how relatively joyous my sister and brother-in-law were looking, both sporting aprons and sweaty brows, with their sense of achievement making them glow.

"The gang's all here," said Bud as he, Big Stan, Neal, and Shorty all presented themselves at the sliding doors from the deck.

"Come on in," I called, and a general excitement began to bubble as the men from The Mob placed an insulated chest they called an 'esky' out on the deck; they filled it with bags of ice, which they then studded with dozens of bottles of beer. It was quite an operation but – apparently – essential. There were compliments aplenty for the display of pizzas and cookies and, with some urging from Bud and me, it was agreed we'd move all the platters to the table out on the deck, which was a relief.

I felt rather pleased with myself when I also managed to seat myself beside Shorty, and I engaged him in conversation – speaking quietly. It wasn't that I didn't want anyone else to hear, but I didn't want to overwhelm what was turning out to be a not-bad dinner party, and certainly didn't want the general conversation taking a specific direction, until I was ready.

Our chatter turned out to be exactly what I'd hoped; Shorty was a man desperate to impress me with his ability to tell a good story, which was something I'd been relying upon. It seemed he just couldn't help but witter on about all sorts of things – an excellent sign, as was his seeming inability to stop fiddling with one of his jacket pockets, which appeared to have something heavy in it.

As the various conversations ebbed and flowed, I could sense that Thelma was getting more and more tense. At about ten to nine, she made a great show of getting up, then said, "If you don't all mind, I'm off out to stretch my legs. Won't be long. Besides, I've had my fill of your wonderful food, thank you, Siân, Todd."

As agreed, Bud and I began our charm offensive by saying the evening wouldn't be the same without Thelma, and then we got her caught up in a drawn-out series of "proper goodbyes" with the Mob, who "might not still be here when you get back". Eventually Bud received a text, which allowed us to shift gears.

Thelma seemed annoyed, and confused, when I said, "Please stay just a moment or two longer, Thelma – I have a little presentation I wanted to make, and I'm sure you'll find it interesting. Your walk can wait. In fact, maybe a few of us will join you for a stroll when I've finished. Now…let me just get this laptop sorted out."

I brought the laptop to the outdoor dining table, and set it up so it was facing me. I fiddled about until I got the result I wanted, then I encouraged everyone to have a fresh drink – not that Big Stan, Neal, or Shorty needed much encouraging…and nor did Todd, as it turned out, who appeared to be in a surprisingly mellow mood; pizza and beers can do that to a person, I've found.

"It's been a lovely evening, and it's not over yet," I opened. "Though, of course, none of us can forget the tragedy that's hanging over us." I raised my bottle of beer and added, "To those who cannot be with us." I sipped – a clear head was going to be critical.

Bud knew what he needed to do, and said, "I bumped into the fire chief, you know, Winnie's cousin, when I was out on a beer run, earlier. He said they've got a bit of a clearer idea of exactly what happened at that house your chums were renting. And Frank Tipton helped, too."

As I'd guessed, the three members of The Mob looked eagerly toward Bud. Thelma fiddled with her watch, and Siân and Todd looked a bit surprised.

"What happened?" Big Stan even put down his beer.

"Who's Frank Tipton?" Neal sounded confused.

"Tall bloke, hangs around Winnie's Place," said Shorty. I wondered how much "hanging around Winnie's Place" he'd had to do himself to know that. I suspected he'd done his best to entertain the locals with his yarns.

"That's right," said Bud, "we met him the other evening. He rebuilt this deck we're sitting on, and did the same job down at the place where your men, sadly, died." Bud looked at his own beer. "Sorry, it's hard to talk about dead people without actually talking about them having died," he added.

Big Stan threw a massive arm across Bud's shoulders, "Don't worry, mate. We understand." I felt relieved for Bud when Big Stan decided his bottle of beer was more important to him than continuing to hug my husband.

Bud pressed on. "Yeah, well, Frank was telling me he'd talked to the fire people, and because of what he said to them, they now have a new theory of what happened."

Neal leaned forward. "What happened? How do you mean?"

Bud also leaned in, and spoke quietly, respectfully. "Frank Tipton was able to confirm that this house and the house that burned down had exactly the same floor plans as each other. The fire department had gone public with the information about there being a candle in a bucket that burned down until kindling caught fire, and they had also said they believed the bucket had been in the corner of the upper living room." He pointed toward the farthest end of our open-plan interior. "Over there."

Everyone turned and craned their necks to see the spot. "But the problem they had, you see, was working out why the three men wouldn't have spotted it, and stopped the fire before it took hold. When Frank had talked to them about the similarities between the two houses, they saw it differently."

"How so?" Shorty's brow furrowed.

Bud stood and walked to the balustrade running along the edge of the deck. "If you look down, you'll see there's another deck below us, but it's set in a bit, as is the footprint of the floor beneath us. The bottom level of the house is smaller than this upper level. The thinking is now that when the upper floor of the burned house collapsed onto the lower floor, it crashed down onto the bucket, which wasn't sitting in the corner of the upper floor at all, but out on the deck on the lower floor."

Neal stared at Bud, then his father. "I don't get it."

Big Stan gazed at his beer as he replied, "The fire didn't start inside the house, son, but outside. Which means anyone could have set it…and that Ditch, Lennie, and Dan didn't have a chance to know it was happening. They might not have known about it until it was too late for them to get out. Think about it – if that deck down there caught fire right now, how would we all get out? This deck would go up in an instant too, right?"

We all stared at Bud who was still standing at the rail. He waved an arm. "If that deck down there caught fire now, we'd all know about it and head for the front door. It's never used, but there is one."

Bud pointed, and everyone's head turned, seeing he was right: there was, indeed, a "proper" front door to the place. However, it was set into the far corner of the house, on the right, where it didn't naturally attract any traffic when you arrived at the front steps, which were set to the left.

"So why didn't they do that?" Neal still sounded confused. "Do we really know that the other house, the one they were in, also had a door like that?"

Bud replied, "It did. Frank Tipton confirmed that the two houses were identical."

Bottoms shifted in chairs. Siân had long-since pushed away her plate; she was hovering on her seat, ready to clear things away, but knowing the moment wasn't right – at least, that was how I read her weird body language.

She said, "Might they have been…well, you know…might they have drunk too much to really know what was happening?"

"They were drugged," announced Bud, causing a dramatic reaction.

"Ditch never did drugs," said Neal firmly. "Couldn't be drugs. What did they say he'd taken? And how would they know, in any case? Fire makes things like that…difficult, right?"

I was surprised by the belligerence in Neal's tone, which was unusual for him.

"They had a tough time finding anything, you're right," replied Bud calmly, "but I've been told this evening that they finally managed to find something. They came up with lithium."

Big Stan scratched his head. "Like the stuff they mine?"

Bud shrugged. "Same stuff, specialized use: pharmaceutical lithium is used in the treatment of bipolar disease, but it's also used as an additional medicine when a person's been prescribed certain other drugs for depression. And if you take – or are given – enough of the stuff, it can poison you. Kill you."

Neal and his father exchanged a significant glance. *They knew!* Neal said, "All three of them? All dosed up with that stuff?"

Bud nodded.

Neal's darting eyes and mumbled response of, "Oh," spoke volumes…at least, it did for me and Bud, because he'd been able to get some medical questions answered about Ditch. We exchanged a slight nod, which I took as my cue.

I said, "You wanted to know what happened that night, didn't you?" Neal lifted his chin in agreement. I continued, "I'm sorry to say that it looks as though someone poisoned all three of your colleagues with lithium, and set the fire to cover their tracks."

Shorty cleared his throat, rather too dramatically. "Look – I was supposed to be there that night. At the house. And not just me. A load of us were supposed to be there. Are you saying that someone would have poisoned and burned all of us if we hadn't gone out doing our own thing that night?"

Bud turned to me. "Cait."

I replied, "No, Shorty, though the tragedy happened when it did *because* you all went out, though I believe it would have happened soon, in any case."

Big Stan, Neal, and Shorty shared puzzled glances.

Big Stan said, "It sounds like you think you know what happened, Cait. Why don't you just put us out of our misery and tell us?"

"If you're sure," I replied.

I noticed the glint of a challenge in Big Stan's eye. "Go on – we're big boys."

I steeled myself. "When we were all on that dinner cruise, enjoying the sunset above the Sydney opera house, you said the yarns we were about to hear were just a harmless way for your men to have a bit of fun, Big Stan. So Lennie spun his about that rifle he found, you talked dramatically about having seen someone killed right in front of you, Shorty, and poor Ditch briefly mentioned someone having got away with murder. At that time, I really had no idea we'd end up here, just a few days later, with two of those three storytellers dead. It makes a person realize just how fleeting life can be, and how precious it is. But, yes, you're right, you're all big boys, and now's the time for me to speak up. Though you might not like everything you're about to hear."

Big Stan shrugged uncertainly, Neal leaned forward, his young brow furrowed, and Shorty looked…shifty.

"The house that burned down was being rented by you Shorty, Dan Entwistle, and a few other colleagues, right?" I asked.

Shorty nodded. "We took both floors so's we could spread out. Dan didn't want to go out with the other lot for dinner, and I wanted to meet up with this pair. Dan said he had plans. I didn't know what they were, but I wasn't surprised to find out that Ditch had come over to see him. Nor Lennie, I suppose."

I nodded. "Yes, Ditch and Dan were especially close, weren't they? Neal, you said that might have been as the result of Ditch seeking a father figure, and – with Dan being such an active father – I understand that. Though I'd suggest that you, Big Stan, were also something of a father figure to Ditch. After all, you'd been a part of his entire life, and Neal and Ditch spent so much time together as boys that Ditch must have been in and out of your home almost as though he were an additional child."

"He was around a lot, alright," replied Big Stan, "but I was the one who was gone, more often than not. Which isn't to say I don't hope the boy respected me, you know? But we wasn't close, or nothing. It was him and Neal, not him and me."

I pressed, "And you two were really close, weren't you, Neal? I've seen how much his death has affected you. Did you have any idea you'd miss him so much, once he was gone?"

Neal looked miserable. "We was the same age – the idea either one of us would die now didn't occur to me."

"But it should have done, Neal," I replied. "Ditch tried to kill himself a few months ago; he slit his wrists and had to be treated not just for his wounds, but for clinical depression. For which he was prescribed both an anti-depressant and lithium, to augment the functionality of the initial drug. I told you both several times that he'd been trying to drown himself at Manly the other day. You must have realized Ditch was struggling…that he wanted to kill himself."

I saw a tear start to form in Neal's eye; he whisked it away, pretending to lift his bottle to his mouth. "Yeah, alright, I knew he was crook. Like we've said to you, Cait, he was never right after that bloke Bruce Walker died, though who knows why that might have set him off."

"I think I can help with that, too," I said.

Big Stan cocked his head. "What do you mean? How could you know anything about that? The bloke died out in the Bush. Didn't set his brakes right. Killed himself – though not like Ditch tried to…" He stopped speaking.

I said, "I dare say you all feel completely disconnected from the rest of the world when you're out there – just The Mob and the Bush. You must feel…safe, I suppose would be the word. Almost as though you can get away with whatever you want, and – if everyone follows a code of silence – then who's to know anything about it, eh?"

Big Stan stiffened. "Now hang on a tick, Cait. I've told you that I won't stand for no funny business on a job. Nothing wrong with a few beers, but we keep it safe out there."

I replied, "And you've also told me how Ditch was your drone pilot. I believe Ditch saw someone kill Bruce Walker on the camera feed from his drone, and that what he saw affected him so much that he wasn't able to cope with it, psychologically speaking. And I asked myself why, rather than speak out, did he allow himself to spiral into depression to the point where he tried to take his own life by slitting his wrists? Not even his medication had seemed to help, if his second attempt to kill himself – which is exactly what happened at Manly – was anything to go by. Could it have been the death of a man he hardly knew that had disturbed him that much? Surely it was much more likely that it was the identity of the person who'd done the killing that was eating away at him. You see, the killer must have been someone he knew, because only The Mob was on the spot. Maybe someone who'd maybe been his best friend for years? Or a father-replacement, maybe, in his youth?"

Big Stan was on his feet. "Right now, that's enough, Cait. I'm all for being a gentleman, but there's a point where that's not going to work. You can't say things like that about me and my son. Look at him – he'd never hurt a fly. Not on purpose in any case. And me? I know I'm big, and I've had me moments when things have got a bit rough in a pub, yeah. But murder? You're bonkers."

I said, "Sit down, Stan, I didn't mean either of you two, I'm referring to Dan Entwistle."

Big Stan hovered, looking confused, then sat down again and took a deep swig of beer. Neal was still sitting with his mouth hanging open, and Shorty looked…nervous. *Shifty Shorty.*

Neal half-whispered, "Dan? Killed Bruce Walker? And Ditch saw that? Nah. Can't be."

I nodded. "I believe what happened is this: Ditch was having fun with his drones, and he saw Dan Entwistle kill Bruce Walker. I don't believe the two men at the head of the road would have heard Ditch's drone because – as you said, Neal – Ditch had fiddled with the contraption to make it fly quietly, and there's the likelihood that the engine of the vehicle Bruce was using was running the whole time in any case. Ditch must have been deeply shocked; I say this bearing in mind how his psyche reacted. He bottled it all up, said nothing to anyone, and – tragically – reached a point where the only way he felt he could deal with a situation that must have been tearing him apart internally, was to try to end his own life. Twice. I believe that Ditch then made one further decision – to kill himself, and to take Dan Entwistle with him. I believe it was Ditch's plan to use his supply of lithium to poison Dan – I'm guessing in a beer – then overdose himself, and he set up the candle in the bucket, out of sight on the lower deck, as an insurance policy, just to make sure the job was done right on his third, and what he was determined would be his final – successful – attempt at finding peace from his psychological turmoil, in death."

A heavy silence followed, during which I noticed that Thelma had stopped fiddling with her watch, Todd was looking uncomfortably embarrassed, and Siân seemed to have given up any idea of clearing away the dirty dishes.

"But what about Lennie?" Neal bleated. "If you're saying that Ditch killed Dan, then did he kill Lennie too? I don't get it."

Bud said, "Phone records show that Ditch messaged Lennie Orkins on the evening they both died, asking Lennie to join him at the house."

"Ditch *wanted* Lennie to be there when he killed Dan? And something went wrong?" Shorty sounded incredulous.

I replied, "I believe that when Ditch confronted Dan Entwistle with the fact that he'd seen him commit murder, Dan told Ditch that the killing hadn't been his idea…that he killed Bruce Walker under duress."

Big Stan growled, "Someone made Dan commit murder? How does something like that even happen?"

"Did Lennie tell him to do it?" Shorty sounded horrified.

Neal sighed. "Don't talk rubbish, Shorty – this isn't one of your blessed yarns. Why would Lennie tell Dan to kill Bruce? And why would Dan have done anything like that just because Lennie told him to? *Kill* someone? What, like a dare? I…I don't get it. None of this is making any sense to me at all. Is it to you, Dad?"

Big Stan shook his head, but I could see that he shot a glance toward Shorty, who looked as though he had ants in his pants, he was wriggling about so much.

I said, "My thinking is that Lennie must have had some sort of hold over Dan. I'll be honest and tell you that I don't know what that was, but I'm hoping that maybe one of you has an idea about that."

I stared at Shorty, who stopped writhing and nibbled his lip.

Shorty said quietly, "I…I suppose I might know." Everyone else looked at him, too. He picked at the cap of the beer bottle on the table in front of him. "Dan was…you know, he was the big family bloke. Churchy, we all knew that. Everything for the wife and kids, right?" Big Stan and Neal nodded. "And you know him and me go back years?" More nodding. "Well…way back when, before he met the missus, Danny Boy – that was what the girls all called him – was a bit of a lad. Got into all sorts of trouble. Even…oh, I suppose I can say it now, because he's gone…there's a kid up in Queensland who's his son, see? Dan never told anyone, but I knew, because I'd been there when it all happened. He sent the girl money for a while, but stopped when he met his wife. Anyway I…well, Lennie was so good at the yarns, and I wanted to outdo him. Thought I'd dressed it all up so he wouldn't know who I was talking about. But Lennie was sharp, when he wanted to be, and after I'd spun him the yarn, he guessed it was Dan who had the secret kid. From then on Dan had to do whatever Lennie told him to do, or else Lennie would have told Dan's wife about his secret…and Dan's missus isn't someone you mess with."

"Never did know when to shut your gob, did you, Shorty?" Big Stan's tone was sharp.

Neal reached into the esky, and opened a fresh beer, as he said thoughtfully, "So, hold on there…Dan Entwistle had an illegitimate son that Lennie Orkins knew about, and Lennie used that knowledge to get Dan to kill that bloke Bruce Walker…which Ditch saw because of his drone, and that's why Ditch killed all three of them – that's what you're saying, right?" I nodded. Neal added thoughtfully, "So, if Dan killed that bloke Bruce – *if* – then why would Lennie tell him to do that?"

I replied, "I don't believe that Lennie had it in him to kill anyone, but he must have believed that Dan would go through with it if he put enough pressure on him." I paused, and glanced at my sister and brother-in-law. "People will go to extreme lengths to protect their family…might do almost anything, even go as far as murder, if they believe the alternative is to lose that family."

Neal was almost bouncing. "No…no, I don't mean that. I mean *why* why? Why would Lennie *want* Bruce Walker dead? None of us even really knew him."

I stared across the table. "Why don't you answer that one, Shorty?"

Once again, every eye turned toward the man, who now looked terrified.

Big Stan rumbled, "Shorty, mate. What. Have. You. Done?"

A loud shout of, "Oi! Get off me!" came from the front of the house, distracting us all.

Two rather large men in surprisingly formal dark suits rounded the corner of the deck, a man in handcuffs stumbling between them, protesting loudly, "Don't push me, you mongrels. I'm going as fast as I can."

I stood and said, "Come on, folks, budge up, we have a new guest."

Big Stan's mouth fell open. "*Ryan?* Ryan McCready? What the hell are you doing here? I thought you were in Broome."

"I was, and I should have bloody well stayed there," was the defeated reply from the handcuffed man.

The Rare Ones Are The Best Ones

The shift in the atmosphere on the deck was palpable. I'd viewed many pictures of Ryan McCready, and had even expected his arrival, but was still surprised by his appearance. I'd seen him dressed in layers of clothes, invariably yomping up or down something that looked close to being a rock face, somewhere in the Outback or the Bush. Now that he was in front of me I could see he was a tiny man, no taller than me, with a birdlike body that didn't fill out the sweater he was wearing above a pair of baggy jeans.

As he noted who was sitting at our table, any bravado he'd been displaying evaporated. His face became a mask of terror...and defeat.

"What are you doing here, Ryan?" Big Stan sounded bewildered.

Everyone's attention was on the newcomer. Siân and Todd looked completely confused.

I said, "Allow me to introduce Ryan McCready, the man to whom Little Stan of S & S Roads – real name, Stanley Hayes, for those of you who didn't know, by the way. I realize that Ryan is already known to most of you here, but, for those of you who don't know it, Ryan was Stan Hayes's confidant and lifelong partner."

"You're the one who gave his eulogy," said Todd, looking puzzled.

Neal guffawed. "You make it sound like Uncle Stan and Uncle Ryan was a couple."

I replied, "Talk to your father about that, later, Neal. For now, let's stick to focusing on how they were partners in something other than life, shall we, Ryan? 'Partners in crime' is a term that can encompass so much, right?"

"What's she on about, Ryan?" Big Stan's tone was sharp.

I didn't want him blowing his top, so said calmly, "Shorty was just about to tell us why Lennie Orkins wanted Bruce Walker dead, weren't you, Shorty? Please don't let Ryan's presence here put you off."

"Who are they?" Shorty nodded at the two men in suits who were hanging about at the far corner of the deck.

Bud said, "Colleagues of Thelma's, from a government office in Canberra." My husband's voice had the gravitas needed to shut everyone up.

Shorty shifted in his seat, stared hard at Thelma – who completely ignored him – then muttered, "Yeah…well…none of the rest of us knew the Walker bloke when he turned up on the job, but I could tell Lennie recognized him, right off. He didn't say why, at first, but we was off having a beer one night and Lennie told me that he'd seen Bruce Walker at Philip Myers' murder trial. Said Myers and Walker was mates. And he told me that wasn't a good thing. For him. That yarn Lennie used to spin about finding that rifle in a waterhole? Not true. He was given it, and told to hand it to the coppers."

Neal nodded at me and said, "See?" I knew he was referring to our earlier conversation about theories regarding the origin of the rifle. He added, "Who gave it to him, Shorty? Was it the coppers themselves?"

Shorty shrugged. "Not…sure."

I asked, "Big Stan…did Lennie get his job with you because Stan Hayes asked you to take him on whenever you could? Despite the fact that Lennie's love of the bottle tended to get the better of him."

Big Stan rearranged his considerable shoulders, his eyes telling me he was thinking back through conversations, and agreements. "Yeah," he replied, grudgingly, "I suppose he did. Little Stan was always a bit of a champion for Lennie, I suppose.

Especially when he'd let us down in some way – you know, like being in such a state that he couldn't pull his weight."

"He was doing that more and more often," said Neal sadly, "but the clients still loved him – he could entertain a crowd at the drop of a hat."

Siân finally spoke. "So, Shorty, you're saying that Philip Myers really *was* framed for the murder of Lowanna Swan by Lennie Orkins? And that Lennie was told to act by…who? Who wanted Philip framed?"

Todd said, "Shush, love."

Siân snapped, "Don't shush me – you worked for the man…don't you want to know who got him locked up? I certainly do. Thelma – does all this make sense to you? And how does this link up with those lithium leases that Philip owned that you've been going on about that have put my family's lives in jeopardy?"

Thelma Pruitt looked across the table at Siân and said firmly, "I don't feel I'm in a position to speak, so I'll just let Cait continue to take the lead. She's so good at it, after all."

I replied simply, "Oh, come on, Thelma, surely you want to say something."

Thelma tilted her head, and looked puzzled. "Like I said, you're doing such a good job, Cait, that I'd rather let you have the floor."

I turned to face my brother-in-law. "Didn't it puzzle you that Philip Myers never made a greater effort to mount a more robust defense in court than he did, Todd?" I asked.

Todd's sharp intake of breath told me I'd caught him off guard. Until this point no one had really paid him much attention, now everyone looked at him, and his ears turned pink. "I supposed his legal team did the best they could," he replied uncertainly. "The evidence was damning. Though, of course, now that we *know* the rifle was a set-up – then, yes, I suppose they could have gone in harder when they questioned Lennie Orkins."

I agreed. "The court transcript shows how incredibly brief the questioning of Lennie was. In fact, it was even something Joyce Trimble commented upon."

"Joyce was at Philip's trial?" Todd sounded surprised.

I said, "For about a week, isn't that right, Joyce?"

A tinny voice wafted from my laptop. "That's right. I was there for about a week, then I went back to my family in Perth."

There was a show of general surprise when I turned the laptop screen to face the people sitting around the table. I said, "Joyce has been listening in, from Todd's office in Perth. Say hello to Joyce Trimble, everyone. Joyce this is – well, let's allow the introductions to wait, shall we? But, tell me, is there someone at this table you recognize?"

Almost everyone peered at the laptop as I shifted its angle so that the camera took in the whole table. Joyce replied, "I saw the man in the handcuffs at Philip's trial; he was there every day I was, and he sat jiggling both his knees up and down the whole time."

We all instinctively looked toward Ryan McCready's knees, which immediately stopped bouncing beneath the table.

"Anyone else? Other than Todd, Siân, and me, of course."

Joyce said, "Not to look at, but I recognize someone's voice – a woman's voice, though I honestly can't say she looks anything like I remember her."

"Did you recognize the voice of Katrina, also known as Trina, Gagnon?" I asked, staring straight at Thelma.

"That's right," said Joyce. "Her husband, Phillipe, used to play pool with Philip Myers sometimes, and she mooned around after Philip and me all the time, when we were a couple."

Big Stan stared at Thelma. "You *are* her, aren't you? Bloody oath you've changed. Your face. Your body. But not that voice.

Who are you now?" He looked at Bud. "You said this woman was a Canadian friend of yours, but…that's not true, is it?"

Bud sighed. "Sorry, Big Stan, I didn't mean to lie to you. I met a woman who worked for the Canadian government, the widow of a decorated RCMP officer by the name of Dwayne Pruitt who'd died in the line of duty." He glanced at me and smiled sadly, then continued sharing the information we'd managed to gather, between us. "I never questioned the fact this woman was Canadian, because it didn't occur to me that she wouldn't be. But, strictly speaking, I started out as a Swede, the same way she started out as an Aussie. Thanks to my wife's research, I now know that one Katrina Thelma Watson married Philippe Gagnon, originally from Montreal, when he was over here in Australia, working for a few years in the mining business. They went back to live with his family in Canada twenty-eight years ago, where he died, not long afterwards. The widowed Katrina met Dwayne Pruitt and they married, though, by then she was using her middle name of Thelma. Thelma Pruitt is the name on all the diplomas she gained when she studied computing and data analysis, which helped her begin her own career with the RCMP, and she then moved on to undertake other duties on behalf of her country. *That* was the woman I met, worked with, and trusted. Thelma Pruitt."

"She's Australian?" Neal was confused.

"She sounds Canadian," said Siân.

I replied, "She does, Sis. But – in just the same way that you and I have, apparently, been getting more Welsh by the day since we've been spending so much time together – so, the longer she was back here in her native Australia, the more Thelma slipped back into her Strine. No Canadian would call a kettle a 'jug', Thelma. That was when the penny dropped for me, but not – to my shame – until the second time you used that term. Then I recalled all your other missteps: 'as sure as spring comes in

September' is not the utterance of someone who's grown up in a country where spring comes in March…or even May, depending on which bit of Canada you're from. No, that's something you'd pop into your conversation if you're from somewhere down under. As is the delightfully multi-purpose 'yeahnah'. Once I spotted it, I couldn't believe I'd been so dim; I suppose I'd got used to almost everyone around me using Strine so often that I became a bit immune to it. More fool me, because I might have seen through you a lot quicker, otherwise. Joyce and Big Stan had both mentioned the woman with the hypnotic voice who'd been around in the years after Philip Myers was supposed to have killed Lowanna. And your voice, Thelma? It really is remarkable."

We all looked at her, but she remained mute, her eyes glittering in the light of the laptop. She looked away from it.

"Does it matter? Where she's from, I mean." Todd sounded genuinely non-plussed. "Like you said, Bud's Swedish by birth, and she's Australian by birth. So…what?"

"She used to follow Philip around like a puppy," said Joyce, the laptop's speaker sounding hollow in the night air. "Like a bad smell, always lingering."

"You inserted yourself into Bud's life, too, didn't you, Thelma?" I said. "Until your transfer to Ottawa."

Thelma sniffed.

I said, "I know that criminal psychology is my specialism—"

Big Stan interrupted me. "You what?"

Bud said, "Cait's a professor of criminal psychology in Canada. Highly respected. Specializes in profiling the victims of crime. Speaking up for them. When I headed up the homicide detection unit in Vancouver, Cait worked cases with me and my team as a consultant. It's how we met."

Big Stan, Neal, and Shorty all stared at me and my husband open-mouthed for a moment.

Big Stan chuckled and said, "A copper? And a criminology professor? Now I'd never have guessed that. Go on then – it seems you two might know what you're talking about, after all."

I felt my right eyebrow creep up to my hairline as I continued, "So – while I'm no psychiatrist – as a *psychologist* I can say that Thelma has displayed certain patterns of behaviour over the years, both as Katrina and Thelma, that suggest she can become obsessed with a person. Joyce, you mentioned almost stalker-like actions, and Bud talked of much the same sort of thing. I also have to wonder about the frequency with which Thelma 'bumped into' Dwayne Pruitt, the man who became her second husband, while he was on duty. Bud, and even Dwayne himself it seems, had always thought of that as a romantic set of circumstances; I see it differently. Now."

I looked at Thelma and added, "I can quite see the attraction of your subsequent data-mining role with the RCMP. And to be able to worm your way into CSIS? That must have been like hitting paydirt for you. How wonderful to be able to keep tabs on whomever you wanted, whenever you chose, wherever in the world they might be…even if they were languishing in an Australian prison, for example. Handy, too, when it came to being able to create so-called 'files' about people by simply collating data from across many existing sources. Nice work, by the way. Though that list of names of consortia you gave me? You had to make up some nonexistent names in a hurry, right? A step too far for you, I fear. You couldn't have imagined I'd find out about Kejoka, after all."

Thelma adjusted herself in her seat and leaned back a little, casually hooking an arm over the edge of the backrest. I noticed the two men at the end of the deck tense, but they relaxed again when she did the same. She still didn't speak.

Todd blustered, "I'm sorry, Cait – this is all very interesting, but what's it got to do with poor Ditch Early killing two men and taking his own life? Let alone Philip Myers being framed for killing Lowanna Swan? Please – stop giving us the dots and join them up for us, will you?"

"Fair enough," I said. "You remember when Thelma saw the photo on your laptop of Philip and Cindy Myers dancing together at your wedding?" Todd and Siân nodded. "And do you recall how she looked truly shocked, and commented quite disparagingly upon how skinny Cindy Myers was?" Siân again nodded, but Todd looked a little more vague. "That shock was an indication she was seeing a photo of Philip she'd never seen before, which, in itself, was a notable reaction, as was her tone when referring to his wife. But the thing is…how would Thelma Pruitt, from Canada, know that was a picture of Philip Myers dancing with his wife? A woman she was even able to name. I wondered if Cindy Myers' name might have appeared in the files Thelma claimed to have been given regarding Philip, but – at least in the information she passed to me – his wife wasn't mentioned; everything about Philip pertained to the period around the death of Lowanna Swan and, of course, Cindy was dead before Philip's trial took place."

"So…how *did* Thelma know about Cindy?" Todd sounded cross.

"Joyce told me that Thelma, when she was known as 'Trina', had been obsessed by Philip, and followed him about. I'd even go so far as to question the nature of the car accident that Joyce had, which kept her in the hospital for some time, where 'Trina' was a devoted visitor. I suspect that when Joyce and Philip broke up, Trina thought she finally had a chance with him…but Philip married Cindy very soon afterwards, and that's when Trina and Philippe Gagnon went to live in Canada. Interestingly, records show that Trina married Phillipe Gagnon thirty-four years ago; that was just after the death of Lowanna Swan, when Philip Myers buried himself in work, digging up a fortune in opals across the artesian basin. We know that Trina had been on the scene before Joyce and Philip were dating: who's to say she wasn't already on the scene when Philip was secretly falling in love with Lowanna Swan, too?"

Big Stan spoke gruffly. "I'm not a clever man, Cait. Hard-working? Yes. Clever? No. What's this one —" he jabbed a thumb toward Thelma — "following Philip Myers about like a love-sick puppy got to do with the death of a poor girl who could point out opal deposits on a map?"

I took a deep breath. "Joyce told me that Philip confided in her that, when his wife had died, 'Trina' visited him…one last time. She turned up at Philip's home believing she had another opportunity to be his choice, but he rejected her once again. 'Thelma' was a widow by then, you see, and Philip was a widower — she felt she really had a chance…that he'd finally choose her. But Philip Myers dashed her hopes, once and for all. So, having waited for almost twenty long, long years, Thelma decided to have her ultimate revenge on Philip: if she couldn't have him, no one would. She decided that he deserved to lose his freedom. And that was when she put her plan in motion to get him convicted of a murder he never committed."

A bat flew past, making everyone jump. Everyone except Thelma, who stared at me with eyes that lacked any emotion whatsoever.

From The Depths

"I'm done like a dog's dinner," said Ryan McCready quietly, covering his face with his cuffed hands.

Big Stan was close enough to the man that he was able to reach his shoulder, which he rubbed. "What are you doing here anyways, mate? And –" he stared at Bud, then me – "and what's the handcuffs about, eh?" He chuckled, then added, "Haven't seen you in them things since that time when you and Little Stan got hauled away from that big blue in that pub just outside Darwin. A brawl to remember, mate. But that was a long time back."

I felt sorry for Big Stan – I knew he was in for a few shocks.

I said, "If Ryan feels able to talk to us, I'll let him explain. Ryan? You know it's all over, don't you?"

The man's eyes spoke of utter defeat. "I knew it was falling apart, but…but we reckoned maybe we could tough it out. I had to give it a go, for poor old Stan's sake."

"Do you mean for my dad, or for Uncle Stan?" Neal's usually carefree expression had dissolved; he looked truly worried.

"Nah, not this big galah here," replied Ryan, managing a hint of a warm smile, "my Stan, your Uncle Stan. Though, to be fair, I called him Hayes to his face, because I didn't ever like the Big Stan, Little Stan thing. Not fair, really. I mean, look at this one – how's anyone going to be anything but little when compared with him? Your dad's a good bloke, Neal, and don't you forget that. Ever. Heart in the right place, bloody hard worker, and he never dobbed his mate in. Right, Stan?"

Big Stan nodded his big head, looking sadly at his beer. "Right."

"Good on ya, mate," said Ryan. "But he's gone, now, and I will be soon…no fighting this lot in their fancy government suits. So say whatever you want, now. It's all over. And, no, I'm not going to dob no one in, either, so I'll just speak my piece, and let them lot over there cart me off to wherever it is they want."

"Dad?" Neal grabbed his father's hand, only to have it shaken away.

"Not your turn to speak, son. Mine. So listen up." We all did. "Ryan is right – there was a time when I should have asked questions, and I chose not to. Then…well, it's like this, son: you get to a point when you know you can't go back and do it different, you just have to keep going from where you are. Like cutting a road through the Bush, really. Someone else sets you a spot on the map where you have to start – and you don't get to ask why. But, with Little Stan – and I'm sorry Ryan, mate, but that's who he'll always be to me – he dropped me at a starting spot, and I could only think about where he told me we could go, when what I should have done was ask him why we was starting where we was. Sorry, son."

Big Stan looked at Bud and me with soulful eyes. "I didn't *know*, see? I was just a kid. Good few years younger than this one is now, and even more green, if that's possible."

He reached over and tousled his son's hair. The rarity of such an action was made clear by Neal's shocked, and somewhat confused, reaction.

Todd leaned forward. "What did you do?"

Big Stan opened another beer, and drank. He wiped his mouth with the back of his hand and said, "Me and Little Stan worked our backsides off to get set up, we really did. But a bit of hard yakka never hurt no one, so we pushed on. We traveled about, word spread, and we made our little roads using equipment we hired or – if Little Stan could talk them into it – with equipment our clients hired for us to use. But we both knew we'd never make a real go of it unless we got our own stuff.

Then, one day, Stan comes into the pub and says, 'I've got something to show you.' I'll never forget it: I walked outside, and there was a digger on a trailer, hooked up to a ute that was big enough to pull it, and another ute with a pop-up camper trailer already attached. All brand new. We was set. Little Stan always did the books, handled the cash…and I'll admit a lot of them early jobs was done for cash, you know? Didn't want the government getting their hands on our money, right? So I told myself we'd really been doing that well…and didn't ask any questions…and we just kept going. It was still hard work, of course, but that was when things turned around for us; we could promise to be in places by certain times, and know we'd be equipped to do a job. He did all the client stuff, and I gathered the crews together – and we got bigger, and then…then he died. And I reckoned the business could be stuffed because I didn't have the contacts, see? He'd known everyone; I'd avoided them – but I told myself it was all for you, son…so I've put another load of hard yakka into getting to know the clients this past year, and that's why we took that suite at that posh hotel over by the station here – because they've all said, at the conference, that they'll keep using us, which is the best news ever."

Neal smiled at his father. "It is, Dad."

"But you really never knew where Stan Hayes got that early injection of cash?" I pressed Big Stan, without a hint of a smile.

He shrugged his bulky shoulders. "Like Ryan said, I didn't ask, and he didn't tell. Life was…busy…distracting. I met my first missus just about then – not your mother, Neal, the one before her. Loved her fancy stuff, she did, and I was off making the money she spent to make us a good home." He paused, and smiled ruefully. "Horrible place, it was. Frills and dainty china all over the place, I was terrified to move whenever I went home, in case I broke something. But she was happy, and I was never there…then she emptied my bank account and shot through with the bloke who did her hair, if you can believe it. After that disaster, I met your mother and we made a proper go of it…once I tracked down the first one to sign the papers so I could get married again."

"Hayes loved you, mate," said Ryan, quietly. "Trusted you with his life, he said. And I knew he trusted me with it, too. He knew you'd never ask, and he knew I'd never tell. But he's gone now, and I can't find the joy in life any more. Never had to do a day's work, me, because of what we did back then – and now? I reckon I've been looking for a purpose all me life, looking for…something that whole time, and I'm never going to find it. Because he's gone. I know that now. Not even with the boat and the all the prospects he left me. I haven't got the heart for any of it, somehow."

Thelma shifted in her seat, and we all glanced at her. She was looking…less, somehow, yet she still had an incredible tension in her body. I wondered how, and when, it might be released. She'd stayed quiet for a lot longer than I'd imagined she would have done; as Ryan spoke, sounding and looking more and more hopeless, I couldn't believe it would be long now.

I prompted, "If it makes things easier for you, Ryan, I'm pretty sure I could tell your tale for you, but hearing it from you, in your own words, would be better, I think. What had taken you and Stan Hayes to the town of Katherine, thirty-five years ago? Am I right that you two had no idea about who Lowanna Swan was at that time?"

Ryan nodded. "Not a clue. We'd heard about her, of course – everyone in the mining business had. You didn't have to be a dedicated opal hunter to know about the girl who could sell you an X on a map so you could make your fortune. But she wasn't someone people had seen, she was just a name: The Girl with the Opal Fingers. So when we saw her dead at a roadhouse outside Katherine, we didn't know who she was. She was just some Aboriginal girl. The person standing over her told us she'd burst into their room and had tried to rob them of the big bag of gold they had with them. They said it was self-defense. We…we believed them."

"I think what you mean is that you chose to believe them, Ryan," I said. "You took the gold the killer offered you in payment for helping them hide the body, right?"

Big Stan growled, "You bought that story? You want us to believe that?"

Ryan stared at the table. "Me and Hayes? A right couple of galahs we was. We had no idea how to hide the body so it wouldn't be found. Birds. That's how her cousin found her body so fast; followed the birds. Anyways…you're right, we took the gold we was given and changed it into cash as quick as we could; who wants to cart gold around, right? Too heavy. Spent a day or two changing it up at various places, so as not to arouse too much gossip. Not that we needed to rush away. No one put much effort into working out who'd shot the girl after they found the body. As soon as her father showed up a few days later, that's when we found out who the dead girl was…and we realized that we'd been lied to. We tracked down the…killer…and they talked us out of saying anything by giving us a map they said could make us a fortune, if we were prepared to work for it. Worth maybe even more than even the gold we already had. I always wondered if the killer started that rumor about Lowanna's father, Guy Pamkal, murdering his daughter themselves; handy for them for folks to think that he'd killed her, see? Then? Then we took off."

I was happy to let my disgust show when I said, "So Ryan, you and Stan Hayes took your blood money and got on with your lives, never wondering about how what you'd done would impact those who'd lost Lowanna?"

Ryan McCready sank further into his chair. "Right. Yeah, that's right. We…we was shocked when we heard about the father killing himself a couple of years later. We told ourselves he might have done it anyway; we talked about it sometimes…wondered if he'd been driven to it by the loss of his daughter. But we found out, on the grapevine, that he'd really been brought to the edge because he'd lost his source of income. Talk was he disappeared into the bottom of a bottle, and didn't care as much about his kid being killed as about her not being around to earn him a living anymore. I'm sure it didn't help matters that no one cared enough to try to find out who'd killed her…not that we wanted them to, of course, because that might have led back to us. But, yeah, I reckon he shot himself because he knew the life he'd planned to afford, by selling his daughter's talents, had gone forever…not because the girl herself was dead."

Big Stan's voice cracked when he said, "And what about letting a person get away with murder, Ryan? Did you and Little Stan ever talk about that? Ever talk about how Lowanna Swan never got any proper justice?"

Ryan shook his head.

I said, "But surely you and Stan Hayes knew something was very wrong when the rifle that killed Lowanna turned up again, twenty years later…and got Philip Myers convicted of her murder. How did you think that had happened?"

Ryan stuck out his chin. "Don't know. But…we knew the killer kept the rifle." His eyes flicked toward Thelma.

Thelma's tone was menacing. "You're pathetic, Ryan. Always were. Just because your beloved Stan's gone, you're ready to give it all up. Can't help but tell, can you?"

She stood, thrusting back her chair.

Everyone flinched.

The two men in suits bounced to attention, and took a half-step in our direction.

"Keep your hair on, you two," called Thelma. Her voice was still enchanting, but her glittering eyes betrayed her anger. "I'll take it," she said, glowering down at me, "but not without you all knowing whose fault everything really was. That Lowanna Swan? She got what she deserved. She was trying to take Philip away from me. He was mine. She was nothing. What did she have that I didn't? Her father hardly let her out of his sight, so she must have seduced Philip when they met just because she couldn't get her hands on anyone else. I followed Philip across country from Darwin to Katherine. I had to know where he was going, see? And why. Then I saw them. Out in the Bush. Getting up to all sorts. In the darkness. In secret. Never noticed me, of course. No one ever did. They talked about their plans, and I knew what I had to do. Stop her, somehow. I followed her back to that roadhouse. Fleapit of a place. Saw she had Philip's rifle in her pokey little room. Had no idea how she'd got it, but knew it was his. I'd seen it often enough at his place, when I'd been...you know, just checking in on him."

Thelma paused, stared directly at the laptop and said, "Boy, oh boy, you and Philip liked to talk dirty on the phone, didn't you, Joyce? Or, at least he did."

Joyce wasn't the only one to look completely puzzled, but she was the only one who swallowed hard...with embarrassment, I judged.

"Of course – your lip-reading ability," I pounced. "No wonder you'd acquired and developed those skills before your time with CSIS, Thelma. They must have come in handy on many occasions; maybe across a bar, where Philip was planning to meet up with Joyce...or maybe even Lowanna, before her."

Thelma sniped, "A right little Miss Clever Clogs, aren't you? Yeah, you can have that one. And you're right – no one ever imagines there might be a lip-reader watching them. Anyway – as soon as I saw Philip's rifle propped up in the corner of Lowanna's room, I knew exactly what to do; I climbed in through her window, and I was ready for her when she came out of the bathroom. Looking so loved-up, she was." Thelma paused and chuckled cruelly at her remembrance. "Neither of us said a word. Neither of us had to. She would have seen on my face what I was going to do, and I could tell she wasn't going to let me. She turned to go back into the bathroom – like that was going to save her. I shot her. Twice."

Siân gasped. "But didn't anyone hear the shots? Call the police?"

Thelma's chuckled wryly. "Call the cops? Yeahnah. If you've never been to a scummy roadhouse like that one was, you'll never understand what you could get away with; someone as drunk as a skunk shooting off a rifle for fun? Happened more than you might think. Often enough that no one thought to mention it when a copper finally got around to asking. Besides, those roadhouses? People move on so fast they don't leave a mark, or a memory. No one ever sees, hears, or says, anything."

"Except for me and Hayes," said Ryan ruefully.

"Yeah. Except you two," replied Thelma, shaking her head. "They were outside, near their ute, having some sort of…argument…fight? I don't know…all over each other, in any case. They saw me coming out with the rifle and pushed past me, into the room. Saw the body, then they saw the bag of gold I was carrying. I reckoned Lowanna had it so that her and Philip could make a go of it together. After that? Let's be honest, shall we, Ryan…you and Stan Hayes didn't take much persuading to help me, did you? You two bought my story so fast my head spun. You got your fortune, I got my freedom…my chance to have the life I deserved with my Philip. But then you wanted more, didn't you? Once you found out who she was you came looking for more gold – but I managed to fob you off with one of those maps she'd had with her at that motel. I gave one to you and Hayes, and I kept one for myself. I'd seen Lowanna giving Philip some of them out in the Bush; maps with opal deposits marked on them…the opals Philip went off to dig up over the next few years, making it impossible for me to follow him. My boyfriend at the time, Phillipe, hadn't even noticed I'd been away for a week when I got back, idiot that he was; he'd been off at a dig site at the time, so I suppose that was fair enough. But my Philip had dropped off the face of the earth, as far as I could find out. So I married the man who wanted me…had to have someone, right? Had to bide my time until Philip came back to Darwin. And Phillipe Gagnon? He was a steady earner at least, and didn't want much more from me than to keep a clean house, and put a meal on the table when he wasn't at a dig site. When Philip finally came back, I knew it was my chance to be with him at last…but then there was you, Joyce. You? Not me? *Again?* Still, we had some good times, right? Some nice nights out together. And, yeah, sorry about that accident you had – I wanted you out of the picture, just for a little while. I hope your leg doesn't bother you these days."

I stood up too – Thelma was still a head taller than me, but I wasn't prepared to have her continuing to tower over me while I sat. I said, "So you bought off Ryan McCready and Stan Hayes with a pile of gold and a map to an opal deposit – where they opened up a mine which they called Kejoka, using Stan Hayes' family's names."

"You just can't help yourself, can you?" Thelma sneered. "You always have to be the one who's worked it all out, and joined up all the dots that dim-witted brother-in-law of yours was on about, right? Yeah, right, Kejoka. Opals weren't my interest at the time, but I've managed to make something of my map since then; there are a lot of people who want the joy of looking for opals, even if they're acting on someone else's behalf, as they always have been, for me. Since I got the place opened up, anyway. I managed to find idiots who'd dig from me, even though I made all the arrangements from Canada."

I nodded. "You have a photo of it as your laptop screensaver," I said. "I could only see a part of what I think was the name plate, with seven short dashes, a long one, four more short ones, something that was pretty definitely the bottom of a capital letter G, five more short ones, and a semi-circle. Would that be KATHEWAGAPRU by any chance?"

Thelma gave me a slow round of applause. "See? Can't resist, like I said. Yeah – Katrina Thelma Watson Gagnon Pruitt. Nicely done, Cait. Should I give you your gold star now? Fancy telling me the value of the opals I've got out there? No? Well, so far, it's a couple of hundred thousand dollars. Nice, right? But not as nice as the mine Stan and Ryan got their hands on, eh, Ryan? I hear you've pulled a couple of million out of Kejoka so far…though it took you a while. I understand Stan Hayes roped you into helping with that mine, Big Stan." She glanced at the shocked-looking Swan men. "Needed brute strength to get that one started, he did…and you were just the brute to do it for him. Did you even know that Stan Hayes managed to sneak that much opal out of that place? That look on your face tells me you didn't. And did you never suspect that him and me kept in touch with each other for all those years, Ryan? Nah, didn't think so. He was a slippery one, Stan Hayes. You might have both loved him, in your own ways, but that man loved nothing more than money."

"*You* killed Lowanna Swan?" Todd was as wide-eyed as I'd ever seen him.

Thelma laughed, musically. "You're just getting that now? Thick as two short planks you, Todd. God help the investors – you're bound to screw up Philip's last remaining mines."

Todd bridled. "I can find out about lithium – I'm an engineer."

"Not lithium, Todd," I said.

Todd spluttered, "But she said…lithium…consortia…that we're in danger…that threatening email I got…" He was squeaking by the time he'd finished.

"Thelma's an expert at data-gathering and covert surveillance, Todd. It wouldn't have been too difficult for her to be keeping an eye on what Philip Myers was getting up to in prison. Keeping tabs on who he was reaching out to. She's the one who sent the threatening email to you – and sent one to Joyce, too, a year ago. There are no nefarious consortia out for your blood. No lithium. Just opals, Todd," I said. "My money's on Lowanna Swan having given Philip maps showing a host of deposits, and the only mines and rights he didn't sell when he needed to liquidate his assets to cover his legal fees would have been the ones she marked out for him. Philip loved Lowanna for his whole life, Todd…he wouldn't have sold those mines. Thelma was spinning us a yarn about the lithium and the consortia – she wanted to be able to manipulate you. Ryan, tell me, was the plan for you to ride in as a white knight, prepared to put up the money needed to save Todd, Siân, and their kids, from a living hell? Splash the cash, and buy up everything Todd believed would prove a threat to his family for cents on the dollar? At Thelma's request, of course."

Ryan nodded.

Siân said quietly, "So Philip never knew what had really happened to Lowanna, but he mined the opals she'd sort of bequeathed him, and then built his empire…I get that. Which is terribly sad. However, I do think he really loved Cindy, Cait, and she always appeared to love him too, which is good. But I still don't understand why Philip didn't fight harder to keep himself out of prison. Why didn't he call witnesses who could exonerate him? He knew he hadn't killed Lowanna. He could have tried harder."

I reached for my sister's hand. "Sorry, Sis, I don't believe he wanted to. I think he felt he deserved to be locked up. You see, assisting someone to commit suicide was illegal in Western Australia until a few years ago. He'd have been charged with murder if it had come to light that he'd helped Cindy to die."

"She killed herself," said Todd firmly, addressing the table.

"Todd, Cindy's autopsy report proves she'd already been dead for approximately twenty hours before Philip called it in," I replied.

Todd spoke quietly, mechanically, "He was out. Getting drunk. We all knew that…he told us."

My sister gasped. "Was he? Was he *really*, Todd?" Siân stared at her husband as she spoke. "You *knew*, didn't you?"

Todd sounded defeated. "No. No, I didn't *know*. Really I didn't. But she *was* real crook, love. It wouldn't have been…easy for her. I *didn't* know. He…he made sure none of us could know. Not for certain. But…but he was never the same after she went."

I could see my sister's mind working. She glanced at me, then glared at Thelma. "He really did kill himself, didn't he? Philip killed himself in prison – for some reason – and you made up some rubbish about non-existent consortia managing to somehow get him murdered because you thought we'd be frightened by that idea. Why would you do that? I've been terrified for my children's safety all this time. Because of *you*. That's unforgiveable."

I said, "Bud got word a couple of hours ago: Philip Myers had been diagnosed with, of all things, pancreatic cancer. The same cancer his wife had. Two months ago. I dare say the irony wasn't lost on him. There was never any doubt at the prison that he'd killed himself. The idea that he'd been murdered? All Thelma."

My sister and brother-in-law grabbed each other's hands. I wanted to hug my sister, but knew I had to press on, so I allowed the topic to rest where it was.

Neal spoke quietly, "So you're the person who shot the girl with the opal fingers, Thelma. That's...awful. To just shoot someone down like that? I don't know how anyone could do that. But I still don't understand how this all connects to Ditch, or Lennie, or Dan."

"Exactly," said Shorty – too quickly. "Who was that Bruce bloke who died, anyway? And why on earth would anyone want him dead?"

Thelma stood behind her chair fiddling with its back, and Ryan stared up at her. I noticed...something...pass between them, but I couldn't work out what the spark meant.

He turned his attention to me. "Any chance I can get these cuffs off so I can have a smoke?"

"It's bad for you," said Siân.

Ryan cracked a smile. "You're kidding, right?"

Bud nodded, and one of the large men wearing a snug, slightly shiny suit wandered over, released one of Ryan's hands, and attached the cuff to his chair.

"We've got the front covered too," said the man with no name, then he ambled off.

Fiddling around in his pocket, Ryan magicked up a packet of cigarettes and a fancy brass lighter. He popped open the cap, flicked the wheel, and lit a cigarette, drawing on it with relish.

Siân snapped, "Do not drop ash onto the floor, or the plates with the pizza crusts. Here, use this." My sister slammed an empty bowl that had earlier held pretzels in front of the bemused man.

Ryan mugged a salute with his free hand, his cigarette hanging from his lips. "Good luck with that one," he said to Todd.

"Are you purposely not answering our questions about our mates, Cait?" Neal sounded angrier than I'd ever heard him. "You've said that Ditch killed himself, and that he killed Lennie and Dan, because Lennie told Dan to kill Bruce Walker, and Ditch saw Dan do it. All of which I find almost impossible to believe, by the way. But *why*? I asked you ages ago. *Why* did Lennie tell Dan to kill Bruce? And if you're telling us it's because this Thelma person told him to – then why did she do that?"

I replied, "Bruce Walker was working for Philip Myers. They were old friends – and, let's be honest, if there's something everyone at this table understands, it's the power of a long-standing friendship. Philip obviously knew he hadn't killed Lowanna, but couldn't work out how his rifle had ended up being presented in court in such a damning way. He needed proof that he'd been framed by Lennie. His friend, Bruce Walker, did something that Philip couldn't do for himself; he got a job with your company, Big Stan, so he could try to get that evidence, or else get Lennie to confess, and explain why he'd done what he'd done. The only thing that can have happened is that Bruce somehow gave himself away to Lennie. I reckon Lennie would have fed word back to Thelma, and she probably told him what to do about it…threatening him with the idea of the perjury charges he'd face if he didn't get rid of Bruce. Perjury carries a significant prison sentence."

"But how did Philip Myers find out that Lennie had framed him?" Neal was agog.

I replied, "As I said, Philip knew he hadn't killed Lowanna, but he didn't know how his rifle – a rifle he'd sent to Lowanna with Bruce, for her protection – could have ended up in a waterhole so far from where her murder took place. He also couldn't be sure if Lennie had told the truth in court – about finding the rifle as a kid, then rediscovering it at his grandfather's death. Then Philip was assigned a new cellmate… Richard Richards, or Ricky 'Carver' Richards, as you knew him, Shorty. You told us on that dinner cruise that Carver liked to think you were his mate…but that you'd cross the road to avoid him. But did you always? Or did you two ever find yourselves sharing a few beers, and swapping the odd yarn? And there was you, the one person Lennie had told about his lies…maybe that was too good a yarn to not tell?"

Shorty sat back in his chair, his eyes darting. "I…I don't know. I mean me and Carver we did have the odd session, yeah, but I don't remember ever telling him anything about what Lennie told me he'd…" Shorty's voice trailed to a whisper.

Big Stan grabbed Shorty's sleeve. "Lennie told you *years ago* that he'd lied about finding that rifle?"

Shorty's hand shook as he reached for his beer. He took a draught. "He…he let it slip a long time back, yeah…we was drunk…him more than me. He had a bar of gold…pure gold, a proper bar. Big, you know? Not something you dig up out of the ground. He kept it in his backpack. No idea why he wanted to lug it about with him, but he always did. Anyways…I spotted it one night, then out it comes, and he's stroking it, and polishing it, and he tells me how he got it. Told me a woman showed up at his place one day with an old rifle. Told him a yarn to spin, and said all he had to do was hand in the rifle at the local cop shop. She offered him the bar of gold to do it. Loved gold, did Lennie. A bit too much, if you know what I mean. He'd have done anything for gold. And did. Anyways…yeah, he told me all this not long after he'd been and gone and done his party piece at the trial. Not that he'd ever thought it would come to that, he said. Of course, he regretted having told me anything at all the next morning. I said I'd never dob him in but…well, yeah…he…he got me my work with you, to keep me sweet after that, you know? But, like I said, I never would have dobbed him in. And I didn't. Though, maybe you're right, maybe I might have mentioned something about what Lennie had told me when I was sucking down a few beers with Carver. He scared me. Best thing I could ever think of to keep him from boiling over was to keep him laughing. With yarns." He stuck out his chin.

Big Stan stood and leaned over the table, towering over Shorty, his clenched knuckles resting on the tabletop. "So let me get this right. This Carver bloke tells his cellmate Philip Myers that he knows why Lennie Orkins fitted him up with the rifle – which he only knew because you told him about it, Shorty. Then Myers sends this Bruce character to come to work for me, so's he can find out more about Lennie. Lennie cottons on – and he was a wily one, when he was sober, was Lennie – so he uses the knowledge he has about Dan Entwistle's illegitimate kid – which he only knows about because you told him, Shorty – to get Dan to bump off Bruce Walker. Poor Ditch sees this happening, can't believe his eyes, which gets him all messed up in his head, and he ends up trying to kill himself, then finally manages to do it, and takes both Dan and Lennie with him. And all of this is because you didn't know when to keep your gob shut, Shorty. Or when to open it and dob a man in." Big Stan shook his head. "Sometimes dobbing a bloke in is the right thing to do, mate."

Shorty's expression couldn't have been more miserable.

"Too right, Dad," said Neal firmly. "All of those deaths because of you, Shorty. Think about that when you're trying to sleep. Poor Ditch."

"None of this was my fault," whined Shorty unconvincingly, shifting about in his seat.

The atmosphere was a mixture of tension, and depression. I knew it was time for me to call over the men from Canberra, but I hadn't been able to predict how much fight was in Thelma.

With one, unexpected movement she grabbed the lighter Ryan had left on top of his cigarettes. She pulled a fat bunch of paper napkins off the pile in the middle of the table, and set them alight. She divided the bunch, darted through the open slider, threw a handful at the dress-curtains at the window, and the other at the curtain hanging to one side of the door itself. The fabric at both openings immediately burst into flames.

All hell broke loose, with everyone leaping from their chairs, and shouting or screaming.

Big Stan pushed past us all, heading to the kitchen, through the flames, knocking down Thelma on the way. Neal grabbed the massive, ice-filled esky cooler from the floor and hurled it at the slider curtain. The two large men in suits came running toward us, but got caught up with Ryan as he dragged the chair he was handcuffed to away from the slider, squealing in terror.

The flames were already licking at the kitchen ceiling.

I could see that Big Stan was filling jugs of water as fast as he could and throwing them around the place, to little effect. Siân and Todd stumbled along the deck toward the front of the house. Thelma knocked Bud down as she ran out of the kitchen, heading toward the far side of the house along the deck.

Big Stan managed to get out of the kitchen through a pall of smoke as we all fell back. The flames were quickly taking hold. Neal grabbed his father and helped him along the deck as the man succumbed to a fit of coughing.

"I'm calling it in," said Shorty, fumbling with his phone. "Where are we again?"

I turned and realized that Bud had got himself up off the floor, and had gone after Thelma.

Ryan stood no real chance of escaping with the chair attached to his arm, so I shouted to the men in suits, "She's gone the other way. Go around – catch her at the front!"

They turned, and shot off. Neal was tending to Big Stan who was hunched over, still suffering from a massive fit of coughing. Shorty was shouting on the phone. Siân and Todd were cowering at the front corner of the deck beckoning for me to join them. Ryan was awkwardly dragging his chair away from the fire.

I decided to get to the front of the house. Maybe Thelma and Bud would have already got right around it?

But if she went that way the men in suits would get her…so…maybe the lower deck…

I rounded the corner to see four men in suits running in different directions at the front of the house. "The lower deck!" I screamed, pointing. "Try the lower deck!"

I ran down the front steps and onto the bottom deck just behind two of the men, who were a lot faster than me.

"There she is," said one of them, pulling a gun – which surprised, and frightened, me.

Thelma was straddling the rail surrounding the back of the lower deck. Bud was within a few feet of her. The man with the gun was hovering six feet or so in front of me, his body preventing me from passing him.

"Where can you go, Thelma?" Bud was using his calming voice, even though he was shouting over the confusion above us. "There really is nowhere to run."

"You're kidding, right?" Thelma was laughing. "There's hundreds of square miles of forest out there for me to disappear into. Then all I have to do is get back to the city, and I know exactly how to blend in when I get there. Australia's a massive place, Bud – I could manage to live out the rest of my life without anyone knowing where I was. Have you got any idea how many people do that in this country? It knocks even Canada into a cocked hat on that front. Off the grid? Easy here. And I've got enough cash, and even some of the original gold, stashed away to be able to make it work for me." She turned from Bud and stared at the man standing in front of me. She shouted, "And you can put that gun away, mate, unless you want to lose your job and your pension – I'm not armed. You'd get done for shooting me, and you know it."

I could see Bud's feet moving, inch by inch, as he approached Thelma, his arm outstretched. "Come on now – you've no idea how far the drop is. You might think you could make it in the long term, but what about that first jump?"

Thelma laughed, "It's no more than a few meters here, Bud, mate."

Bud managed to grab her arm, and then her shoulder, and, for a moment, I thought he might be able to pull her off the railing. But she grabbed at him with both hands and shouted, "Come for the ride, Buddy Boy! Something soft for me to land on."

I couldn't move.

Thelma had gone, and Bud had disappeared with her.

Over the edge.

I think I screamed. The bloke with the gun certainly turned to stare at me. Then he ran to the railing where they'd disappeared, and – to my amazement – leaped over it. Then his colleague pushed past me and did the same thing.

Siân grabbed at me as I began to run toward the spot where Bud had disappeared. The smoke seemed to be tumbling like a waterfall from above, engulfing the lower level of the house. I was aware that the sirens in the distance were coming closer. My sister was shouting something at me as she tried to pull me away.

"He went over, Siân. Thelma dragged him over. Right here," I screamed.

I pushed her off and peered over the rail. My head didn't swim. I didn't feel the knot in the pit of my stomach that I usually do when I look down. All I could focus on was Bud.

He was lying on the ground about ten feet below me. His body was horribly crumpled.

I managed to get my foot above my hip and onto the rail, then pulled myself forward to try to roll over the top.

Siân was at my back, grabbing me. She dragged me off the rail. "Cait, come away. Look up. The fire's coming through the deck above us. It's not safe to be here."

I screamed down, "The fire. Bud, the deck might collapse. The whole house might come down on you. Bud…move!"

As my screams died away, I saw Neal and Big Stan Swan scrambling toward Bud. I had no idea how they'd got to where he was, but the pair picked up my husband and began to carry him back the way they'd come. Big Stan was still coughing uncontrollably as he held onto Bud's feet, and Neal was doing both the heavy lifting and the steering, with his arms cradling Bud's shoulders.

Siân and I stumbled toward the front of the house. I could see a narrow path beside the lower deck leading to the walking trail below. I tried to get down, but had to reverse as Neal and Big Stan carried Bud toward me.

Two fire engines appeared and began to tackle what was now a fully engulfed house. An ambulance arrived, and the paramedics immediately tended to Bud. He was put onto a gurney by the Swan men.

My heart slowed just a little when I could see that Bud was conscious, but gasping for air. He…he didn't look at all good. I tried to hold his outstretched hand, but was swatted back by the paramedics.

There was so much noise, so many flashing lights, so much smoke, and shouting…

"Cait!"

I snapped out of my panic to see my sister's face. "They think he might have a collapsed lung – they're taking him to the hospital. Do you want me to drive you?"

I nodded. *Collapsed lung?* I struggled to focus. "Did they get Ryan? Where did Thelma get to?"

"Cait, let the professionals deal with Thelma bloody Pruitt. Get in the car. I'll drive. Todd, you too, get in and shut up. And grab Cait's bag from the floor there – I snatched it off the deck. She might need it. Come on, Sis, just for once, let me be in charge."

Cold As Ice

I sat in the small waiting room with Siân on one side of me, Big Stan on the other, and Neal facing me.

The father and son had been brought to the hospital in a second ambulance. They'd X-rayed Big Stan upon his arrival, and he'd taken the news that he had a significant amount of scarring in both his lungs surprisingly well. The doctor who'd spoken to him had – so Neal told me – suggested the condition was probably the result of being exposed to too much airborne dust and soil out in the Bush during his unmasked years of roadbuilding. All they could do was treat him for the immediate effects of smoke inhalation, and tell him to see his own doctor as soon as possible. I had a feeling that wasn't going to happen, though the glint in Neal's eye when he told me about it made me suspect he'd intervene.

Big Stan had a cannister of oxygen beside him, and a mask in his hand from which he was gulping air, making him sound like a poor Darth Vader impersonator.

Shorty had insisted he was brought in to be checked out, too. He had a grazed knee, but was otherwise just fine, and was sitting across from me, looking grubby, and utterly miserable.

Neal had a massive sticking plaster on his face, where Bud had – apparently – lashed out with his arm when he'd been carrying him.

We sat there like that for an hour, no one speaking, all just…waiting.

I heard bustling, looked up, and there was Winnie with a tray covered with plastic wrap, followed by Timbo, who was still in his firefighter's uniform, and carrying a massive thermal cannister. She was a real sight for sore eyes. He was grimy, but looking happy.

"The food here is non-existent," she announced, "and there's not even any decent coffee, so I brought some for this lot." She nodded toward Timbo. "My heroes. You can have what's left now that the firefighters have had at it."

"Fantastic, Winnie – thanks ever so much," said Siân, leaping up. "This is just what we all need. Right – coffee for everyone, with loads of sugar, whether you usually take it or not."

I sipped at mine as Timbo and Winnie handed around cups and dug through whatever it was she had in her basket of goodies. She kept reaching up to pat Timbo on his broad shoulders, and he beamed at her constantly. The young man clearly valued her admiration. I was grateful for the sweetness and heat of the coffee; I felt chilled to my bones, and that wasn't because the hospital was cold.

"You should at least have a banana," said Winnie, shoving one in my face. "They're good for you, aren't they, Timbo? Look at him – what a fine young man. So brave. My grandson, and my hero. Everyone's hero."

I saw Timbo smile down at Winnie, and I stood, pulling at his cumbersome sleeve. "A word, if I may, Timbo," I said, smiling, and dragged him aside just a little.

"You look done in, Cait," he said. "We managed to get it all under control. The house is gone, but the fire didn't spread at all. We got there fast, and tackled it like a good team should." He gave me a confident wink, and a broad, even-toothed grin.

I managed to pull him down so I could whisper in his ear. "If I get wind of any more small fires breaking out unexpectedly in this area, I'll be having a word with your fire chief, Timbo. Tonight, you've all done a good job – but if you think you can carve yourself out a role as a local hero by starting fires you then have to rush off to put out, you can think again. You've been lucky so far – no one has been injured. But even small fires can quickly get out of control around here, and one or more of your colleagues – or even you – could be badly hurt, or worse. You saw what happened to those men who died in that house. Stop now, before that happens to someone else. Your grandmother will still love you, and she'll continue to think highly of you; why not focus on your prowess in the pool, instead of at the fire hall?"

Timbo sagged beside me. "I'm…I'm not as good a swimmer as my parents wanted me to be. Never will be. No matter what Gramma says. But this firefighting? I'm…I'm good at this."

I shoved him. Hard. "Listen to me – not one more fire. Got it? You have no idea who I am, I know that, but trust me when I say that I can, and will, keep tabs on what goes on around here from now on – from wherever in the world I might be. Got it? Stop. Now. Save the reputation you have."

His lip quivered. His chin puckered. He nodded, and whispered, "I understand. Sorry." He was dragged away by his grandmother, who insisted he returned to be with his firefighting colleagues, who were about to leave.

I heard a door open, looked around, and a woman in scrubs appeared.

I hustled toward her, with my sister a step behind me. "She's the wife, I'm the sister-in-law," she said. "News about Bud Anderson – right?"

The doctor nodded. "As the paramedics suspected, he's suffered a collapsed lung. He had a nasty fall. We're carrying out checks for a concussion too. No broken bones, except one rib – about which we can do little other than manage the pain. The lung? It should heal well; he's generally fit and healthy. We've addressed the immediate problem, relieving the stress within the lung, and he was lucky – just a portion of it collapsed. We'll need to keep him here for a day or two, but then we'll pack him off to Sydney. They'll monitor the lung there as it heals."

"Can I see him now?" I didn't know what I'd do if the doctor said no; I was already working out how to get past her and through the doors behind her if she declined.

A tired smile prefaced her assent. "Give us ten minutes to get him into a proper bed, then you can sit with him. He's groggy and he really needs to rest, as – I dare say – do you. But I can't imagine that will happen until you've seen him." She looked at her watch. "Ten minutes. Someone will fetch you."

Siân nodded and steered me away. "Right then, Sis – get that banana inside you, and finish this coffee, then go to the toilet and get yourself cleaned up a bit. We can't have your husband seeing you like that, can we? You're covered in smudges. Todd and I will wait here until you decide you need some sleep. Though where we'll do that, I don't know."

"I've organized a couple of rooms for you in town," called Winnie. "Just show up here – they're expecting you." She shoved a card into my sister's hand.

I nodded my thanks and munched on the banana, which seemed to be incredibly sweet.

"You're a nurse, Siân," I mumbled as I chewed – apparently, I was ravenous. "Tell me honestly – will Bud be alright? I mean is this collapsed lung something he can make a complete recovery from?" I knew I was out of my depth.

My sister smiled. "Yes, if he does what he's told. But he won't be able to fly for quite some time. Maybe months. When we've all wrapped our heads around this, we'll look into what you need to do about your flights home, and talk to the doctors about how long you'll have to stay in Australia. We'll help you sort out any visa issues, too. There'll be bridges to cross, and we'll help you do that."

My heart sank. "I'm due to be teaching in two weeks, when term starts. I'll be letting them down again."

Siân grabbed both my shoulders. "Your husband's in there – safe. Yes, you might have lost all your luggage in the fire – all of us did – but you're safe, too. As are we all. Work's just work. You've told me they can't get rid of you, because you have tenure, so get a substitute in for a term. Be with Bud. He'll need you, and – let's be honest – you need him."

I did my best to pull myself together. "I didn't mean I'd leave Bud to go back to work." I couldn't believe that my sister had imagined I'd contemplate such a thing. "You and Todd should go home, to Perth, though. Tomorrow…today…like you planned. Get back to the kids. There's no fear of any secret consortia being out for Todd's blood any longer…that was all just rubbish, made up by Thelma to frighten you. But I know you'd rather be with them than with me, in any case. And I'll be fine, as long as I know Bud's healing well. We'll stay in Sydney until he's better then…well, maybe we could drive from there to Perth to spend some time with you until he's able to fly back to Canada. I mean, there's no other way to get there from here, so we've got no choice."

"You could sail." Big Stan was close beside me, dragging his oxygen tank. "There are cruises from here to the Pacific Islands – then on to Hawaii, then to where you live. I know because I looked into doing the trip myself, as a honeymoon for my little Kookie. Don't know when ships do that, exactly, but I know it's possible. You should look into it. Can't think that driving from here to Perth is something Bud should be doing if he's a bit crook. Don't think you've worked out what this country's really like, yet. 'Big' doesn't come close."

"Forests as far as the eyes can see, that's for sure," I said.

"Cities that glitter at night, and gleam in the sun," said Siân.

"The Bush and the Outback, where a man's got less of an advantage than the rest of nature," said Big Stan.

"And don't forget the beaches, and the sea," said Neal, popping up beside his father. "Australia's a bit of everything," he said.

"And it's good people, too," I added. "Thank you for your help, Neal, Big Stan. That whole building could have come down on Bud…on all three of you. You saved his life, and risked your own. Thank you."

"No worries, Cait," said Neal. "Couldn't leave Oscar like that, could I?" He winked.

"They got her!" Todd's shout made us all jump. "One of the blokes in suits out there just told me." He jabbed a thumb toward the doors. "They managed to nab Thelma – she got tangled up in some chain-link fence that was put across the trail to prevent rocks falling – or something like that. Anyway, the paramedics patched her up out there, in an ambulance, and now they're taking her directly back to Canberra. Ryan McCready too. I…I don't even know what will happen now, but I do think we should try to get some sleep. Oh – is that coffee? I could do with a cup, if there's one going."

"I could do with another one, too," called Shorty, finally rising from his bucket chair with a groan. He grabbed his back. "I think I've hurt myself a lot more than this bunch thinks I did," he said, adopting a pathetic puppy look.

I said, "Maybe your back's bad because you've been lugging around that bar of gold you helped yourself to when you volunteered to sort out Lennie's belongings." Shorty's hand twitched toward his pocket. "Yes, the bar of gold that's weighing down that side of your jacket, Shorty. Tell you what, given how much trouble you've caused, why not try to come up with the name of a suitable organization that could do with a nice donation? Maybe this hospital? Or what about the local fire service? Or how about the families left behind by Dan Entwistle and Ditch Early? You and Lennie, between you, owe them that much, at least."

Despite the condition of his throat, Big Stan bellowed, "You've got a *what* in your pocket? From where? That's blood money, that is, Shorty...come 'ere..." He strode across the room, dragging his tank, not smiling at all.

"Mrs. Anderson?" Both Siân and I looked around.

"I'm Bud Anderson's wife," I said to the nurse who'd entered the waiting room.

She smiled. "You can come through, now."

Siân kissed my cheek and said, "We'll be here when you need a lift to the hotel. Go on – and don't forget – no hugging."

"No hugging – not for a while." I turned to the nurse. "Please take me to my husband."

All Together Now

Lying on the hospital bed, Bud looked pale, despite his tan. He was attached to an alarming number of machines, and his eyes were closed above an oxygen mask. In that moment, I literally felt my heart skip a beat, then he opened his eyes, and smiled.

I leaned over him, touching his hair as gently as I could. "How do you feel, Husband?"

"Not down and out yet, Wife." His voice rasped through the mask.

"Good. I don't know what I'd do without you. You know that, right?"

"I do. But you'd be okay. You were for all those years before you met me."

I shook my head. "No, I wouldn't be. And no, I wasn't. But you're going to get well, and we'll work together to make sure that happens in the best way possible. They've talked to you about your diagnosis, and prognosis?"

Bud didn't nod, but I could see his eyes smile. "They have…but I don't think I took it all in. Did they talk to you?"

"Yes, and you've been lucky; just a partial collapse of one lung, and you're already on the mend. There'll be follow-up assessments done in Sydney. It…it could have been much worse."

"I think it's best if you get back to Vancouver, for work. I'll be alright on my own. I'll fly back home when they say it's safe."

I chuckled. "If you think you're getting rid of me like that, then you're very much mistaken, Mr. Anderson. Your wife will be with you at all times. My choice."

Bud's eyes wrinkled. "Thanks. I'll get better faster because of that. But you're back to teaching next month. How will you sort that? You've been away for so long already."

He was speaking slowly, breathing deeply. The nurse had told me he'd been given some strong painkillers.

"Not your problem." I replied with as much of a smile as I could muster. "You're my priority, they'll understand. And Marty will be happy to stay longer at Jack and Sheila's place; they love him almost as much as we do, and you know how Marty feels about playing with their dogs all the time – so no worries on that front. I'm sure they'll keep looking in at the house for us, and the garden will have to get along without your attention for a while. This is what we have to be doing for now, so we'll do it. Just like we had to work as a team to help me recover from my problems in Budapest. We can do it, Bud. Together."

"I love you, Cait."

"I love you, Bud."

"And…um…did they manage to get Thelma? The doctors couldn't help with that one." Bud managed a wink.

I smiled. "She's on her way to Canberra, though how it will all be handled there, I don't know. Maybe you can make a few calls to find out more, when you're able to. I'm sure they'll want justice to be served – but who knows how they'll choose to achieve that in this instance? What she said in our presence won't count as an actual confession, will it? So maybe we'll have to give evidence at some point about what we know, and what she said. Though I believe that Ryan McCready might prove to be her undoing, in the end. I didn't see any fight left in him, did you?"

"Not a bit of it." Bud's head sank back further into his pillows.

"We got to the truth of Lowanna Swan's murder, Bud, and we both know we'll follow this through to make sure that justice is handed down. But don't let that worry you for now."

Bud's eyes widened a little. "Thank Big Stan and Neal for me? They're good men, Cait. Didn't hesitate to help me, did they? I'm so grateful."

I nodded. "Me too, Bud. They're outside, in the waiting room. I'll tell them what you said. But you should rest now. That lung of yours needs time to heal. I'll be here, when you need me. I'll find somewhere for us to stay in Sydney where you can recuperate…and we'll be able to see the sun setting over the opera house all the time until you're better. Properly better. Who knew that an evening on a dinner cruise would lead us here, eh?"

Bud was almost asleep. "Not me for one," he managed.

"And not me for two."

I kissed his forehead, gently, and knew that however long it took him to get back to being one hundred percent, everything would be manageable, and even wonderful, because we'd be together.

Acknowledgements

As always, so many people have played a part in this book ending up in your hands, and I'm going to do my best to thank them all.

First of all, my thanks to The Mob. Yes, The Mob exists, though I have taken all sorts of liberties when "recreating" them for this book…with their permission. When you said you'd be fine with being in a book, and that you didn't mind if you turned out to be goodies, or baddies, or a mixture of both, I bet you didn't think it would happen. Well, it did, and here you are! I hope you enjoyed my yarn as much as I enjoyed all of yours. Thanks for the laughs, the happy memories, and the insights into a way of life I couldn't have imagined. (Dear Reader: The Mob in the book and The Mob in real life are not one and the same. The *real* Mob is made up of warm, funny, hardworking people, who are generous to a fault.)

My thanks, too, to my real-life sister who lived in Perth, WA, for many years; she's nothing like Siân, really, though I have given Cait's sister some of my own sister's hobbies and passions. Her insights have been so valuable, as ever, with this book.

I'm delighted that Mum will be one of my earliest readers, again. This isn't something I take for granted, and am always grateful for her feedback.

My husband put up with rather more than usual while I was working on this book. Let's just say that a broken ankle can even put a crimp in the abilities of someone whose job essentially requires them to sit and type. Without his support, and without him looking after me while I write (able-bodied, or not) it would take immeasurably longer for me to start plotting a book, let alone finish writing one. Thank you.

To my editor, Anna Harrisson, and proofer, Sue Vincent: thank you both for all your hours of diligent effort. Dear Reader:

we have worked as a team to make this the best possible version of this book; if you find any errors, please accept our apologies (because none of us want anything to sneak past us) and please let us know, because sometimes we can fix them.

Of course I want to thank every blogger, reviewer, librarian, bookstore worker, and fellow reader who might have helped you make the decision to try this book. I hope you've enjoyed your time with Cait and Bud, and that you choose to keep checking in on their adventures.

Cathy Ace
November 2023

About the Author

CATHY ACE was born and raised in Swansea, Wales, and migrated to British Columbia, Canada aged forty. She is the author of The WISE Enquiries Agency Mysteries, The Cait Morgan Mysteries, the standalone novel of psychological suspense, The Wrong Boy, and collections of short stories and novellas. As well as being passionate about writing crime fiction, she's also a keen gardener.

You can find out more about Cathy and all her works at her website: www.cathyace.com

Made in the USA
Monee, IL
20 September 2024

66113972R00173